Faery Rebels

SPELL HUNTER

R. J. Anderson

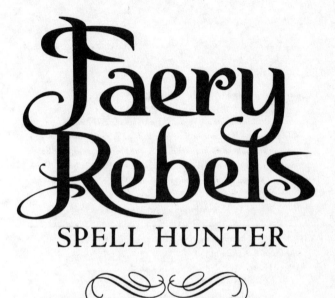

Faery Rebels

SPELL HUNTER

HarperCollins*Publishers*

Library of Congress Cataloging-in-Publication Data

Anderson, R. J. (Rebecca J.)

Spell Hunter / by R. J. Anderson. — 1st ed.

   p. cm. — (Faery rebels)

   Summary: In a dying faery realm, only the brave and rebellious faery Knife persists in trying to discover how her people's magic was lost and what is needed to restore their powers and ensure their survival, but her quest is endangered by her secret friendship with a human named Paul.

   ISBN 978-0-06-155474-2 (trade bdg.)

   [1. Fairies—Fiction. 2. Magic—Fiction. 3. Supernatural—Fiction.
4. Interpersonal relations—Fiction. 5. Conduct of life—Fiction.] I. Title.

PZ7.A54885Kn 2009   2008027469

[Fic]—dc22   CIP

                                                          AC

Typography by Amy Ryan

09 10 11 12 13   CG/RRDB   10 9 8 7 6 5 4 3 2

❖

First Edition

To my father,
the voice of Aslan;

To my mother,
who taught me to do what is right
and not give way to fear;

And to my brother Pete,
who may not believe in faeries
but always believed in me.

One

"I only want to go out for a little, little while," the faery child pleaded. "Just below the window, on that branch. I won't fly away and I won't tell anyone, I promise."

"Oh, Bryony, you know you can't." Wink's voice came from the other side of the sewing table, muffled by a mouth full of pins. Her red hair had come free of its knot, falling in bedraggled ringlets, and her cheeks were pink with the room's oppressive heat. "None of us can. It isn't safe."

"But the Gatherers go out all the time," said Bryony. "And so does Thorn."

"Thorn is the Queen's Hunter," Wink told her with unusual sternness, "and without her and the Gatherers we'd all starve. But they only go out when they have to, and they don't stay out any longer than they have to, and you and I don't have to, so there."

Bryony jumped up and dragged a stool over to the window, hopping up on the seat for a better view. If she looked straight out, there was nothing but leaves and branches. But if she craned her neck and peered all the way down, she could just see—

"Oh, Bryony, do sit down," said Wink wearily. "You're blocking all the fresh air."

Bryony made a face and plopped back onto her seat, a wobbly construction of twigs and dried grass that felt as though it might come to pieces any minute. "But it's hot in here," she muttered. "And so *ugly.*" Like most of the other rooms inside the Oak, the apartment she shared with Wink was plain-walled, clumsily furnished, and cramped. Not like the garden she had glimpsed through the open window, its velvety stretch of lawn framed by shrubberies and dotted with bright flowers. *That* was beauty.

"Why don't you go down to the kitchen?" said Wink distractedly, eyes fixed on the seam she was pinning. "I hear the Gatherers found a bees' nest this morning. If you wipe dishes or sweep the floor a bit, they might let you have a piece of honeycomb."

"I'm not hungry." Besides, Mallow was in the kitchen, and no one would dare offer Bryony such a sweet bargain when the Chief Cook was around. Except perhaps Sorrel, who was old and kindly and more than a little absentminded—but

Bryony had not seen Sorrel in days.

"Polish the looking glass, then," said Wink.

Bryony perked up. The full-length mirror on its carved stand was the one lovely object in the room, a relic from the Days of Magic. It had belonged to the previous Seamstress, who was Bryony's own egg-mother and namesake, and Bryony had spent many hours in front of it, whispering secrets to her own reflection. There were no other children in the Oak, so the white-haired girl in the mirror was the closest thing to a playmate she knew.

She rose and stepped toward the glass—but even as she moved, the window caught her eye again. Between the branches of the great Oak glowed dazzling gems of blue sky, and the leaves whispered promises of a breeze she longed to feel. A robin lighted on a nearby twig, cocking its head at her, and Bryony felt a sudden urge to dive through the window and leap upon its back. Together they would soar far away from the Oak, to a place where she too could fly free. . . .

With a flick of its wings, the robin vanished. *Another chance missed*, thought Bryony, and frustration swelled like a wasps' nest inside her. "It's not fair," she burst out. "Why can't we go out? Just because the Queen says it's not safe—how does she know? She never leaves the Oak either!"

Wink snatched the last pin out of her mouth, looking shocked. "Of course she doesn't leave the Oak! She's the one who's kept us all alive since the rest of us lost our magic. If it weren't for her protection the Oak would sicken and die, and all sorts of horrible creatures would come crawling inside to gobble us up. She doesn't dare go out, because if anything happens to her, it'd be the end for all of us!" Her voice trembled on the last phrase, as though she could already see the disaster happening.

Bryony leaned on the windowsill, staring out at the sky. "It's still not fair," she muttered.

Her words were followed by a heavy pause, then a sigh from Wink. "I suppose you're old enough to know," she said. "I didn't like to tell you before, but—"

"I already know about the Sundering," interrupted Bryony, who had spent a whole afternoon dusting bookshelves to get the story from Campion, the Oak's Librarian. "A long time ago someone put a curse on everyone in the Oak, so we couldn't do magic anymore. And everybody got confused and scared and a lot of faeries died. And then Queen Amaryllis came, only she wasn't called Amaryllis yet and she wasn't a Queen, but I can't remember that part—"

"Her name was Alder," said Wink softly.

Bryony ignored the interruption. "And she still had her magic because she wasn't in the Oak when the Sundering happened, so she had to become Queen because nobody else was clever or strong enough anymore. And she made lots of different rules to try to keep people safe from the crows and

4

foxes and things outside, but they kept making silly mistakes and getting killed anyway, and finally she told everyone that it wasn't safe to go out of the Oak, ever." She finished the last sentence in a single breath, and turned defiantly to look at Wink. "See, I told you I knew."

"Oh . . . yes," said Wink, flustered. "Well, I suppose—"

"Except that it's still a stupid rule," Bryony went on hotly, "because I'm not silly and I'm *not* going to be killed, so there!" With a flash of her wings, she hopped onto the windowsill.

"Bryony!" Wink shrieked. "Get down!"

But Bryony did not hesitate. Crouching on the window ledge, she studied the distance between herself and the nearest branch. Then, just before Wink's flailing hands could seize her, she leaped.

Wings outspread, she landed neatly as a dragonfly. As she straightened up, flushed and proud, she was rewarded with a touch of summer breeze, lifting the sticky hair away from her forehead. It felt wonderful.

"Bryony, come back! No, wait. Stay right there, and I'll get help—but no, I can't leave you—oh, what shall I do?" Wink fluttered back and forth by the open window. But she was clearly too frightened to climb out of it herself, which meant that Bryony could count on at least a few more minutes of freedom.

Eagerly the faery girl scrambled up the branch to its

very tip. She wrapped her arms about a supple twig and hung there, enraptured. Below lay the garden she had always longed to explore: the barely tamed wildness of the rose hedge on the east, a stout line of privet to the west, the flower-stippled lawn, and in the distance the daunting bulk of the House.

There had been faeries in the Oak for more than four hundred years, Campion had said. That made the House a latecomer, and a rude one at that. No one had invited it to settle here, but its stony face, blank windows, and arrogantly peaked roof did not allow question, let alone argument. Rumor said that it was full of monsters, but Bryony had never seen one. Perhaps she would see a monster today?

"Bryony, oh, Bryony, *please,*" Wink entreated, but her voice was faint now and easy to ignore. Bryony slid down the twig and straddled the end of the branch, kicking her bare heels. How had she borne it so long, shut up in the Oak like a prisoner?

Her thoughts were distracted by a scuffling noise below. Bryony peered over the edge of the branch to see an enormous creature, with sun-browned limbs and a round, hairless face, standing at the foot of the Oak. As she watched, it leaped up to grasp the lowest branch and began climbing the tree toward her.

It must have been right underneath me the whole time, she thought with a thrill that was half delight, half terror. *And now it's coming up. Should I run? Should I fly? Or should I stay here, very small and quiet, and hope it doesn't see me?*

The monster had hair almost as pale as her own, but yellower and cropped close to its head, exposing a pair of oddly rounded ears. Its eyes, when it lifted them upward in search of the next branch, were as blue as Wink's. And despite their enormous size, there was something familiar about its features. . . .

It was a child, Bryony realized, her excitement rising. Just like herself. A real playmate at last!

Meanwhile, Wink had stopped dithering and begun to lose her temper instead. "Bryony, if you don't come back in the Oak this very minute—"

"Shh!" said Bryony. "You're going to frighten it away!"

That stopped Wink short. "Frighten . . . what?"

"The monster, of course," Bryony told her impatiently, without taking her attention from the child. It was only a couple of branches below her now, and although it did not appear to have seen her, it paused and tipped its head to one side as though listening.

Several heartbeats passed in silence. Then she heard Wink say in a strained whisper, barely audible above the rustling of the leaves, "Bryony. Don't . . . oh, please, whatever you do, *don't move.*"

Bryony had lived with Wink all her life, but she had never heard that particular note in her foster mother's voice before. Wink didn't just sound nervous, or even worried: She sounded terrified.

Bryony's confidence wavered, and she began to wriggle backward, very cautiously, toward the Oak. She could hear the monster's labored breathing as it resumed the climb, and her own breath quickened as she realized how close it was now, close enough to seize her in that grubby hand, to tear off her wings, to cram her into that red, half-open mouth. . . .

Then the child looked up, and its gaze met hers.

The fear within Bryony burst like a soap bubble. She saw astonishment on the creature's face, but no hint of malice or hunger. In fact, if she had not been assured all her life that faeries were the only real *people* in the world, she might have taken the alertness in those eyes for intelligence.

Impulsively Bryony stretched out her hand. The other child's teeth gleamed as it pulled itself level with her branch, and its huge fingers reached out toward hers. . . .

All at once Bryony felt herself seized from behind and wrenched into the air. Throat tight with terror, she could not even squeak as her captor dragged her down the length of the branch and tossed her through the window into the Oak. Bryony tumbled to the dusty floor, flinging up an arm to protect herself—only to realize that it was Thorn standing over her, panting and furious.

She had been rescued by the Queen's Hunter.

Thorn's dark hair was windblown, her tunic and leggings streaked with dirt. Her face a scowl of concentration, she slammed the window shut and leaned against it, listening intently. Then she spun about and snapped at Bryony, "You ignorant, selfish little gnat. And you, Periwinkle—" She stopped, the anger fading from her face. "Wink?"

There was no reply. Bryony turned and saw Wink lying on the rug an arm's length away. Her eyes were closed, her face colorless.

"Oh, blight," said Thorn wearily. Reaching down, she hauled Bryony to her feet and shoved her into a nearby chair. "Sit there, and don't move. I'll ring for the Healer."

"She has merely fainted," said Valerian, straightening up from the sofa where Wink lay. "I will give her some chamomile tea when she wakes, but she will need rest and quiet to recover."

"Well, she won't get much of that with this one underfoot," said Thorn with a glance at Bryony. "All right, girl, come with me. You can explain yourself to the Queen—"

"That will not be necessary," said a lofty voice, and they all turned to see Bluebell, the Queen's attendant, standing in the doorway. "Her Majesty has sent me to investigate. Am I to understand that this child actually"—she paused and gave a little shudder—"crawled *out* of the Oak?"

"Yes, and in another two heartbeats she'd have been

down that human boy's gullet," said Thorn. "If there weren't so few of us already, I'd say it was no more than the silly chit deserved."

"Human?" said Bryony, testing out the strange word.

"But this cannot be," said Bluebell, looking alarmed. "Every morning the Queen renews her spells of protection about the Oak for this very purpose: to keep the humans at bay."

"It works on grown humans, no doubt," said Thorn. "But children are chancy little weasels. And speaking of which, this one"—she pointed at Bryony—"has obviously grown too wild for Wink to manage. Someone else will have to take the brat."

"I shall consult Her Majesty," said Bluebell, and Bryony's stomach squirmed. What if the Queen sent her to live with someone like Thorn? Or, even worse, Mallow?

"I'm sorry," she burst out. "Let me stay with Wink. I'll be good from now on—"

"You," said Thorn, whipping around to glare at her, "shut up. The trouble you're in right now, you'll be lucky if the Queen doesn't clip your wings and make you scrub the chamber pots until you're fifty."

Bryony's eyes grew huge. She sat back in the chair, hands clasped meekly in her lap.

"Well," said Bluebell, "that seems a little extreme— the Queen is merciful. But clearly the child needs to be educated."

"Leave her to me," said Thorn. She strode forward,

seizing Bryony by the elbow and yanking her to her feet. "I'll put some fear into her."

"If you plan to beat her—" began Bluebell, but Thorn cut her off.

"I've got something better than a willow switch," she said, "believe me." And with that, she pushed Bryony toward the door.

Panicking, Bryony dug in her heels, but Thorn merely grabbed the back of her tunic and lifted her into the air. The fabric bunched beneath her wings, and Bryony kicked and twisted, but Thorn marched out of the room with her, undaunted. When they reached the landing she dropped Bryony back onto her feet and said, "Six winters ago your egg-mother went out of the Oak in the middle of an ice storm and froze herself to death. By the time I found her, she'd already given up the last of her magic and vanished: There was nothing left but a pile of old clothes—and you. The first intact egg we'd found in Gardener knows how many years, and we all held our breath for fear you wouldn't hatch. D'you think the Queen a fool, making rules on a whim? You could have died out there today."

"He wasn't going to hurt me," Bryony protested. "He only wanted to play—"

"So do cats," said Thorn. "And they eat you afterward. Now you can walk, or I can carry you over my shoulder like a dead shrew, but either way you're going down that Stair."

"What are you going to do to me?"

"You'll see," said Thorn. "Now move."

With dry mouth and leaden feet, Bryony obeyed. Thorn prodded her down two full turns of the Spiral Stair to the next landing, then across the walkway and around the curve of the hall to an unfamiliar door. There Thorn rapped with her knuckles and waited, fingers drumming on the hilt of her bone dagger. When it became clear that no one would answer, she put her shoulder to the door and shoved it open.

The room smelled stale inside, and the air was cloudy with dust. Thorn lit a lamp and carried it over to a narrow cot heaped with blankets, where a faery lay on her back, open-eyed and still.

"Look," said Thorn. "Do you recognize her?"

Of course Bryony knew who it must be. But the figure in the bed looked so wizened and frail, so unlike her former apple-cheeked self, that it would have been easier to believe her a stranger. Her once ageless skin had turned white as ash flakes, showing the veins beneath. Her arms and legs were gaunt, and her scalp bore only a few clumps of grayish hair. She smelled of comfrey ointment but even more strongly of decay, and Bryony stumbled back from the bed, clapping her hands to her mouth.

"That's right," said Thorn. "It's Sorrel. She used to slip you treats from the kitchen, didn't she, when Mallow wasn't looking? She wasn't even that old, you know. Only a hundred and ninety."

"What . . . happened to her?"

"We call it the Silence." Thorn drew the blankets back up over Sorrel again. "First you become short-tempered—sometimes even violent. Then you get confused, and babble nonsense. Soon you're too weak to move, too cold for any fire to warm. Finally you end up like this." She gestured to the figure in the bed. "Not moving, not responding. You lose your hearing, your sight, every sense and feeling. Eventually you just . . . fade . . . away."

Bryony swallowed. "But I thought . . . we didn't get sick."

"So did the rest of us," said Thorn, "until this started happening. Did you never wonder why there are so few of us? I suppose not, as an empty Oak is all you've ever known. But when I was your age, there were twice as many of us—and that was even after things got so bad the Queen had to order everyone to stay inside."

Bryony's head swam. She closed her eyes, trying to shut out the image of Sorrel's wasted body. "You mean they all—died like this?"

"Great Gardener, no," said Thorn. "But even a few is too many. It was bad enough when we only had to worry about faeries doing fool things out of doors and getting themselves killed; more often than not their eggs got smashed or eaten by the crows before we could find them. But when the Silence takes a faery, it's even worse, because then there's no egg at all."

Nausea overwhelmed Bryony. "I didn't—I never knew—"

"Of course you didn't," said Thorn flatly, "because Wink didn't want to give you nightmares. I always did say that woman was too softhearted."

"But—" Bryony was still struggling to understand. "Where does the Silence come from?"

"Ah, that's the question," said Thorn. "Nobody knows, not even the Queen. But I've seen this happen a few times now, and you know what I think?" She beckoned Bryony closer, bent, and hissed in her ear, "It's the *humans*."

Shocked, Bryony jerked away. "Got your attention now, haven't I?" Thorn said. "Think about it. The House was built just over a hundred years ago . . . and the Silence came not long after. Do you really think that's just coincidence?"

She was right, Bryony realized, looking down at her own hands in horror. She had reached out to the human child— the *boy*. What would have happened if she had touched him?

"There are only forty-six of us left now," Thorn pressed on, "and with those humans right on our doorstep, staying in the Oak is our best hope of staying alive. So if you don't want to end up in the same nutshell as Sorrel—"

Bryony could bear it no longer. She whirled, stumbling

on the rug, and rushed from the room as fast as her legs would carry her. As she dashed back up the Spiral Stair, she tried to think of her toys, her books, Wink's mirror—anything but the terrible thing Thorn had shown her. . . .

She flung herself through Wink's door and collided with someone tall. Staggering back, she looked up into the austere face and grave gray eyes of Valerian—and with that, Bryony burst into tears.

"You needn't worry about the child now," said Thorn's voice from behind her, as Bluebell clucked reproachfully and Valerian stroked Bryony's hair. "She won't do it again."

Two

ryony sat back on her haunches, wiping her brow with her forearm. All morning she'd been scrubbing the floor of the Dining Hall, polishing each cobble until it shone, but she was still nowhere near finished. As usual, Mallow had given Bryony the most grueling chore she could find.

But the window behind her stood open, the sound of gentle rainfall mingling with the fragrance of wet grass and new-turned soil, and Bryony inhaled deeply as she worked. Nearly seven years had passed since she stepped out of the Oak and met the human boy, but she had never forgotten that bittersweet taste of freedom. And though her dread of the Silence had kept her from venturing out again, she still often found herself thinking about it.

Everything had changed after that day, much of it for the worse: She had been taken away from Wink and given to Valerian, who had filled Bryony's days with work and study and left her no chance to be idle. When she had learned how to read, write, and do her duty to the Queen's satisfaction, she had been moved into a small room of her own near the foot of the Spiral Stair and told that she must carry out whatever tasks the older faeries gave her, until she was old enough to be given an occupation of her own.

Since then Bryony had done everything from carding rabbit wool to digging out new privies, but all the while she knew what she really longed for: to be a Gatherer. It was hard work, she knew, with no time for exploration or flight; it was also dangerous, for a faery with a basket on her back was an easy mark for predators if she did not remain alert. But neither of those things would trouble Bryony, she felt sure, if only she could go outdoors again.

Gatherers were chosen for their strength and endurance rather than their wits, but Bryony felt confident she had enough of both to be a good candidate. The only question was, would the Queen feel the same? Or would her magical Sight tell her to place Bryony in some other position, and she would simply have to make the best of it?

Until recently Bryony had not troubled herself with such questions, since she was still too young to do a grown faery's work. But over the winter she had shot up like a sapling, her spindly child's frame filling out, and now she was a fly's length taller than anyone else in the Oak. She had also worked hard to prove herself dutiful at all her tasks, no matter how unpleasant. At any time the Queen might summon her to an audience, and Bryony was determined to be ready.

She bent again to her work, wielding the brush with renewed vigor. One more hour, she told herself, and she'd be finished. Then she could have a bath and pick out a book from the library, to reward herself after yet another of Mallow's miserable chores well done.

"Bryony! Where are you?"

The voice came faintly down the corridor, muffled by echoes. But it sounded like Bluebell, and Bryony snapped her head up to listen. If the Queen's attendant was looking for her . . .

"There you are!" exclaimed Bluebell, bustling into the Dining Hall. "What are you doing here? The kitchens are empty, and we've all been waiting for you this age! Mallow said she gave you my message an hour ago."

Of course she did, thought Bryony with a spark of anger. No doubt it had pleased the Chief Cook to leave her scrubbing the floor when she should be getting ready for the most important moment of her life. She flung the brush into the bucket and stood up.

"Oh, dear Gardener," said Bluebell, "you can't go before

the Queen looking like that!" She whisked Bryony around and gave her a little push toward the door. "To the bath, and then off to Wink—hurry!"

There was no time for argument. Bryony took off at a sprint, vaulting tables as she went, and raced down the corridor to the bath chamber. The water in the great tub was cold, but Bryony gritted her teeth and plunged in, scrubbing at the dirt beneath her fingernails. She soaped and rinsed her hair, then leaped out of the bath again, snatching up a towel to cover herself as she fled. Rushing back along the empty tunnel, she took the Spiral Stair two steps at a time, arriving breathless and dripping at Wink's door.

She had barely knocked before it flew open, and a pair of fluttering hands tugged her inside. "I thought you'd never get here! Quick—put these on!" Wink said, and she thrust a white shift and a length of silky, thistle-colored stuff into Bryony's arms.

Bryony wormed her way into the petticoat, then the gown. It smelled of dust and rose petals, and the fabric was so fine that it seemed to weigh nothing at all. The sleeves were mere puffs, the neckline low and square, and the skirt fell in soft folds from the bodice to brush against her ankles.

"It's too short," fretted Wink, bustling around her and twitching various bits of the dress into place. "I knew it would be, even after I let it out—you can breathe, though, can't you? Only don't breathe *too* much," she added in haste as Bryony began to inhale. "You'll split the seams, and Campion will never let me hear the end of it. Whatever took you so long?"

"I didn't know," said Bryony.

Wink picked up a comb and set to work on her hair. "You mean—Mallow didn't tell you? Of all the spiteful things to do! Well, she'll be sorry when—"

"Is she ready yet?" asked Bluebell from behind them, and Bryony turned to see the Queen's attendant standing in the doorway, one foot tapping with impatience.

"Oh, I wanted to put her hair up. Well, never mind," Wink said, and she handed Bryony a pair of slippers.

Bryony bent to put on the shoes. Like the dress, they were too small, but she would have to manage. Already Wink was tugging her toward Bluebell, who looked her up and down and sighed. "I suppose it can't be helped. Here." She held out a long, downy-plumed feather.

"What's this for?" Bryony asked.

"You're to give it to Her Majesty," said Bluebell. "It's part of the ceremony. Now hurry!"

Bryony stopped short at the entrance to the Queen's Hall, gazing up at the festive tapestries hanging from the rafters. Though worn with age, their colors were a wonder, as were the intricate patterns of birds and flowers they depicted. No faery alive knew how to dye such tints anymore, much less make pictures from them, and the sight of them brought a lump to Bryony's throat. It seemed so wrong that this marvelous craft, like so many other creative things her people had done in the past, was now lost to the Oak forever.

Bluebell cleared her throat loudly in Bryony's ear, then announced, "Her gracious Majesty, Queen Amaryllis, invites her subject to approach."

The far end of the high-vaulting chamber was taken up by a semicircular dais. Atop this stood a chair carved with twining vines, and in it sat the Queen of the Oakenfolk. Her silken gown flowed about her feet, and her hair was the color of honey wine, crowned by a circlet set with emeralds. Her features were lovely, but her eyes held no warmth, and her expression gave nothing away.

"Go on," whispered Bluebell, poking Bryony in the back.

Until now Bryony had felt strangely calm. After she had kept the Queen waiting for Gardener-only-knew how long and then shown up with damp hair and an ill-fitting gown, there had seemed no way that her situation could be any worse. But then she remembered why she was here, and how badly she wanted to be a Gatherer, and as she took her first step, she stumbled.

Whispers ran up and down the hall, and Bryony's cheeks glowed with humiliation. Deliberately she squared her shoulders and walked forward, holding the feather before her. *Just not the scullery*, she prayed silently, *anything but the scullery* . . . because no matter how disappointed she might be at not being a Gatherer, it would be far worse to end up apprenticed to Mallow.

She had just reached the end of the carpet when the Queen spoke, her voice chill and remote:

"Kneel."

Bryony dropped to both knees, wincing as the seam beneath her armpit ripped. She could sense the Queen's searching gaze upon her; it was not a comfortable feeling.

"Faery," said Queen Amaryllis, "do you this day give me your service?"

"I do," said Bryony.

"Give her the feather," hissed Bluebell, and Bryony rose awkwardly and walked forward to offer her plume to the Queen.

"I accept your service," said Amaryllis. "And do you give me your honor?"

Bryony wasn't sure exactly what that meant, but it sounded harmless enough. "I do," she said.

"I accept your honor," the Queen said, then, in a lower voice, "and do you give me . . . your name?"

Bryony froze. In addition to the common-name inherited from her egg-mother, each faery was born with a secret name that belonged only to her—and whoever knew that name could command her absolutely. Was this really how the Queen made sure of her subjects' loyalty? Would it be considered treason to refuse?

In the end she could think of only one answer that was not an outright denial, and her voice shook as she replied: "My name is Bryony, Your Majesty."

A sigh rippled through the hall, and Amaryllis sat back with an enigmatic smile. "I accept your name. And now I call upon the wisdom of the Sight, that I might declare to you the nature of your service. . . ."

There was a long pause while the Queen's hyacinth-blue eyes slid out of focus and then sharpened again. "Bryony," she said, "you are apprenticed to Thorn."

"What?" yelped a familiar voice from the back of the hall, but it was quickly hushed into silence by the other Oaken-folk. Up on the dais Bryony's knees buckled, and her head spun like a dropped acorn; it was all she could do to keep from falling. "I . . . beg your pardon?" she said weakly.

"So the Sight has told me," said Queen Amaryllis, "and so it shall be. You will be trained as my new Hunter." She spoke with confidence, but an ember of uncertainty flickered behind her eyes. "May the Gardener protect you and give you success, Bryony of the Oak."

In her wildest imaginings, Bryony had never anticipated this. The most dangerous task in the Oak—and yet it was also the most free. Gatherers were forced to plod and dig, and hide in burrows for safety; but the Queen's Hunter flew, protecting herself by speed and skill alone. The task required not only a strong body and a steady hand but sharp eyes and quick wits as well—and best of all, it meant leaving the Oak on a regular basis, not just during the growing season but all year round. Thorn would be a hard mentor, Bryony knew, but right now not even that thought could diminish her joy.

"Your Majesty," she stammered, bowing deeply to the Queen. "I can hardly tell you—" But Amaryllis only shook her head, averting her gaze to the crowd below.

"You are dismissed," she told them in a clear voice. "Thorn, come and claim your apprentice." Then without another word she rose, beckoned Bluebell after her, and swept out of the hall.

Bryony wandered back down the aisle, still dazed. As she neared her fellow Oakenfolk she heard whispers, many of them scornful or pitying; few seemed to think she would succeed in her new position, and some even doubted she would survive. Mallow especially looked smug, as though she thought Bryony's new occupation a fitting punishment—but her smirk faded as Thorn shoved past her and planted herself by Bryony's side.

"Well?" she said to the other faeries. "She's my apprentice, not yours, so off with you."

Grumbling, the others filed away. Only Wink paused, dabbing at one eye as though she had something in it, before hurrying out after the rest.

"Gardener's mercy," muttered Thorn. "What a cuckoo's egg this day's turned out to be. All right, girl"—she turned to Bryony—"get out of that frippery you're wearing and put on some proper clothes. We're going outdoors."

Wink wrung her hands when she saw the damage to the gown, but she also lost no time in finding a tunic, waistcoat, and breeches for Bryony to wear. Bryony could only suppose that it must be the privilege of Hunters to have their wardrobe provided without cost, for not only did Wink refuse to bargain with her, she apologized for the ill-fitting clothes and promised to make her better ones soon. This was pleasant. However, Wink also kept sighing and giving her mournful glances, which was not nearly so pleasant, and Bryony was glad to finally get away.

She found Thorn by the Queen's Gate, near the foot of the Spiral Stair. Together they hauled the heavy door open, climbed the ladder of roots, and emerged from the Oak into a misty gray afternoon. The sunlight filtered dimly through the veil of cloud, and the air smelled of earth and green things. Thorn stalked straight out across the lawn, her bow and quiver dangling at her side; but Bryony lingered, gazing up at the colossal bulk of the Tree. She had never viewed it from this angle before, and the sight of it filled her with awe.

The Oak was at least five centuries old, and in happier days it had sheltered more than two hundred faeries within its hollow heart. Even by human standards it was huge, and Bryony supposed that only Queen Amaryllis's spells had kept the humans from trying to live there as well. Carriers of the Silence or not, it was almost enough to make her pity them, for how could their House of dead stone compare to the majesty of the living Oak?

"Stop dawdling and move," snapped Thorn. "We've work to do."

Bryony hurried to catch up with her. Picking their way through the damp earth of the flower beds, they ducked beneath the privet hedge and skidded down the dew-slick incline into the field beyond. The grass grew long here, mingled with weeds and wildflowers, and nearby she could hear the gurgling of the brook from which the Oakenfolk drew their water.

"Right," said Thorn. "Lesson number one: How not to get killed." She shielded her eyes with one hand and squinted upward. "The first thing to do when you leave the Oak, always, is to look out for predators. Most birds and animals ignore us, but foxes will eat us if they get the chance, as will cats, owls, and especially crows." She lowered her hand and turned slowly, scanning the field in all directions as she went on. "There's one big, ugly crow in particular—Old Wormwood, we call him—that you'll need to watch out for. He killed Foxglove, the Hunter before me, and he's been hungering for another taste of faery ever since."

Bryony glanced apprehensively at her weaponless hands. "So what do we do if we see him?"

Thorn snorted. "You have to ask? We hide, of course. In the Oak, if we can get there quick enough, or down the nearest burrow we can find."

"Oh," said Bryony, feeling oddly disappointed.

"Sky's clear," said Thorn. "Right, then, follow me." And with that, she spread her wings and took off.

Inexperienced as she was, Bryony did not falter. She leaped blindly after Thorn, trusting her instincts to take over—and they did. A heart-stopping dip, a few wobbles, and she was airborne. *This is it*, she thought, terrified and exhilarated all at once. *I'm flying!*

At first they glided in a straight line, skimming low over the grass toward the nearby wood. Then Thorn banked away from the trees, and Bryony carefully followed her example. When her teacher angled upward, she did likewise, tentative at first but gaining confidence with every wing stroke.

As Thorn led her through a series of simple maneuvers, Bryony's nervousness melted away as she realized how quickly she could move through the air, how the mere flick of a wingtip could send her veering off in another direction. She could dive, she could roll, she could even hover in place, like the dragonfly her wings resembled. All her life she had yearned to fly, but she had never expected it to be so *easy*.

No longer content to follow Thorn's example, Bryony

began to zigzag across the field. Distantly she heard Thorn shout, and reminded herself to watch for crows. But when a quick glance showed none in sight, she launched herself skyward again.

Soaring on an updraft, she noticed for the first time a line of tall poles at the southern edge of the field. They were linked by dark ropes—a barrier of some sort? The topmost strand was dotted with sparrows. Curious, she glided closer. . . .

"Stop!" came a cry, and Bryony glanced back to see Thorn speeding through the air toward her. "*Never* touch those wires!" she snapped, grabbing Bryony by the arm and wrenching her around. Startled, Bryony dropped like a stone, dragging Thorn down with her. They tumbled into the grass, perilously close to a patch of nettles, and for a few moments they were both too winded to speak.

"Don't ever go off like that without me again," said Thorn, panting. She clambered to her feet and began brushing herself off. Still dazed, Bryony stared up at the poles towering above her.

"What . . . are they?" she asked.

"I don't know what they're called, or what they do. They're human things. All I know is that there's magic in them, and if you touch them, you'll be dead before you hit the ground."

"But the birds—"

"Is your head made of solid wood?" exploded Thorn. "You're not a bird! And neither was Henbane. One of those ropes came down in a storm, she went to look, one touch, and zap! There was nothing left of her. Not even an egg."

"You saw it happen?"

"No, but Foxglove did—my old mentor. What, did you think I was making it all up out of my head?"

Thorn's tone was sardonic, and Bryony felt her face burn. "No," she said. "I just wondered how you knew."

"Valerian keeps a book," said Thorn. "Every time one of our people dies, it's written down: the name, and the way she died. And if you don't want your name to be next, you'd better listen to me when I call you. The *first* time, d'you hear?"

"I hear you," said Bryony, wincing as she rose. Her whole body ached, especially the wing muscles.

Thorn glanced up at the sky again. "We've been out here long enough," she said. "Best to head back, before the crows start getting interested." She stomped off through the grass.

"Have you ever fought one?" asked Bryony, hurrying to keep up with her. "A crow, I mean."

"If I had," said Thorn, "I wouldn't be talking to you now."

"And what about humans? How do you deal with them?"

"I don't," said Thorn flatly. "And neither will you, if

you've half as much wits as a rabbit. When they're mucking about in the garden, or cutting the grass with that noisy wagon of theirs, we lie low and wait until they're gone." She gave Bryony a sharp look. "Unless you have some other idea?"

Bryony shook her head.

"I didn't think so. Now if you're ready to use your wings properly instead of playing the fool with them, it's time we were flying home."

From that point on, the weeks blurred together as Bryony spent day after day with Thorn, learning the Hunter's craft. At her mentor's command, she ran, climbed, and flew about the Oakenwyld, ever more aware of its dangers, but growing bolder nonetheless. Flying was still her greatest pleasure, but soon she began to enjoy her lessons for other reasons as well: her pride in her growing strength and agility, the excitement of hunting prey, and the bargaining power her new skills gave her. Now at last she could barter with her fellow faeries as an equal and get things like proper candles and whole bars of soap, instead of having to make do with the stubs and scraps she had earned doing chores.

On days when bad weather or human activity kept them inside the Oak, Thorn taught Bryony to make her own weapons, then to use them. Once she had crafted her first bow and arrows she fired at targets until she could hit the center eight times out of ten before moving on to mice, frogs, and flying insects. Her fingers grew calloused, her muscles wiry; her senses of smell, hearing, and vision became acute.

Thorn taught her how to gut a kill and cut it up quickly before the crows could come to investigate. She showed Bryony the best hiding places the Oakenwyld had to offer, and the secret hedge tunnel into the Oak that only the Hunters and Gatherers knew. And as Bryony listened and learned, and practiced her new skills, she felt more and more certain that the Queen's magical Sight had not deceived her: Of all the tasks in the Oak, this was what she, Bryony, had been meant to do.

One summer evening Bryony and Thorn were coming home from a successful hunt, their packs heavy with squirrel meat, when Bryony spotted a dark shape perched at the top of a nearby tree. It was a crow, a big one—and its yellow eyes were fixed hungrily on them.

"It's him," hissed Thorn. "Old Wormwood. Run!"

She and Bryony leaped toward the shelter of the hedge, but the crow swooped down to block their path, croaking. One black wing knocked Bryony off her feet, and by the time she struggled upright Thorn was trapped beneath the crow's scaly talon, yelling as its beak stabbed at her. A moment later Old Wormwood tossed his head back and swallowed, and Bryony felt sick; then she realized that Thorn had managed to shove her pack in front of her, and the crow was gobbling up their store of meat instead.

There was no time to think, only to act. Bryony flung her pack aside, snatched the bone knife from her belt, and launched herself at the crow. As she dropped astride his back, the reek of dust and carnage made her head reel; her knees skidded across his slick feathers, and she tumbled off before she could even strike a blow. But she landed on her feet, and when Old Wormwood flapped about to face her, Bryony was ready for him. With all her strength she drove her dagger into his shoulder, and the great crow shrieked.

The next few heartbeats passed in a frenzy of black feathers and thrashing wings. Bryony's bone knife snapped, and she staggered back with the useless hilt still in her hand. Her leg stung like fire, but she ignored the pain as she scooped up a pebble and hurled it at the crow's head. It glanced off his skull, and with a squawk Old Wormwood leaped into the air, wings beating.

Thorn clawed her way up the slope and disappeared among the roots of the hedge, leaving her pack behind. Bryony threw another stone to keep the crow at bay, then darted after her. Exhausted, they lay together in the darkness, watching Old Wormwood peck at their abandoned packs. When nothing remained but a few shreds of leather, he gave a querulous caw and flapped away.

Thorn was the first to crawl through to the far side of the hedge. She moved stiffly, one hand pressed to her bruised ribs. "You midge-wit. You could have been killed!"

Bryony limped out to join her. Her leg still bled where the crow's talon had scratched it, but fortunately the wound was not deep. "I know," she said.

"You attacked him. A full-grown crow." Thorn shook her head in disbelief. "Why didn't you run?"

"I don't know," said Bryony. "It just—it seemed like the only thing to do."

"You," said Thorn shortly, "are mad." She shouldered her quiver and began walking toward the Oak. Bryony followed, but they had only gone a few paces before Thorn stopped. She bowed her head, and purple tinged her cheeks as she muttered, "And I suppose . . . I owe you my life."

"Oh," Bryony said, and then, "well," but she couldn't think of any other reply.

"Just *never* do anything as flea-brained as that again!" snapped Thorn, and stomped away.

"I wounded him, though," said Bryony, catching up to her. "He'll be stiff in that shoulder from now on."

Thorn gave an incredulous snort and kept walking.

"If we fight together," Bryony continued, "we might even be able to kill him."

Her teacher whirled on her, seized her by both shoulders, and shook her so hard, her ears rang. "Don't you *ever* think about that again. It's impossible, even for you. Do you hear me?"

Bryony heard the words, but the warning in them scarcely registered. Only one phrase echoed in her mind: *even for you.*

Her head felt light; coming from Thorn, that could be no idle flattery. *Impossible, even for you.*

Not impossible, she thought as she watched the older faery stalk away. *All I need is a better knife.*

Three

"You're making that edge too thin," said Thorn.

Bryony scarcely heard her, all her concentration focused on chipping her new knife into shape. This was her latest of several attempts at crafting a fighting blade, but deep down she knew it would fail like all the others. The more she honed the edges, the sooner they crumbled; the sharper the point, the more readily it would snap.

"This is useless," she said at last, throwing the flint down. "Why don't we have any real weapons?"

"Made of metal, you mean?" asked Thorn, brushing a curl of wood from the stake she was whittling. It was raining, so there was little for either of them to do but sit in the East Root and wait for the clouds to move on. "Why should we?"

"Why shouldn't we? There are metal things in the Oak."

"Only what's left over from the Days of Magic. Lanterns, bits of jewelry, a few tools. But most of that's brass or copper, too soft for weapons. Anyway, the Queen doesn't like too much metal around: You never know what it might be made of."

"What do you mean?"

"Cold iron," said Thorn impatiently, and when Bryony still looked blank she went on: "It stops magic—if it's pure, that is. But there isn't much iron around here anymore; these days you mostly find steel."

"Steel," said Bryony. "That's iron mixed with . . . ?"

"Gardener knows," said Thorn. "All I know is that if I happen to bump into some, I can still fly afterward, and that's good enough for me."

It had never before occurred to Bryony to think of flying as magical, but now she realized that it must be. "So we still have some magic after all."

"Well, it isn't much use, since we can't control it," said Thorn. "Now and then one of us manages to cast a spell by accident—I saw Foxglove change size once, trying to get down a mouse hole. But it always wears off in an hour or two." She gave a little snort and added, "You can't use it to kill Old Wormwood, if that's what you were thinking."

Bryony pushed the heels of her hands against her eyes. "There has to be *some* metal we could use," she said.

"Not in the Oak," said Thorn. "Unless you'd like to

march up to the House and ask the humans for it?"

Bryony's mouth flattened as she picked up a new flint and bent once more to her work. Much as she had learned to respect Thorn, there were times when the older faery's black humor went too far.

But then a thought struck her: Did either of them really *know* that humans carried the Silence? After all, Bryony herself ought to be dead by now, if getting close to a human was all it took. What if Thorn had been wrong, and the disease came from some other source? In which case going to the House for metal might not be such a bad idea after all. . . .

I need to talk to Valerian, Bryony decided. The Healer had treated several cases of the Silence by now: If anyone knew how the illness worked, she would.

"What would you ask of me?" said Valerian. Her manner was formal but courteous, and she seemed only mildly surprised to find Bryony at her door.

"Knowledge," said Bryony.

"And what have you to offer in return?"

"Herbs, any kind you like." It would be easy enough to pick them the next time she and Thorn went hunting, and no doubt Valerian would appreciate not having to wait for the Gatherers to get around to it.

Valerian's brows rose. "Agreed. I'd like chervil, if you can find some; if not, I can always use more comfrey or willow bark. Your question?"

"Is there any way to protect yourself against the Silence?"

"None that I know," said Valerian. Then, at the look of disappointment on Bryony's face, she added, "Why do you ask? It's been years since Sorrel died, and you shouldn't be in any danger, not at your age."

"At my age?" Bryony was startled. "You mean you have to be older?"

"Quite a bit older, I'd say. I'd hesitate to give an exact number, but so far, all the Oakenfolk I've seen taken by the Silence had been born well before the Sundering." She gave a sad smile. "Even if they were too confused to remember it."

"But they all had some contact with humans," said Bryony. "How much does it take?"

Valerian frowned. "I beg your pardon?"

"It's just"—Bryony hesitated, then plunged in—"now that I'm spending so much time outdoors, I'm afraid that one of these days I might end up crossing paths with a human again. So I need to know how serious—"

"What makes you think the Silence has anything to do with humans?" Valerian sounded genuinely perplexed.

"You mean it doesn't?"

"I can't think how it would," said Valerian. "None of the Oakenfolk I've treated had ever gone near a human—at least, not in my lifetime. In fact, one of my earliest cases was so terrified of humans that she refused to open her window even in summer, for fear of seeing one. And Daisy was such a timid little thing I can't imagine she'd ever been different, even before she lost her magic."

Bryony sagged against the door frame, relieved. So it wasn't true, this thing she'd grown up believing. Her instincts had been right, and Thorn was wrong.

Which meant that as long as she didn't let the humans catch her, she could sneak right into their House to look for metal, and no one would even know. . . .

"Are you all right?" asked Valerian. "Do you need to lie down?"

"No," said Bryony. "I'm fine."

Outside Bryony's window the Oakenwyld lay shadowed, a sliver of moon barely visible in the cloud-streaked sky. Leaning on the sill, Bryony stared out across the garden, her stomach tight with anticipation.

Even if she could find some shard or snippet of metal inside the House, could she really escape with it undetected? And if the worst happened and she was caught, what might the humans do to her?

Bryony drew a deep breath and let it out. Then she climbed up onto the windowsill and dove headfirst into the darkness.

Her translucent wings snapped open, and she glided down to the surface of the lawn, bare feet almost brushing the grass. At this hour most of the Oakenfolk were in bed, but she paused and glanced back over her shoulder just in case. If anyone knew that she was out at night, alone . . .

But the great tree's trunk remained dark, its windows closed. Reassured, Bryony turned and resumed her flight toward the House. As its gray bulk loomed up in her path her resolve began to falter, and for a moment she almost turned aside; then she remembered what she had come for—*metal, the humans have metal*—and made herself carry on.

Soon the lawn beneath her gave way to stone pavement, and she drew herself up sharply, landing just outside the House's back entrance. A pair of doors inset with glass panes towered above her, glowing with muted light. What would she find on the other side? Summoning courage, she pressed her face to the bottom pane and peered in.

At first she could make out only dim shapes. She cupped her hands against the glass, squinting through the sheer curtains. What she saw then made her gasp, and she let her hands drop, stunned. The ugly stone House, where the human monsters lived . . . inside, it was *beautiful*.

Never in her life had she seen such magnificently crafted furniture, with its fluid curves and dark wood polished to a sheen. The Oak's finest tapestries were crude compared to the pattern of twining leaves that covered the humans' sofa, and no hand-knotted rug of Wink's could rival the plush carpet that flowed across their floor. Even the walls were impossibly smooth and straight . . . were they really painted blue, or had it just been a trick of the light?

Wait. The light. Where did it come from? She had seen no fire, no candles, yet the whole room shone with radiance. Bryony darted back to the window, intent. Ah, there was the source: a pair of lamps set on either side of the sofa. But how could the flames inside them burn so steadily? And why did their papery shades not catch alight?

Magic, she thought in dismay. *The humans have magic.*

Bryony sat down heavily on the doorstep. She knew, now, that the humans could not be monsters. They might still be dangerous, but they were not animals, living by mere instinct. They were intelligent. They were *people.*

All at once a shadow passed over her, and she leaped up in panic before realizing that she was still safe, that the dark shape remained on the far side of the door. In fact, with such bright light coming from inside the House, and nothing but darkness in the garden where she stood, it would be difficult for the humans to see her unless they already knew where to look. Silently rebuking herself for her cowardice, she crouched by the window again.

"Did you see?" The voice sounded hollowly from the other side of the glass. "We had a letter from Paul today."

The speaker was an older female, her hair a loose cap of brown curls streaked with silver. She picked up a tray from the tea table and padded out of sight again, adding as she went, "He's sounding much happier lately. I wonder if he's met someone?"

They speak our language, thought Bryony in amazement. *How could they have lived so close to us for so many years, and we never knew?*

"I doubt that," said a deeper voice, and Bryony craned her neck to see a second human enter the room and sit down in one of the armchairs. She frowned a moment, bemused by the square jaw, flat chest and heavy hands; then she realized that the two humans were a mated pair, and this must be the male. What a strange-looking creature he was! But he also reminded her of the boy she had met climbing the Oak, all those years ago. Did he live in the House, too?

"Well anyway, he's enjoying the choir," offered the woman, "and they've made him captain of the rowing team this year."

"Beatrice," said the man, waving a folded piece of paper at her, "I can read."

His mate made a clucking noise and was silent. Eventually the man let the page fall to his lap and leaned back in his chair with a sigh.

"Away for Christmas," he said dolefully.

"Oh, George, he's young. At sixteen, would you have given up an opportunity to go to Paris just to sit at home with your parents? At least he'll be well looked after, and we'll have him for the New Year."

"I suppose." He tossed the envelope onto the tea table. It skittered across the surface and tumbled to the floor. Bryony read the address written on it quickly—*George and Beatrice McCormick*—then ducked back into the shadows as the man approached.

"Do you need help with those dishes?" he asked, stooping to retrieve the letter. "I'll dry up, if you like."

"All right," said the woman, and then as if it were nothing she added, "Thanks."

Bryony took a step back, appalled. How could the human *thank* her mate, just like that? Putting herself forever in his debt, all for the sake of a few dishes?

On the other hand, she realized as the shock subsided, the man had seemed just as unconscious of his own strange behavior—offering help without being asked for it, and not even taking the time to bargain. Did he really value his own services so little? Wasn't he afraid that his mate would take advantage of him?

Or was it possible that these two humans had reached some sort of understanding, and no longer needed to bargain with each other at all?

Part of her wanted to stay and find out. But she had wasted enough time already: She could see no useful metal here, and she dared not go into that room in any case. With a last wistful glance through the glass, Bryony backed up a few steps and launched herself up to the next window.

She flitted from kitchen to dining room, to the top level of the House and down again, amazed and fascinated by the things she glimpsed inside. But nowhere did she see anything like a faery-sized knife. Eventually, however, she found a room that looked more promising. It was dimly lit, but as she peered through the gap in the curtains she could see what appeared to be a study. The walls were lined with bookshelves, and across from her stood a desk with papers stacked upon it. And there, beneath the radiance of the swan-necked lamp, sat an earthenware pot holding a few pens, a ruler, and—

"Oh," she whispered reverently.

At first glance it looked like a spear, a pole of gleaming silver just a little shorter than Bryony herself. But instead of the diamond-shaped spearheads that she and Thorn carved, it bore a long, angled blade. The point looked wickedly sharp, and Bryony clapped her hands with excitement. If she could pull that blade free of its shaft, it would make a perfect knife.

The room stood deserted: She had her opportunity, if only she could find a way inside. Bryony crouched, jammed her hands into the crack beneath the window, and yanked upward. For a moment she felt nothing except the sting of scraped knuckles, and she feared that it might be locked. But then came a creak, and the window shifted. It took a few more tooth-gritting efforts, but at last she had made a gap wide enough to squeeze through.

Now was her last chance to turn back. At present she was safe, the humans nowhere in sight, but once she entered the House, anything could happen. If they had magical lights, they might have magical traps as well. Was it worth the risk?

She would just go in a little way at first, she told herself as she lay down upon the sill. That way, she might still have time to escape if anything went wrong. Wriggling through the gap, she clambered to her feet on the far side and waited, every muscle tensed. But nothing happened, and she began to wonder if the humans might not be so magical after all.

Her sensitive wings quivered against her back, eager to taste the air; she hesitated, then spread them wide and glided down to the desk. With both hands she seized the knife on its silver pole, and tugged.

It lifted easily—too easily, for as it came free the whole container tipped over. Scrambling to keep her feet as pens and pencils clattered about her, Bryony did not see the worst of the danger until it was too late: The earthenware pot tumbled off the edge of the desk and crashed to the floor below.

"What was that?" exclaimed the woman's voice from the other room, and her mate replied, "It sounded like it came from the study."

Footsteps in the corridor—too fast, too close. There was

no time to reach the window. She had to find a place to hide. Bryony ran to the other side of the desk, looking frantically in all directions. Seeing below her a basket half filled with crumpled papers, she hurled the knife into it point-first, then leaped after it. She just had time to crouch down and tug a scrap of paper over her head before she heard a snap, and the room flooded with light.

"What is it, George?" asked the woman.

"Something's knocked over my pens," the man called back. "A mouse, I suppose." He paced around the desk, his shadow darkening the basket, and Bryony cringed.

"Oh, good." His mate sounded relieved. "As long as that's all. I'll put out the traps before we go to bed."

"Mm," said the man dubiously, and Bryony heard a scraping noise followed by clinks as he picked up the pot from the floor and dropped his writing tools back into it. Then he put out the lights and left the room, shutting the door behind him.

Bryony pressed her face against her knees, swallowing. He had come so very close to her hiding place, so close that she could smell him—but by the Gardener's mercy he had not scented her. She must get out of the House at once.

Breathing hard, she flung herself from one side of the wastebasket to the other until it tipped over, showering her with crumpled wads of paper. Then she dragged her stolen knife into the moonlight and began to examine it.

The blade was loose, jiggling in its socket. She fiddled with the shaft until she figured out how to twist it apart, and her new knife dropped onto the floor at her feet.

Finally she had the perfect weapon: a slim silver triangle lighter than flint, stronger and more resilient than bone. Its far end bore a slotted tab where it had fit into the barrel—a perfect core for a hilt.

Leaving the two pieces of the barrel lying next to the overturned basket, Bryony crawled out the window and flew back to the Oak, her glittering prize clenched between her teeth.

That night she didn't sleep at all.

Four

Once Bryony had rounded out the grip and bound it with hide and twisted gut, her new knife fit so comfortably in her hand that it might have grown there. Alone in her room, she practiced slashing, stabbing, and even throwing the blade, with a sack of dry grass for a target. Soon she felt ready to try it on a real quarry, but Thorn was never far away when they went hunting, and Bryony dared not risk anyone finding out about her visit to the House, not yet. She would just have to wait for a chance to hunt alone.

As autumn faded into winter, however, Thorn became increasingly reluctant to go outdoors. Not because of Old Wormwood—there had been no sign of him in weeks—but if the weather was not too cold for hunting, it was too damp, or else too windy. Now most of their lessons took place inside the Oak, as Thorn taught Bryony how to tan hides using the brains of the animals they killed. It was a messy, smelly business, and though Bryony had no doubt the knowledge would be useful, it seemed a poor substitute for fresh air and freedom.

By the time the first flakes of snow drifted from the sky, Bryony had lost all interest in tanning, rendering tallow, and the other mundane tasks Thorn was teaching her. She felt restless, ready for a new challenge; more and more her thoughts turned to the House, and the odd creatures who lived in it.

Of course there was no real reason for her to go back there, not now that she had her knife. And yet she was tempted, for the House was so enticingly different from the Oak. The furnishings, the carpets, the draperies—they had all complemented one another in a way that she found strangely satisfying, like a well-cooked meal for her senses. And then of course there were the humans, who had done it all.

How was it that her people knew so little about humans? Before the Sundering took their magical powers, the faeries had freely explored the world beyond the Oak, and made note of everything they learned. The library was full of their observations about every creature imaginable, including the most dangerous predators. How had humans escaped their notice?

Unless—the thought came to her slowly but with the

force of a revelation—there *were* books about humans somewhere in the Oak, and people had just forgotten where to find them?

There had been a time, long before Bryony was born, when the library had bustled with activity. The well-worn seats of the chairs that ringed the central table, the creased spines and ragged pages of the books upon the shelves, bore witness to an enthusiasm for learning that was now almost unknown among the Oakenfolk. There was even a tall bookcase designed to show off the latest additions to the collection—but now it held nothing but dust, for there were no authors in the Oak these days, any more than there were painters or musicians. Somehow the faeries' creativity, like their passion for scholarship, had died.

The Oak's Librarian was also responsible for the archives and storerooms, so Bryony was not surprised to find her desk empty. Most likely Campion was with the Gatherers, making sure her records of the Oak's winter stores were accurate, or else polishing up the lanterns and other ancient decorations for the Midwinter Feast. Bryony picked up the mallet and rapped the brass gong upon the desk, sending a deep metallic note reverberating through the room and into the corridor.

When Campion appeared a few moments later she looked harried, with a streak of dirt across one cheek and her hair in disarray. "You wanted something?" she said.

"I'm looking for books about humans," said Bryony.

Campion looked wary. "Did the Queen send you?"

"No," said Bryony. "I just wanted to find out more about them."

The Librarian relaxed visibly. Stepping behind the desk, she took down her catalog and began turning pages. "Well, I do have a few volumes in a special collection," she said. "If you had a particular subject in mind . . ."

"Special collection? Why aren't they on the main shelves?"

Again that shrewd look from Campion, as though she was trying to decide what to make of Bryony's request. "Because they're . . . special," she said. "And rare. I can't give them to just anyone."

"Look," said Bryony, exasperated, "I thought helping people find books was supposed to be your duty, but if you want me to bargain, I will. I have a nice piece of squirrel fur, freshly tanned and just the right size for a bedspread. You can have that, if you like. But then I'll want to see all the books you've got, not just one or two."

Campion blinked, as though taken aback by the hand-some offer—or perhaps just by Bryony's boldness. With a furtive glance at the door she said, "Well . . . all right. But," she added as she led Bryony toward the back of the library, "this stays between us. You're a Hunter, so I suppose you have good reason to know, but I don't think the Queen would be pleased if everyone started reading them."

At the back of the library, almost invisible in the shadows between the shelves, stood a narrow door. Campion unlocked this with one of the keys at her belt, and let Bryony into a closet where a single chair sat beside a tall case bulging with books. "There," she said.

"Which ones?" asked Bryony.

"All of them," said Campion with a touch of impatience. "There's a lamp and a tinderbox on the top shelf. Keep the door closed while you're reading, and let me know when you've had enough. I'm going back to the storeroom." And with that she disappeared, leaving Bryony staring up at the shelf and wondering where to begin.

It seemed she had found something to do over the winter after all.

After that, Bryony visited the secret closet as often as she could. Campion became accustomed to her presence in the library, and even began leaving the key for her as a matter of course. By Midwinter, Bryony had read every book on the shelves, some of them twice over.

One thing at least had become plain: The Oakenfolk's attitude to humans had changed drastically since these books had been written. It seemed that before the Sundering, faeries had not only been well informed about the habits of human beings, they took a keen interest in them. Naturally the Oakenfolk would have been bolder when they still had all their magic, but even so, Bryony was amazed, for the books seemed to cover every possible aspect of human life and society.

Among other things, she learned that human beings did not have magic after all. All the marvels she had seen in the House were the work of clever minds and skillful hands, nothing more. Furthermore, humans did not eat faeries, or hunt them for sport—in fact few of them even believed in her people's existence. All they knew of faeries were ridiculous tales, which Bryony read with mingled amusement and disgust: stories where men tricked faeries into becoming their mates, or where human children were stolen away and replaced by hideous changelings. There was even one about a faery hiring a human midwife to help her give birth—how absurd, when everyone knew that faeries hatched from eggs, and that the Mother would have to die before her egg-daughter could be born!

She also read that human men and women sometimes swore vows to each other, becoming mates for life. This might be why the pair in the House had felt no need to bargain, and had seen nothing unusual about *thanking* each other. Still, it seemed strange to Bryony that anyone would commit themselves to another person so completely. Surely it was better to be free, and not in debt to anyone?

Learning about humans was fascinating, yet the more Bryony read about them, the more mystified she became. Sundering or not, it didn't seem to make sense—if her fellow faeries had once been so interested in humans, why were they so ignorant and fearful of them now?

For weeks the Oakenwyld lay brown and barren, while the faeries' winter stores grew ever more scant and fresh meat harder to come by. Each night Bryony puzzled over the books until her head ached, but she came no closer to answering her question. She considered asking Campion what she thought, but it would be hard to do that without explaining her visit to the House, and she was not sure she could trust the older faery with the secret. Eventually she gave up, handed in the key, and went back to studying the habits of crows instead.

At last spring arrived, heralded first by a scattering of snowdrops, then by the crocuses that raised their golden and purple heads at the base of the Oak. The animals crept out of their winter homes, and the air lightened with birdsong. When the sun came out, Bryony was quick to follow, reveling in the chance to stretch her wings. She had shot a vole and was skinning it by the Queen's Gate when Thorn stamped up and said:

"I've no more to teach you."

Bryony looked up sharply. "What?"

"I said, I've no more to teach you." Thorn shook back her dark hair with a brusque movement of her head. "You know the work as well as I do now, and the Oak only needs one Hunter, so as far as I'm concerned, you may as well take over."

Bryony was stunned silent. She had not expected this so soon. Thorn might not love hunting as Bryony did, might even be glad to give it up, but she was a thorough and exacting teacher. If she believed that Bryony was ready . . .

"You're good," said Thorn. "If you ask me, it's unnatural, and I think you're mad for actually wanting to do this filthy work. If you end up in a crow's belly, I won't be surprised. Still, you're better at this than I'll ever be, so—here." She unstrapped the leather band from her arm and held it out to Bryony.

"Oh," said Bryony faintly. Her head was whirling, and as her fingers closed around the band she felt very young and small again.

"I'll be moving out of the Hunter's quarters this week," continued Thorn. "I'll let you know when you can move in."

Bryony nodded, too distracted to speak.

"The Queen will want to see you, too. She'll ask if you'd like to take a new common-name. I'll let her know that I've approved you, and she'll call on you in a day or so."

There was an awkward pause. "All right," said Bryony,

since Thorn seemed to be waiting for an answer.

Still Thorn remained, looking down at her. "You know," she said at last, "you're sitting in almost the same place I found your egg."

"Oh?" said Bryony.

Thorn cursed, made an abrupt turn, and plunged back into the Oak, slamming the door behind her. Bryony sat back on her heels. What was all that about?

Part of her was tempted to go after the older faery and ask. But the half-skinned vole would attract crows if she left it for long, so after a moment Bryony sighed and picked up her flint again. Thorn could look after herself, and surely would: but Bryony was the Queen's Hunter now, and she had work to do.

The crescent moon glowed wanly in the cloud-choked sky, and a mist had settled over the Oakenwyld. Bryony slipped out of her window and dropped to the ground, grimacing at the cold slickness of the grass beneath her feet. Not the most pleasant night to be out, but something strange was going on at the House, and she could not resist the temptation to investigate.

If it had only been idle curiosity on her part, she would have resisted it. But for all her studies she had still not been able to figure out what had gone wrong between her people and the humans, and going back to the House was the only way she could think of to learn more. Whatever had made the Oakenfolk so fearful of human beings, it seemed to have happened around the same time as their other misfortunes— the loss of their magical powers, the fading of their creative abilities, and worst of all the deadly arrival of the Silence. Could all these things be connected?

It was a complicated question, and she didn't expect to be able to answer it tonight. But she could at least find out one thing: Why were the humans up so late? They had put out the lights and gone to bed at the usual time, but now the House was lit again, and she could see their shadows moving about inside. Something urgent must have wakened them—but what?

Landing on the cobbled veranda, Bryony crouched and peered through the door. She was surprised to see the human woman—Beatrice—sitting upon the sofa in her dressing gown, eyes puffy and cheeks wet with tears. Nearby stood her mate, barefoot and disheveled, speaking to an odd-shaped object in his hand:

". . . impossible to tell at this point, yes, I understand. But when can we see him?"

There came a long pause.

"I see. All right, then. Good-bye." The man set the object back on its hook, his face ashen. For a moment he stared at the wall; then he turned to his wife and said, "Apparently it's . . . quite serious. We should . . . they think we'd better come at once."

Beatrice made a choking noise, and her shoulders began

to shake. The man looked down at her helplessly, then reached out and put his arms around her, holding her as she wept. Bryony watched them, puzzled by this excess of emotion, until the two humans drew apart and walked slowly from the room, putting out the lights as they went. Moments later Bryony heard the front door slam, followed soon afterward by a rumbling and a crunch of gravel, and she realized that they had left the House together.

As she walked back toward the Oak, Bryony was frowning. What could have happened to upset the humans so much? Something terrible had happened to "him"—their son, Paul, probably—but if the disaster had already taken place, why were they rushing off in the middle of the night? It wasn't as though they could do anything about it.

She was still musing over the strange ways of humans when the wind shifted, and a familiar dank odor blew past. Bryony spun around, her hand dropping to the metal knife she carried at her belt. *He's back*, she thought—and that was all she had time for before the crow swooped down and knocked her to the ground. She rolled with the blow, leaping up just in time to avoid being pinned; then she ripped her new dagger from its sheath and flung herself at her enemy.

He flew to meet her, beak snapping, but Bryony dove at the last minute. She ducked beneath his outstretched wing, zooming so low that the wet grass brushed her chest; then she twisted about, and slashed straight across the back of both his legs.

He shrieked and stumbled, ragged wings beating the ground. Bryony was sure she had crippled him—but then he hopped upright again, and with a croak launched himself into the air. Bryony hesitated, looking up at the black shadow rising above her. Surely he couldn't be retreating so soon? And even if he were, could she afford to let him go?

Bryony sprang from the ground and flashed after the crow, wings buzzing furiously. In a heartbeat she had passed him and swung about to hover in the air, waiting to see what he would do.

She did not have to wait long. With a mad gleam in his eye he turned on her, and she was forced to flee. But even as the crow pursued her, Bryony felt no fear. A crow in full health was a swift and deadly flier, but she had wounded this one, and now he could barely keep up with her.

Bryony darted across the yard and into the shadow of the Oak, weaving her way easily between its wide-spaced branches. But just before she reached the trunk, she veered aside—while the crow, dazzled with pain and rage, smashed straight into it. She heard an awful crunch, a slithering sound followed by a thump, and then silence.

A shaft of golden light shot from the Oak as its topmost window burst open. Bryony caught a glimpse of Queen Amaryllis's fair, furious face and raised a hand in salute before circling back to find out what had become of her enemy.

Now that the frenzy of their combat had subsided, Bryony was disappointed to see that the crow lying crumpled across the Upper Knot Branch was not Old Wormwood, after all. It was a smaller crow, too young and inexperienced to be a good fighter—no wonder she had defeated him so quickly. Exhilaration fading, she lighted beside him with dagger drawn, ready to stab him the instant he moved. But there was no need, for his eyes had gone dull and his wings hung limp as rags. She prodded him gingerly with one foot, then jumped back as he slid off the branch and tumbled to the ground below. Her enemy was dead.

Only then did Bryony notice that her arm was bleeding. Light-headed, she folded to her knees as Bluebell exclaimed from the window above her: "Great merciful Gardener! Is that *Bryony*?"

"Go and fetch her," said Queen Amaryllis's voice. "Bring her to me."

A moment later Bryony felt someone tugging her to her feet. "Ugh," said Bluebell, and the supporting hands were hastily withdrawn. "She's filthy."

That was, unfortunately, true. Crows were dirty creatures at the best of times, and not all the blood on Bryony was her own. She turned her head, discovering at the same moment that her neck ached dreadfully, and saw Bluebell regarding her with wary, almost fearful eyes.

"One moment," said the Queen. "What is that weapon she carries?"

Bluebell bent to inspect the dagger still clutched in Bryony's hand. "It appears to be made of metal, Your Majesty. A strange sort of knife."

"Metal? What kind of metal?"

The Queen's attendant touched the blade gingerly, her nose wrinkling in distaste. "Steel, my lady. Safe, I think."

"Bring it, too," said the Queen. Then she paused and added, "Have her bathe first." She pulled back her shining head and closed the window.

"You heard Her Majesty," said Bluebell. "You had better come with me."

Sometime later, bandaged from wrist to elbow and freshly dressed in the cleanest tunic and breeches she could find, Bryony followed Bluebell up the last turn of the Spiral Stair to the Queen's chambers.

As Bluebell, with lamp in hand, led her along the corridor Bryony stole quick glances into the rooms they passed. The first archway revealed a small audience chamber draped in scarlet curtains; next came a private bath with fixtures of polished stone and a mirror even larger than Wink's; and last and most interesting, a library littered with open volumes and scribbled sheets of paper, as though the Queen had been interrupted in the middle of some urgent study. Only one last door remained, and it was closed. Bluebell stopped and gave the brass knocker a respectful tap.

"Enter," came the Queen's voice from within.

Bluebell opened the door. "Your Majesty, Bryony is here."

"Very well. You may leave us."

The Queen's attendant bowed her head and retreated. Bryony was left standing alone in the doorway, gazing about the chamber and thinking how much it reminded her of the House—though the furnishings here were older, and beginning to look a little worn. There was a wide feather bed with a post at each corner, and a table with two chairs upholstered in delicate needlework. The window, twice the size of any other in the Oak, looked straight out at the House—but it was closed now, the curtains drawn.

On the room's far side stood a dressing table topped by an oval mirror, and there sat Amaryllis, combing her hair. She did not look up as Bryony approached and performed the ritual curtsy. Only when she had finished did Amaryllis put down her comb and turn gracefully in her seat, drawing her dressing gown about her.

"Precisely what did you mean by your reckless behavior?" she inquired.

Bryony met the Queen's blue eyes with her own black ones. "To kill a crow, Your Majesty."

"And so you did," replied Amaryllis. "But why were you out so late at night?"

Bryony opened her mouth and shut it again, her color deepening. How could she explain without admitting that she had been to the House? At last she said, "Your Majesty, I hoped to rid our people of a dangerous enemy. And . . . I wanted to test my new weapon."

"Ah, yes." Amaryllis held out her hand. "Show me this metal knife of yours."

Bryony drew the dagger from its sheath and held it out to the Queen, who took it in her long, white hands. "It appears," she said dryly, holding the sharp edge up to the light, "to be effective. How did you come by it?"

Bryony bit the inside of her lip, unsure of how to answer.

"I asked you a question," said the Queen. Her tone was mild, but as she spoke her shining wings lifted and spread wide, a wordless reminder of her magical power.

"I stole it," said Bryony. "From the House."

"Where the humans live."

"Yes."

"Do you intend to make a habit of disobeying my commands and risking your life?"

Bryony straightened her shoulders. "Your Majesty, I needed a better weapon to fight crows with, and I could see no other way to get it. Yes, I risked my life then, and I risked it again tonight, and I will continue to risk my life as long as you call me your Hunter, because that is my duty."

The Queen was silent a moment. Finally she said, "Disobedient you may be, but you are also courageous. I know of no Hunter who has ever killed a crow. Very well, you have my pardon—this time. But beware, child. You are no match for a human, and I do not wish you to enter their House again. Am I understood?"

"Yes, Your Majesty."

"Good." Amaryllis folded her wings and turned back to the mirror, laying the knife down on the dressing table. "How then shall I reward your bravery?"

Bryony drew herself up. "Your Majesty . . . I would like to change my name."

"Is that all?" asked the Queen. "But that privilege has always been yours; surely you knew that. Tomorrow, when I confirm you publicly as my new Hunter, you may choose for yourself whichever common-name you please."

"But you wouldn't let me choose just *any* name," said Bryony. "Not the one I really want." She gestured to the blade upon the table.

The Queen sat back in her chair, regarding Bryony's reflection with narrowed eyes. "Do I understand you rightly? You must know that none of our people has ever taken such a name."

"I know."

"You are determined to be different, aren't you?" the

Queen murmured, and then in brisker tones, "Very well. I shall announce your choice to the others tomorrow. But should you die in battle, that name will not pass to your egg-daughter."

"That's all right," said Bryony. "I wouldn't want it to. Your Majesty, may I withdraw? I am . . . tired."

"You may." The Queen picked up the dagger, turned, and held it hilt-first out to her. "Here is your weapon: I give it to you. And if anyone should ask how you came by it, you will tell them so—that you received it as a gift from me."

Which would satisfy the other faeries' curiosity about where the blade had come from, without letting them suspect that their Hunter had visited the House. Looking into Amaryllis's level eyes, Bryony felt a surge of admiration: No wonder she was the Queen. "I will," she said, taking the knife with care.

"Then you are dismissed," said Amaryllis.

Bryony curtsied and backed out of the room. Bluebell met her in the corridor, clucking disapproval at the weapon in her hand. "Really, Bryony—"

"No."

"'No'? 'No' what?"

"From now on," said Bryony firmly, "you can call me Knife."

Five

"This will hurt a little," warned Valerian, her scissors poised above the line of stitches in Knife's arm.

"It can't hurt any worse than it did when you put them in," said Knife. "Go on."

Valerian sighed and set to work, while Knife stared at the wall of the Healer's room and tried not to flinch. She hadn't reckoned on this when she became a Hunter. Oh, she had known that the work could be dangerous, and that she was bound to get injured now and then. But after living all her life in the safety of the Oak she'd had very little idea of what being wounded felt like, or how long it would take to recover. Even now, with her first battle scar still livid and tender upon her skin, it was hard to believe how close she had come to death, or how fortunate she was that the injury had not been worse. Skin and muscle would heal, given time, but if it had been her wing . . .

Knife repressed a shudder. Best not to even think about that.

"Do you think," said Valerian, putting down the scissors and looking at Knife with her searching gray eyes, "that you may have done enough now, at least for a while?"

"Done enough what?" Knife said, not quite meeting the Healer's gaze. She hopped off the table and stretched her arm experimentally. The skin pulled a little, but it already felt better without the stitches.

Valerian wiped her hands on a towel and began untying her apron. "I think you know what I mean, Knife. Not that I mind having new and interesting injuries to treat, but if you wanted everyone in the Oak to know that you're a good Hunter, I think you have already proven that quite sufficiently."

Knife blinked. Was Valerian actually trying to have a *conversation* with her? The idea was so bizarre, so unfaerylike, that it took her a moment to think of a reply. "I know that," she said. In fact she had known it for some time, for as soon as the news that she had killed a crow had reached the rest of the Oakenfolk, they had become much more respectful toward her. It had taken them a few days to adjust to her new name, but not even Mallow dared to order her about anymore.

"Then why," asked Valerian in a voice edged with impatience, "do you keep taking such terrible risks?"

There was no easy answer to that question. "Because I have to," Knife replied, and it was true, although she knew Valerian would never understand. How could she explain to someone who had spent decades quietly holed up in the Oak, content with her books and her surgeon's kit, that being a heartbeat from death was the only way to truly feel alive?

"Well," said Valerian, "try not to do too much with that arm for another week or so. A few stretching exercises each morning and night, and this ointment"—she handed the pot to Knife—"worked well into the skin, should help it heal. But come and see me, if you please, before you do anything too strenuous."

Knife nodded.

"Then I give you good evening," said Valerian, and let her go.

Days passed, and the pain in Knife's arm subsided; Valerian examined the scar and reluctantly pronounced her fit for duty. By then the Oakenfolk were clamoring for meat, tallow, and other necessities, and Knife found herself so busy that she had no time to visit the House or even think about the humans. All her spare moments were spent on exercise and weapons practice, trying to get her weakened muscles back into fighting shape; by the end of the day she was so exhausted that she simply fell into bed and lay there senseless until morning.

When the workers arrived, however, backing their metal wagons into the House's front drive and filling the once-quiet Oakenwyld with their appalling mechanical din, it was impossible not to take notice. At first the Oakenfolk were terrified, and it was all the Queen herself could do to reassure them. Then, as the pounding and screeching went on day after day, their fear turned to resignation, and finally to impatience.

"What are they doing in there, anyway?" demanded Campion one night at supper. "Knife, you should know, if anyone does. Have you seen anything?"

Knife was tempted to ask the Librarian what she was prepared to offer in exchange for the knowledge, but she knew bargaining would be futile when she had so little information to offer. "They're changing the inside of the House," she replied shortly, helping herself to a third serving of roasted finch and shoving the empty platter back down the table.

"What for?"

"I don't know." She had watched the downstairs bathroom being gutted; she had also noticed that the study had been moved to the upper floor. But the humans—*her* humans—were still away from the House more often than not, so she had no idea why these drastic changes were necessary.

"So many humans in the Oakenwyld now," said Linden, one of the Gatherers, with a shudder. "Too many."

"They'll be gone soon enough," came Thorn's voice flatly from the end of the table. "And your bleating isn't going to make them move on any sooner, now, is it?" She pushed back her bench and stalked away.

"What's she so angry about?" asked Knife, but her only answer was a series of shrugs. Only Wink looked troubled by Thorn's outburst, but a moment later she returned to her meal as though nothing had happened, leaving Knife wondering if she had seen that anxious look at all.

Eventually the commotion in the House subsided, and the workers packed up their wagons and drove away. Over the next few days Knife made a survey of the renovations and found that outside the front step had been replaced by a wooden ramp, while inside the former study now contained a wardrobe, a chest of drawers, and a double bed. The workers seemed to have done something to the stairs as well, but as no window overlooked the staircase, Knife could not be sure. All that noise, all that fuss—why?

Fortunately, she did not have to wait long for an answer. That night George and Beatrice returned to the House together, and Knife crouched beside the back door, watchful and listening.

"He'll be out on the fifth," said the man, methodically buttering a scone.

His wife stopped with her teacup halfway to her mouth. "He—said that?"

"They told me. When I stopped to see him today."

"But he didn't speak to you?"

George's jaw tightened. "No."

"You told him he's coming home?"

"I told him. He just looked at me."

Beatrice lowered her head, the lines around her mouth deepening.

"He'll be all right once he gets here," said her husband. "You'll see."

"It'll be nice," said Beatrice, with desperate brightness, "to have him home again. Won't it."

"Yes," said George in a thin voice, "very nice."

"You're wanted by Her Majesty," called Bluebell from the top of the Spiral Stair, and Knife, four turns down on her way to breakfast, stopped short. "What?" she said.

"I said, the Queen wants you. At once."

Grudgingly Knife turned around and trudged back up to the landing where Bluebell stood. "Why?" she asked.

Bluebell ignored the question. Instead, she walked briskly along the corridor, pulled aside the curtains, and ushered Knife into the Queen's private audience chamber.

"I have summoned you," said Amaryllis from her throne, "because I have just received news that the crow known as Old Wormwood has returned."

Knife was startled. How could he have come back to the Oakenwyld without her knowing it? But the Queen went on:

"One of the Gatherers reported that a large crow attacked their party just after dawn, as they were heading toward the wood. They were fortunate enough to find places to hide before it could harm them, but two of the workers had nervous fits and had to be carried back. I would prefer that this not happen again."

"You want me to kill him?" asked Knife.

"I would not ask you to take such a risk," said the Queen. "He has killed one Hunter already; I do not wish to lose another. No, your task will be to escort the Gatherers whenever they go out. Their work is vital to our survival, and nothing must be permitted to hinder them."

Guard duty. Inwardly Knife groaned, but she kept her voice polite as she said, "For how long?"

"As long as the threat remains. I trust you will still be able to carry out your own duties while you wait for the Gatherers to finish theirs?"

"Yes, Your Majesty."

"Then you are dismissed."

Knife bowed and left the room with every appearance of calm, but her thoughts were in turmoil. The Gatherers had spotted Old Wormwood before she did—that was a serious blow. It was the Hunter's task to watch for predators, and she had failed in that duty. . . .

"Did the Queen tell you?" said a timid voice at her elbow, and Knife turned to see Holly, the Chief Gatherer, standing there.

"About Old Wormwood?" she said. "Yes."

"He's huge." Her eyes were haunted. "And fast—I've never seen a crow move that fast before. He pecked a hole straight through Linden's basket." She shuddered visibly before going on: "So will you be coming with us tomorrow? The others—we all want to know."

"I'm coming," said Knife.

"You'll meet us right at sunrise? And you'll stay with us all the way to the forest and back again?"

"I'll bring my bow," Knife told her. "And I'll keep close watch. I won't let the crow get near you."

Color rushed back into Holly's face, a pink wave of relief. She bobbed a curtsy and hurried back down the Spiral Stair.

Knife followed in gloomy silence, fingers drumming on the sheathed blade at her side. There was no help for it: Her duty was clear. She must put her curiosity about the humans aside, and concentrate on the task the Queen had given her.

The double load of work would be exhausting, and now it might be weeks before she found out what had happened to Paul.

It would be so much easier if she could put the humans out of her mind, convince herself that they didn't matter. But she couldn't forget the woman's stricken face, or the man's voice cracking on the words *very nice.*

Perhaps she was getting too attached to the humans.

Over the next few days Knife carried out the Queen's command, watching over the Gatherers as they worked. Once she had seen them safely across the open field, she busied herself with her own duties, hunting when they foraged and dressing her kills while they unloaded their baskets at the Oak. All the while she kept an eye out for Old Wormwood, but there was no sign of him.

Sometime during that week—though when exactly, Knife never knew—Paul arrived at the House. Despite her weariness, Knife did everything she could to catch a glimpse of him, but he always seemed to be in his room with the curtains drawn, or the lights turned out, or both.

"He doesn't say a word to me all day," Beatrice sobbed. "Never a single word. He looks through me like I'm not there."

"There's no excuse for it," her husband said, setting down his teacup with unnecessary force. "There's nothing wrong with his tongue, or his brain. It's just stubbornness, that's all."

"George, don't," implored the woman. "Be patient with him. He's been through so much—we don't know what might be wrong."

And I don't even know what he looks *like,* thought Knife in frustration. *A blight on Old Wormwood, and the Queen, and all her precious Gatherers, too—this has been the longest week of my life.*

That week, however, came to an abrupt and spectacular end when Knife, with eight weary Gatherers in tow, climbed up the slope at the Oakenwyld's western border to find a peculiar obstacle blocking their way to the Oak. Through a gap in the hedge Knife glimpsed a flash of sunlight on polished metal, the black-edged curve of an enormous wheel. With a chopping motion she directed the others to lie flat, and crawled beneath the bushes to examine the monstrous machine more closely.

She assumed it was some new gardening tool that the humans had left on the lawn, but as soon as she emerged from the hedge she realized her mistake. *Great Gardener. It's him.*

He sat upon a silver throne, a book laid open on his knees: a young king, uncrowned and plainly dressed. He was slim, with broad shoulders and long arms wiry with muscle, and Knife thought he must be nearly as tall as his father when he stood. The wind blew his pale hair across his brow; he shook it back with an impatient movement of his head—

And froze, staring. At her. At Knife.

She couldn't move. Her mouth worked dryly; her hand quivered on the hilt of the dagger at her hip. All the while those blue eyes regarded her unblinking, while wonder dawned on Paul McCormick's face. She was only just out of reach; one lunge would put her in his grasp. But he did not move.

"Paul!" came a shrill cry from the direction of the House.

He turned his head toward the sound, and the spell shattered; Knife dove back through the hedge to find the shivering Gatherers waiting for her.

"I'm coming to bring you in," Beatrice shouted across the lawn. "It's time for tea."

"What do we do?" whimpered Clover, her nails digging into Knife's arm. Knife grimaced and shook her off.

"Just wait," she breathed. "He'll be gone in a moment."

They all went still, listening to the crunch of footsteps on the fresh-mown grass. Just visible on the other side of the hedge, the woman's stocking-clad legs appeared. "There now," she said, and the wheels of the silver throne turned toward the House.

"You were right beside him," whispered Holly in Knife's

ear. "So close—to a *human*. Weren't you afraid?"

"No," said Knife distractedly, watching Paul's seated figure shrink toward the House and finally vanish through the back door. She turned to the others. "It's safe now. Pick up your baskets and let's go."

"Did he see you?" squeaked another voice.

Knife ducked under the hedge and began walking toward the Oak, not looking back.

"Of course not," she said.

Six

Knife lay on her bed, staring at the gnarled ceiling of her room. Somewhere in the back of her mind, Paul was still sitting in his wheeled throne, looking at her.

She couldn't believe she had just stood there like that, right in front of a human. Perhaps it was the shock. She had been too astonished to feel afraid, or even to move. And fortunately he had been just as astonished, or she might not be here right now.

Yet it wasn't just shock that had made Knife linger by Paul's side: It was fascination. This was the boy she had met when she first stepped out of the Oak eight summers ago, after all, and part of her had always longed to see him again. . . .

She flopped over onto her stomach, rubbing her eyes.

Stupid girl, she told herself. *He might not want to eat you, but he could still stomp you flat in an instant. Or worse, he could put you in a cage and keep you there until you die. He's human, and you're a faery—you're nothing alike.*

A soft tapping sounded at her door. "Hello?" she said, but there was no reply.

Mystified, Knife rose, lit her candlestick, and went to answer. She stepped out onto the landing and looked around, but all the doors were closed. Had she imagined that knock?

Then her foot struck something solid, and she bit back a yelp as it skittered away across the floor. Some crawling insect—? But no, it was just a small parcel, with her name printed on it. When she picked it up and tore off the wrappings, it turned out to be a book.

More puzzled than ever, Knife went back into her room and sat down on the sofa to examine it. Easing open the cover, feeling the worn leather flake and crackle beneath her fingers, she began to read.

I have never before tried to keep a diary, but Laurel says it is a worthy exercise; and as there is no one whose writings I admire more, I should be foolish not to take her advice. Still, even as I pen these words, I find myself at a loss for what to say. Had I a remarkable friend like Dr. Johnson, I should have no lack of diverting incidents to record, but alas, I am no Boswell.

Knife stared at the tiny, elegant handwriting. Dr. Johnson, Boswell . . . Those were *human* names. The writer must have lived when the ties between the Oak and the human world were closer—and if so, this diary might help her find the answers she'd been looking for.

> *Nevertheless, for the sake of my imagined reader I must give myself a proper introduction: Heather by name, one and forty summers of age, born in the reign of good Queen Snowdrop, and now appointed Seamstress of the Oak. I have an apprentice, named Bryony. . . .*

That confirmed it, thought Knife with a flare of excitement. She had never heard of Heather, but she knew her own egg-mother's history well enough: The old Bryony had become the Oak's Seamstress in the last few years of Queen Snowdrop's reign, then served for nearly a century before dying and passing that role to her own apprentice, Wink. So this diary had been written near the end of the Days of Magic—exactly the time in the Oak's history she needed to know about.

Somehow, thought Knife as she smoothed out the crumpled second page, whoever had sent her this book must have known she was trying to find out about the Oakenfolk's past. Campion, perhaps? But surely it would have been easier for her to just slip the diary onto the back shelf and wait for Knife to find it?

Slowly she turned the diary's pages. The first few entries were disappointingly ordinary: Heather had found a new lace pattern and was eager to try it; she approved of the chemise her apprentice had just made; and so on. It was like living with Wink all over again, and Knife was about to put the book down when the next line caught her attention:

Jasmine returned to the Oak today, much to everyone's surprise. No one dared ask why she had come back, for she was full of black looks and could not give a civil word to anyone. I am sure Queen Snowdrop will want to speak to her; she has always been a difficult creature, and now she is insupportable.

Jasmine . . . The name tweaked at Knife's memory. She felt sure she had heard it before, but where?

Azalea says that Jasmine should be called to account for abandoning her post, but the Queen appears to feel more kindly toward her. Indeed, she has forbidden anyone to question Jasmine, and says that she will by no means allow her to be punished.

Knife frowned at the page. What did *abandoning her post* mean? Had Jasmine been sent on some important assignment? But if so, what?

The only idea she could think of was that Jasmine might have been sent out as an ambassador to another faery Wyld. But the Oakenfolk had not seen or heard from any of their fellow faeries in centuries, so she would have had to search for them first. Curiosity rekindled, Knife read on.

. . . *Jasmine came to my room today, bringing with her a gown which she said was in need of mending. I was tempted to refuse, yet I could not help but exclaim aloud when I saw it, for the bodice was badly torn and one sleeve ripped quite away. The skirt was blackened almost to the knee, as though she had fallen in the mire, and it seemed to me that if this were the gown in which she had returned home, it was little wonder the others had found her ill-tempered. Pity overcame me, and I told her I should have it mended in a fortnight.*

"And how shall I repay you for your services?" she asked.

I knew I ought not to pry, yet my curiosity was too great to resist. "Knowledge," I said. "What misfortune befell you, that you should return to the Oak?"

Her lips pressed tightly together. "I cannot speak of it," she said. "Suffice it to say that I believe I can better serve our people here."

"I beg your pardon," I said, for I saw that I had grieved her.

"No matter," she said. "If curiosity is a fault, it is one I share. But I shall offer you knowledge more suited to your craft—some sketches of clothing I saw when Outside, perhaps?"

"Oh!" I said, much surprised. "Could you?"

"Certainly. I have gained some little skill as an artist, since I went away." She smiled, but her eyes remained bitter. "It would

be pleasant to put the talent to more . . . worthy use."

I could not think what to say to that, and we stood a moment in silence. Then Jasmine continued in a lighter tone: "I shall bring you the drawings soon. A fortnight before the gown is mended, you say? I should not like to press you, for I know that you do fine work; but I fear that I have little else to wear."

"I shall have it ready in a few days," I told her, for now I truly did pity her. She inclined her head to me, and left.

I have always felt inferior in Jasmine's presence, and tempted to fault her for it; but now I see that my thoughts have been unkind, and that she has suffered more than any of us guessed. I think that I shall exhort the other faeries to show her more kindness—but discreetly, for Jasmine is proud even in her disgrace, and would no doubt be offended if she thought I was gossiping about her.

Knife was tempted to read on, but by now she was so tired, she could scarcely see the page. She pulled out one long white hair and used it to mark her place, then shut the diary and crawled into bed.

The next morning Knife found the Gatherers lined up in front of the Queen's Gate as usual, shouldering their baskets and discussing their plans for the day. She could hear Holly's voice raised above the general chatter: ". . . done well these past few days, especially as it hasn't rained until now.

We're well stocked with berries and greens, so . . ."

All at once she caught sight of Knife and stopped, swallowing visibly. The other Gatherers also fell silent and averted their eyes.

"What?" asked Knife, but no one answered until Holly cleared her throat to reply:

"I think we won't be needing you today after all. The crow seems to have moved on, so we should be all right on our own for a while." She looked around at the others. "You agree, don't you?"

They all nodded.

"All right," said Knife, perplexed. "It's all the same to me. I'll be out hunting later anyway; if you need me you can always shout."

Holly looked relieved. "Yes. We'll do that. Everyone ready? Let's go."

Knife watched until the Gatherers had filed out and shut the door behind them. What had all that been about? Surely they couldn't be frightened of her just because she had gone near a human?

Eventually she shrugged, and headed off toward the kitchen. If her services weren't going to be needed right away, she might as well have a proper breakfast—and then, perhaps, she'd pay a visit to the library. Reading Heather's diary had made her curious about the reign of Queen Snowdrop, and she wanted to see what the old histories had to say.

She was surprised, on reaching the kitchen, what a blaze

they had going in the fireplace. Usually the cooking fire was kept modest during the summer months, to keep the inside of the Tree from becoming too stuffy.

Still, that was the kitchen workers' problem and not hers, and furthermore they all kept looking at her askance as though finding her presence unwelcome, so she poured herself a cup of hot chicory and headed off to the library.

Campion was sitting at the desk when she arrived. The catalog lay open before her, and she dipped her pen mechanically into the inkwell as she stroked out one entry after another. Her head was down, her face hidden behind her hair, but the fingers that gripped the quill were trembling.

"Campion, what—" began Knife, but at the same moment she glanced toward the back of the library, and the words froze on her tongue.

The door to the secret closet stood open, and a trail of ashy footprints led into it and out again. The shelves were empty, the precious books on humans all gone.

"What happened?" demanded Knife, rounding on Campion. "Who did this?"

Campion slowly put the quill back in the inkpot and looked up. Her face was colorless, her eyes so full of fury that Knife took a hasty step back, afraid the other woman might strike her.

"You," said Campion in a low voice. "You never thought, did you? You couldn't pretend, even for a moment, to be afraid."

"I—don't understand—"

"Of course not, you're too young to think about anyone but yourself. All you cared about was showing off to the Gatherers. Look at me, not a bit frightened of humans, tra la!" She gave a hysterical laugh. "It never occurred to you, did it, that the Queen might hear how terribly *brave* you were, and start wondering just what had made you feel so confident around humans? Or that she might take—steps—to make sure that no one else would follow your example?"

Nausea crept into Knife's throat. "You mean . . . the books . . . they've been destroyed?"

"Oh, yes," said Campion, biting off the words savagely. "Didn't you notice what a lovely cheerful fire they've got going in the kitchen this morning? All because of you, and I'm sure we'll appreciate the extra heat even more by this afternoon."

Knife closed her eyes, her lips shaping inaudible oaths.

"Those books were priceless," Campion told her. "Irreplaceable. I hope you're happy." She snatched up her quill again and began crossing out entries, while a large tear rolled off the end of her nose and splashed onto the page.

"I'm . . . sorry," said Knife. She felt helpless and, for the first time she could remember, ashamed.

"Yes, well, that's what the Queen said, too," sniffed Campion. "But at least she was doing what she thought was best for all of us. What's *your* excuse?"

There was no answer to that, so Knife bowed her head and turned to leave. But then a thought struck her, and she looked back. "I don't suppose . . . ? What I mean is, if you knew this was coming, then maybe . . ."

The uncertainty in her voice made Campion look up again, the anger in her sharp face easing. "What?" she said.

"Did you send me a package last night?"

"Me, send a package? To *you*? Right now I wouldn't give you a dead slug if you offered me gold for it." Her mouth hardened. "Now get out."

Defeated, Knife left the library. Climbing the stairs to the Oak's ground level, she made her way slowly toward the East Root exit, her thoughts full of black smoke.

The first thing she heard when she emerged from the Oak was Beatrice's tremulous voice: "Paul. Please."

The words came faintly from the far end of the lawn, but there was no mistaking the distress in them. "I just—I want to talk to you. Why won't you speak to me?"

Paul made no reply. His blond head inclined a little as she spoke, but his face remained expressionless. Beatrice pressed her hands to her mouth as though muffling a sob, then hurried back into the house, leaving her son alone on the veranda.

Knife folded her arms and studied Paul critically. He

must be quite proud of that throne of his, since he was always sitting in it. His own mother waited on him like a servant, and pleaded for his favor. And yet for all that apparent wealth and power, he did not seem happy.

Well, he was in good company there, thought Knife with a rush of bitterness. How could Amaryllis have burned those books? She had been a scholar once; she should have known better. . . .

Her thoughts were interrupted by the sound of faery voices. Knife glanced back to see two Gatherers emerge from the Oak, duck beneath the hedge, and pick their way down the slope, heading for the distant wood. Somehow they had become separated from the rest of the group, but judging by their slow pace it didn't concern them very much.

Knife made a disgusted noise. All that fuss about Old Wormwood and the need for extra protection, when the whole time she'd guarded them there was scarcely a crow to be seen. And now there they were, sauntering across the field as though—

She snapped her fingers. Of course! Old Wormwood had never returned at all. The whole story had been a lie, an excuse to keep Knife busy. Somehow Queen Amaryllis must have found out that she'd been watching the humans again, and put her on guard duty to punish her. No wonder the Gatherers out there didn't seem afraid! They knew there had never been any real danger.

It all made perfect, maddening sense. The lot of them must have thought Knife so gullible and perhaps even had a good laugh when her back was turned. She slammed a fist into her palm. Well, they wouldn't laugh again. She'd—

A scream sliced the air, and Knife jumped, her anger forgotten. Out upon the open field, a huge black shape wheeled and dove into the grass. There was a frantic rustling, and the next shriek was abruptly cut off.

"Don't run!" shouted Knife. "Drop your baskets and fly!"

There was no answer. Knife plunged through the hedge and leaped into the air, wings whirring. She drew her knife, wishing fervently that she had brought her bow and quiver instead.

The crow raised its head, and she recognized the limp form dangling from its beak: Linden. A soft-spoken faery, whose shyness and drab coloring made her easy to overlook—but she could carry twice her own weight in chestnuts, and the Gatherers could ill afford to lose her.

At first Knife feared she might already be too late to save her, but as she flew closer Linden roused and began to struggle. The crow's grip on her was cruel, but he had not killed her yet. Gathering her strength, Knife put on a final burst of speed, flashed up to him, and hacked wildly at his tail.

A ludicrous attack, but it did as Knife had intended: Old

Wormwood squawked in alarm, and Linden tumbled free. Knife hastily stuck her dagger between her teeth, then dove and caught the other faery before she could hit the ground.

Laying Linden down on the grass, Knife glanced about and saw Tansy, one of the other Gatherers, cowering a few crow-lengths away. Impatiently Knife beckoned her to come and help, then leaped out of the grass and took to the air again to face her enemy.

She had all his attention now, just as she had hoped. With a cry of defiance, Knife fled back across the field as Old Wormwood took up the chase. She wanted to lure him as far away from Linden and Tansy as she could, but right now she could barely keep out of his reach. Relentlessly the crow pursued her, up the rise and over the hedge into the Oakenwyld.

Knife's wing muscles burned with the effort of flying at full speed, but she dared not slacken her pace. She rounded the House in a turn so tight, her foot scraped the brick, then looped wildly across the garden, but try as she might she could not shake her enemy. She launched herself straight up toward the sun, hoping that Old Wormwood would lose her in its dazzling light, but he was too quick. He soared above her, a looming shadow three times her size. The beating of black wings roared in Knife's ears, and in desperation she lashed out with her dagger. The blade snagged in her enemy's feathers, tearing skin and flesh, and he screamed.

Knife darted away, but the crow thrashed after her, a

scant wingspan behind. His eyes glowed with fury, and his hooked talons raked the air. She had wounded him, but he was still faster, still stronger. Her only hope of escape was to dive low over the garden, then snap out her wings and shoot straight for the Oak. If she timed it just right—

Then she glanced down, and her muscles turned to water. Paul was rolling down the stone path toward the Oak, completely blocking her planned approach. He could not know, she thought wildly, that her own death turned upon his wheels. Unless—

A searing pain shot across her wing as the crow raked it open. Out of control, Knife tumbled through the air, her mind shrieking: *Fool! Fool! Never hesitate!*

Old Wormwood was upon her now, beak wide as if to swallow her whole. Knife's wing was useless; she could barely keep aloft. Soon she would fall, and where the ground leaped up to meet her she would die. But better that than surrender to those cruel claws.

With the last of her strength, Knife slapped her wings flat against her back. Agony drowned her consciousness as she spiraled from the sky and dropped, senseless, straight into Paul McCormick's lap.

Seven

Knife woke in a cold sweat, the torn edge of her wing sizzling with pain. Hunger gnawed at her stomach, and her throat burned with thirst. But the moment she tried to sit up her head spun like a weaver's bobbin, and it was all she could do not to vomit.

How long had she lain unconscious? In the darkness it was impossible to guess. The last thing she remembered was Old Wormwood's talons ripping through her wing, and the ground rushing up to meet her as she fell. . . .

I will never fly again. The realization came to her with cruel clarity, tempting her to weep. To live without the thrill of the hunt, or the joy of soaring through the air . . . short of death itself, Knife could imagine nothing worse.

Yet there was nothing she could do about it. No poultice could heal a torn wing; a hundred stitches would never close the wound. She had been the youngest and the best Hunter ever to serve the Queen—but without the ability to fly, she would be useless. Thorn would take over her duties, and she would go back to being Bryony, a nobody. She would spend the rest of her life trapped in the Oak—

No. She would not, *could* not. If Queen Amaryllis refused to let her go out with the Gatherers, then she would simply run away, and live as best as she could, as long as she could, alone.

Breathing deep to quell her nausea, Knife tried to swing her legs over the edge of the bed. The room was so dark, her wits so blurred with pain, that it took her several attempts to realize that there was no edge—that the soft thing on which she lay was in fact the floor.

Knife's stomach knotted. No wonder it was dark; no wonder the room smelled strange. Instead of lying on her own bed in the Oak, waiting for Valerian to come and tend her, she was in some unfamiliar place, all alone.

But where?

Cautiously, trying not to jar her injured wing, Knife crawled forward into the blackness. She had shuffled only a few beetle-lengths when her hand struck something cold. She felt her way up its smooth surface to find a huge glass bowl, filled with—

Water. Oh, Great Gardener. Clambering to her feet, Knife leaned over the bowl and drank thirstily, then plunged her hands into it and splashed her face and neck. By the time she had finished washing, she felt almost alive again.

Beside the bowl sat a plate heaped with chunks of some spongy, cakelike substance. It smelled peculiar, but it seemed to be food. Tentatively, Knife took a bite and began to chew.

After a few more mouthfuls she no longer felt light-headed, and her queasiness began to subside. Her wing still hurt, but she could bear it. Feet braced wide for balance on the too-soft carpet, Knife set off into the darkness again.

Three or four steps in any direction brought her up against the wall: not wood, not stone, but a tough papery substance. It gave a little when she pushed against it, but as soon as she let go it sprang back. There had to be an exit somewhere. . . .

Knife squinted upward. A faint stripe of radiance crossed the ceiling from one end of the room to the other. Could the door be up there?

Without warning, her prison tipped to one side. Knife tumbled to the floor, scrabbling for a hold as the carpet slid sideways and the water in the bowl slopped over. Then with a bump the room righted itself again.

Knife lay still, afraid to move in case she set off another tremor. But the floor remained steady, and when she lifted her head she found the room lighter.

Automatically she looked up—and choked back a cry. The ceiling had cracked wide open, and an enormous human face stared down at her. Knife scrambled back into the corner, pulling her knees up to her chest and hiding her face against them.

"It's all right." His voice sounded husky, as though it had not been used in a long time. "I'm not going to hurt you."

Knife drew a ragged breath. Her worst fears had come to pass: She was trapped, flightless, a prisoner. The humans had put her in a box, and now they had come to torment her.

"You're still here," the voice went on, hushed with wonder. "I half thought, when I opened the box . . . but you're real." A finger touched her hair, and Knife shuddered. She would not cry out, must not—

"You're frightened." He sounded surprised. "You weren't yesterday." A pause. "All right, I'll leave you alone for a bit."

There was a rustling noise, then silence. Thinking that he had gone, Knife lifted her head—and found Paul still sitting there.

"So you do understand me," he said.

Knife slumped back into the corner, defeated. Hollowly she said, "Let me go."

"But you're hurt."

"I can take care of myself."

His mouth quirked. "Oh, right," he said. "I should have guessed. So what are you, some kind of crow-fighting warrior faery?"

He made her sound like a joke, and Knife's pride flared. "Yes, I am! What gives you the right—" Then common sense caught up with her, and she stopped. Fighting crows was one thing, but arguing with a creature ten times her size? That wasn't courage, it was suicide. "Never mind," she muttered.

"I see you've eaten the bread. What else would you like? Fruit? Vegetables?" He paused, then added, "You don't eat meat, do you?"

"Yes," said Knife.

"Really?"

She nodded.

"All right, then, I'll see what I can find. Later."

"Why not now?" she asked. If she could convince him to leave her unguarded, just for a moment—

"Because my mother's in the kitchen," said Paul. "And she'll want to know what I'm looking for—or worse, offer to get it for me." The words were laced with bitterness.

"You mean," said Knife, surprise momentarily overriding fear, "she doesn't know about me?"

"No. And I'd like to keep it that way, so . . ." He held a finger to his lips. "Don't talk so loud."

Knife sat back a little, digesting this. If Paul was the only one who knew about her, then . . .

"Look," said Paul. "What if I let you out for a bit? You're not going to run away, are you?"

The tone sounded casual, but Knife was wary. Why did he want her to come out? "No," she said, then realized too late that her answer had been unclear as Paul's hand swooped down and snatched her into the air.

She was not used to being touched, let alone swept up completely. Panicking, Knife struggled, but could not get free. As soon as he set her down again she tried to bolt, but her legs would not obey; she staggered a few steps and sat down with a thump.

"There," said Paul.

He sounded so satisfied, as though he had done her a favor. Knife gritted her teeth. If he touched her like that again, she would stab him in the thumb, and blight the consequences—

But the sheath at her belt was empty.

Knife's heart constricted. Where had her dagger gone? She leaped up and turned around, searching the desk where she stood. It had fallen out when he put her down, it must have. It had to be here.

"Lost something?" asked Paul.

Knife ran to the edge of the desk, frantically scanning the floor below. But even there she could see nothing but a few stray hairs and webs of dust. Her box prison sat open at the end of the bed, but it too was empty.

She turned away, feeling sick. Her precious metal blade, the only possession she had ever valued—and she had lost it. How could she possibly escape from the House now?

"What's wrong?" her captor demanded.

Knife shook her head, unable to reply. She sat down and

hugged her knees again, feeling smaller and more frightened than ever.

Paul reached past her to pull a spiral-bound notebook from the shelf. Wrapped in misery, Knife paid little attention until he laid the book on his lap and began flipping through it. Then her unfocused gaze sharpened, and she scrambled to her feet. The Oak!

There it stood, traced in silvery lines upon the page: There could be no mistaking the shape of those wide-flung branches, or that gnarled breadth of trunk. A real drawing, such as none of her people had made in well over a century—and a good enough likeness to make her feel homesick. How had he done it?

"I'd like to sketch you," said Paul. "Is that all right?"

"Me?" Knife was so startled, she forgot to be unhappy. "You mean—draw my picture? Now?"

He nodded.

Her eyes returned to the drawing of the Oak. "Did you do that?"

"Yes."

Knife hesitated a moment longer, then said, "All right."

"Excellent." His face lit. "Just stay as you are, then, and try not to move." He plucked a pencil from the drawer and bent over the page.

Knife tried to watch, but his lowered head blocked her view, so she began to look around the room instead. At first glance it appeared plain compared to the others she had seen in the House, with its bare floor and simple furnishings. But then she looked up, and a shiver of excitement ran through her.

The walls were full of pictures.

The biggest hung over the bureau: a swirling storm of gold, ocher, and blue with a dark shape moving through it. Another frame showed pine trees amid a snowy landscape, overshadowed by distant spires. On the other side of the room a host of tiny figures swarmed against a backdrop of lakes and mountains. And in the far corner, a man looked straight into a mirror at the back of his own head.

Knife studied each of the paintings in turn, fascinated. They were nothing like the tapestries in the Queen's Hall, or the simple pictures of flowers and fruit she had seen elsewhere in the House: These were startling, bewildering, in some cases almost ugly. Yet they seemed somehow *more* than the other pictures—more meaningful, more alive; it was as though they were shouting at her in a language she did not understand.

"There," said Paul with satisfaction. He raised the sketchbook from his lap, and Knife was captivated all over again. In a few spare strokes he had described the angles of her limbs, then traced the outlines of her hair, wings, and clothing; it was almost carelessly done. Yet that very roughness made it seem alive, as though at any moment her figure might leap off the page.

The face, though—that was even more amazing. There were her narrow, slanting eyes, her broad mouth, and pointed chin; he had even captured her wary expression. Not even Wink's mirror had ever caught her likeness so perfectly; somehow he had not merely drawn her appearance, but her essence.

"It's . . . very good," said Knife, when she could speak.

"Is it?" Paul said, and turned the page to look at his drawing again. "Do you know," he said in a slow, wondering tone, "I think you might be right."

Suddenly it was too much for Knife—the fight with Old Wormwood, the loss of her dagger, waking up to find herself a prisoner in the House, and now this. "I'm tired," she said, rubbing her eyes. "I need to rest."

"Oh." Paul sounded disappointed. "I'd wanted to draw you again, but all right." He reached for her.

Knife leaped back, fists raised. "Don't touch me!"

"What?" said Paul. "I didn't hurt you last time, did I?"

"It's not that," said Knife flatly. "I just don't like being grabbed and carried about without so much as a by-your-leave. Would you?"

His face darkened. "Not all of us get a choice," he said. "But if it makes you feel better, here." He held his hand out to her, palm upward.

Knife licked her lips, mustering her courage. The hand was a dry, bleached leaf, she told herself, or the upturned cup of a mushroom. Nothing more. Gingerly she stepped forward, and Paul lowered her into the box upon his lap. She jumped off his hand and lay down, shivering.

"I'll put you back in the wardrobe," said her captor's voice as the lid of the box rasped back into place. "You'll be safe there." Wheels squeaked, and she felt a bump as he set her prison back upon the shelf. The wardrobe door swung shut, muffling her in darkness.

Rest now, she told herself. *You'll need all your strength to escape—* and with that, she fell asleep.

When Knife woke, the room was so black, so silent, that she knew it must be night. She got up stiffly and helped herself to another drink and a few bites of bread. Then she sat down cross-legged, put her chin in her hand, and started thinking.

The pain in her wing had eased while she slept, but that didn't help much. Her metal knife was gone. She was trapped in a box with walls too smooth and high for her to climb. How to escape?

Then an idea came to her, clear and irresistible as a voice calling her true name: The walls of her prison were made of paper.

Knife jumped up, grabbed the drinking bowl by the rim, and tipped it over. Water gushed out, soaking deep into the carpet at her feet. For a few moments she waited, giving it time to seep in. Then she squelched over to the corner of the box, crouched, and began to scratch her way out. The sodden pulp came away easily in her hands, and soon she had clawed a hole large enough to crawl through.

As she clambered out onto the shelf, she could just make out a bar of dim light: the edge of the wardrobe door. Cautiously Knife sidled up to it and gave it a shove. Nothing happened, so she leaned harder. The door flew open, and Knife tumbled out.

It was not a long drop, but the floor was hard. Clutching her bruised elbow, Knife rocked and hissed between her teeth until the pain subsided. When she looked up, the first thing she saw was Paul's wheeled throne, sitting empty beside the bed. Its steely frame glowed in the moonlight, and she wondered again why Paul, of all his family, should be so honored.

Still, even if he was a king by day, he seemed ordinary enough in sleep: eyes closed, mouth slack. Knife watched him warily, but he did not stir, and at last she tiptoed away.

Hurrying down the corridor to the familiar sitting room, Knife inspected every crack and corner in search of an exit. It was no use. The doors were latched, the lone window closed, and the metal grille in the floor too heavy for her to lift. Heart drumming, she fled through the archway into the kitchen.

Crossing the tiled floor, she studied the glossy face of the oven, the smoothly varnished wood of the cupboard doors.

If she could find a way to climb up onto the counter, she might be able to reach the window above the sink. It looked to be slightly open; if she could reach it, it would be easy to slip out.

Knife had not tested her wings since the crow wounded her, but she had to try them now. She would not be able to fly in a straight line, or for any great distance, but—

Holding her breath, Knife moved her wings slowly backward, then forward again. Her injured forewing felt stiff, and the air sliding across its ragged surface made her stomach lurch. She crouched and tried again, harder this time, repeating the motion until her nausea began to settle. Her wings beat faster and faster, lifting her from the ground.

Little by little she rose toward the counter high above, weaving drunkenly through the air, but flying nonetheless. It was working! Just a few more wingbeats, and she'd be there—

Intent on her goal, Knife neither saw nor smelled the cat until it leaped out from the shadows and its heavy paw smashed her to the ground.

Eight

Knife writhed away from the cat before it could pin her, but her head reeled from the force of the blow. Instinctively she grabbed for her dagger, only to find it missing. No weapon to fight with, no wings to fly away— what was she going to do?

Shadows rippled along the cat's body as it paced around her. Knife dropped into a crouch, feinting to one side, then the other. But the cat was not fooled, and its paw lashed out again, flicking her off her feet. Grit seared Knife's arms and legs as she skidded across the tile.

This was impossible, she thought wildly. How could she not have noticed that the humans had a cat? Unless it was a new arrival, and belonged to—

"Paul!"

She screamed his name as the cat pounced, batting her between velvet paws. Again she cried out while the cat tossed her up in the air and caught her again, this time in its mouth. Hot breath steamed over her, and the stench of fish made her gag. Near fainting, she gasped Paul's name a final time and went limp.

"Vermeer!" hissed a voice from behind them, and the cat froze. Cringing, it dropped Knife and slunk away.

Knife lay winded on the tile, watching the ceiling swim in and out of focus. Her wounded wing felt as though it had been dipped in lye, and she could not move for trembling. But her rescuer made no move to touch her, nor did he speak again.

At last Knife's fluttering heart slowed, and she felt her strength return. The room clouded, lurched sideways, sharpened into focus, and she looked up—so very far up—into Paul's face.

"I owe you my life," she said weakly.

"Yes," said Paul, sounding tired, "you do." He leaned over in the chair, reaching out to her; Knife pulled herself upright, staggered two steps, and collapsed into the hollow of his hand.

Knife was barely aware of Paul lifting her onto the counter, and the trickle of running water sounded muffled and far away. Only when he began to dab at her bleeding hands did she blink back to awareness, startled.

"Sorry," said Paul, mistaking her reaction. "Is the water too hot?"

"No," said Knife, "it's just . . . warm." She touched the washcloth wonderingly. "How did you do that?"

"Magic," he said. "Or a hot-water heater, whichever you prefer. Here." He handed her the cloth, and Knife rubbed it cautiously across her face, wincing as soap worked its way into the scratches.

When she had patted and rinsed herself clean, Paul held out his hand to her. The smell of sweat hung heavy around him, and she wrinkled her nose as she stepped onto his palm. Pushing himself about in that throne must be hard work—but why had he bothered taking the time to get into it, when she had needed his help so urgently? Surely he couldn't be *that* proud?

"Do you want to go up or down?" said Paul.

"What?" asked Knife.

"I need that hand to steer the chair, so you'd better decide where I should put you. Unless you want to spend the rest of the night here in the kitchen, going in circles."

"Oh." Knife looked from his face to his knee and back again. "Then I suppose . . . down."

Paul lowered her to the edge of the seat and waited until she settled herself beside him. Then with practiced movements of his hands he pushed the wheeled throne forward, gliding noiselessly around the corner and down the corridor to his room. He half-turned the chair as they entered, easing the door shut; then he rolled up beside the bed, and Knife jumped onto it.

"Why do you—" she started to ask, but Paul interrupted:

"How do you know my name?"

Knife toed the blankets. "Oh. Well. I've . . . heard your parents speak about you. And to you, sometimes."

"So you live nearby. In the garden? The wood? Or . . ." He stopped, his eyes narrowing. "I know—you live in the old oak tree."

Her heart plummeted, but she managed to stay calm. "We live in many places," she said. "Sometimes we use the Oak as a lookout, but—"

"For a faery, you're a terrible liar," said Paul. "What are you afraid of? I'm not planning to chop it down." His eyes became distant. "I thought I'd just imagined you, that day I climbed the oak tree all those years ago. But when I saw you again in the garden, with that white hair and those black eyes—I knew I hadn't been dreaming after all."

Knife sank down onto the mattress and put her head in her hands. So that was it: After centuries of secrecy, the Oakenfolk were no longer safe from humans, and it was her fault. If she had only listened to Wink at the beginning, or at least resisted the temptation to spy on the humans later on, none of this would have happened.

"So what's your name, then?" asked Paul. "Or am I not supposed to know that either?"

I wish I knew myself, thought Knife unhappily. Without her weapon or her wings, the only name that truly belonged to her was the one she could never speak. Unless, of course, she went back to being Bryony—but no. Not as long as she still had a choice. "My name is Knife," she said.

Paul looked incredulous. "Knife? As in, a thing to cut with?"

She nodded, and he made a noise halfway between a snort and a chuckle. "Your mother had quite the sense of humor."

"My egg-mother had nothing to do with it!" said Knife indignantly. "I chose the name my—" Then she realized she had said too much, but it was too late.

"Really?" said Paul. "Why 'Knife'?"

For a faery, you're a terrible liar, he had said. But she couldn't tell him the truth, because that would mean confessing that she had stolen her weapon from his House, and who knew what he might do to her then? Her only chance was to change the subject, and quickly.

"Where did you get that throne?" she blurted.

Silence crashed down between them, and the color ebbed out of Paul's face. "Throne." His voice rasped on the word. "Is *that* what you think this is?"

Knife shifted in her seat, embarrassed without knowing

why. Then her gaze fell to Paul's uncovered legs, so still and awkwardly bent, and her eyes widened as she realized her mistake—

"That's right," said Paul grimly. "I'm a cripple. You thought my parents were fussing over me and pushing me around in this thing because I liked it?" He spat out a laugh. *"I wish!"*

Knife swallowed. She had thought herself the injured one, but he had suffered a far greater loss. "I'm . . ." she began, but Paul cut her off.

"Don't say it." He shoved the chair back from the bed with a savage thrust of both hands. "I'm sick of apologies, and I don't want your pity. The only thing I want to know is, can we make a bargain?"

"A . . . bargain?"

"You're a faery. Isn't it obvious?"

She shook her head.

Paul gave an exasperated sigh and pushed a hand through his hair. "Magic. You have it, I need it. One wish, that's all I want—and then you can go home."

Knife looked at him helplessly. "I . . . can't," she said. "I don't have any magic."

"Look," said Paul. "I know faeries are supposed to be full of tricks and all that, but I'm not that stupid."

"Neither am I!" snapped Knife in frustration. "If I could cast spells, don't you think I'd have vanished in a puff of smoke by now, or at least healed my own wing so I could fly again? Not to mention that horrible cat of yours—believe me, I'd have been delighted to turn him into a toad and save you the trouble of rescuing me."

"If you'd stayed where I put you, you wouldn't have needed rescuing." His mouth twisted. "What a stupid thing to—"

"I didn't know you had a cat. And why shouldn't I try to escape? You put me in a box!" She folded her arms and added resentfully, "I don't understand why you won't just let me go."

"Are you serious? Do you have any idea what it means for a human being to find a real, live faery?"

"About the same as it means for a faery to find a real, live human being, I suppose," said Knife tartly. "Except I don't have a box big enough to put you—"

The last word froze on her tongue as the door creaked open, and Paul's cat squeezed himself through the gap. He sat down, showed his pointed teeth in a yawn, and began to wash himself with great thoroughness, while Knife ducked into Paul's shadow and tried to make herself as small as she could.

"It's all right," Paul said, and offered her his hand again. She climbed onto it, and he lifted her to the safety of his shoulder. Then he whistled between his teeth, making the cat look up.

Knife clutched at his shirt. "What are you doing?"

"Don't worry," said Paul. "I won't let him harm you." He rubbed a finger along the edge of the blankets, and the cat hurried to the side of the bed, watching with rapt golden eyes. Paul bent and scooped up the animal, dragging it onto his lap and holding it there.

"He's a silly cat, really," Paul remarked. "No brain whatsoever." He scratched the back of the cat's head, kneading his way down the spine to the tail, and it collapsed, purring. "He found a mouse once and had no idea what to do. So he sat on it until we came and took it away."

"He seemed to think he knew what to do with me," said Knife doubtfully.

"He probably thought you were some kind of wonderful new toy. He might have killed you by accident, but not on purpose."

This struck Knife as less than comforting, but there seemed little use in saying so. "What did you say his name was? Vermeer?"

"That's what I call him. Because of the way his fur shines in the light."

Not a true name, then, she thought, disappointed. She had hoped that knowing the cat's name would give her power to command it as Paul did. "I don't understand," she said aloud.

"Vermeer was a painter, back in the seventeenth century. Here, I'll show you." He seized the half-slumbering cat around the belly and tossed him onto the bed, then rolled over to the bookshelf. There he took down the biggest book Knife had ever seen and opened it to a full-color portrait of a young woman. Her eyes were wide, her lips slightly parted, and a teardrop-shaped ornament dangled from her ear.

Paul's finger traced the metallic sheen along the earring. "He was a genius with light," he said. "And he used a lot of rich, warm tones in his paintings."

Knife was silent, gazing at the girl's luminous face. The picture was beautiful, and yet somehow it was more than that. It was as though the artist were not merely showing her a girl, but telling her something about the girl as well.

Then in a flash Knife understood: That was what made the other paintings in the room special, too. They weren't just images, they were *ideas.* Excited, she slid off Paul's shoulder and leaped onto the desk, scanning each of the hanging canvases in turn. If she could just figure out what they were saying. . . .

"You like them," said Paul, and when she glanced back she saw a new respect in his eyes. "You really get it, don't you—art, I mean. You're not just being polite."

Knife nodded.

"Do you . . . would you like to see some more?"

She hesitated. He was offering her knowledge, but without magic, what could she give him in return? "I can't pay you," she said.

Paul made a face, as though she was being ridiculous.

"Pay me? What for? I'm not an expert. I just like art."

"But you have knowledge," she persisted. "That's worth something. You can't just give it away."

"Why not?"

"Because—" She struggled for an explanation, and finally threw up her hands. "Because that isn't how it's done!"

"Maybe that's how things work in that oak tree of yours," said Paul mildly. "But you're not there now, are you?"

Knife looked down at the painting of the girl, torn between doubt and yearning. For saving her from Old Wormwood, she already owed Paul a great debt. If she accepted any more favors, she might as well sign herself up as his slave, because it would take her years to pay him back.

And yet . . .

"Yes," she said. "I'd like to see some more. Please."

The tension lifted from Paul's face, and for a moment he looked almost like the boy who had climbed the Oak again. "Let me show you *The Lacemaker*," he said, and began turning pages.

When Knife woke the next morning her body ached, but her mind had never felt more alive. If only she could write down everything she had learned, before she had the chance to forget it!

She and Paul had talked for hours. Once he realized that she was genuinely interested in the art he loved, all the pent-up words of the past few weeks came rushing out of his mouth. He took book after book off his shelves, explaining different painting techniques and styles, pointing out his favorite artists and telling her why their work was important. Now and then he paused to give Knife a sidelong glance, as though he could scarcely believe that she was still listening; but all she ever said was, "Go on," and in the end he did.

When they had finished looking at the pictures, Paul took out his sketchbook again and began showing her how to draw, making quick sketches of her from various angles as he talked about things like shading, perspective, and point of view. For Knife it was a feast of knowledge, and she felt as though she could listen forever; but eventually Paul's voice thinned to huskiness, and when she caught him rubbing his eyes she realized that she had kept him up long enough. Still, when she said good night and climbed back into her damp-smelling box she could not help feeling disappointed that the conversation had not lasted longer. There was so much she could do with this knowledge once she returned to the Oak. . . .

Except that she couldn't, because then everyone would want to know where she had learned it. The Oakenfolk didn't have new ideas anymore; they had a hard enough time not forgetting the things they knew already. Besides, without Paul's books to show them, what good would it be? She had learned a great deal about art last night, but that didn't make her an artist.

Knife sighed as she rolled over and climbed to her feet. She crawled out of her box and sat down on the edge of the shelf, kicking the wardrobe door wide for a view of the room beyond.

Judging by the color of the light fingering its way past the curtains, it was almost noon, but Paul was still asleep. She cleared her throat loudly and rapped on the wooden shelf until he stirred in his nest of blankets, muttered something unintelligible, and opened his eyes.

"Good morning," said Knife.

He pushed himself up on one elbow, his gaze focusing blearily upon her. "You're still here," he said. "You weren't a dream."

"No. Should I have been?"

He ignored the question, pinching the bridge of his nose between his fingers. "I feel terrible."

"Well, I feel hungry," said Knife. "And you promised me meat, remember?"

Paul snorted, but the sound was good-natured. "Yes, Your Majesty."

"You managed to get all this from your mother without saying a word?" said Knife when Paul returned, bearing a heavily laden tray across his lap.

Paul stopped and shook his head warningly. "Not so loud," he mouthed, and Knife cringed. He was right, of course: They would both need to speak quietly if they wanted to keep her presence in the House a secret.

Gingerly Knife hopped onto the tray, sidestepping a glass of orange liquid and sitting down next to a plate steaming with two enormous eggs, a pile of beans in brown sauce, and several strips of fat-marbled meat. It was more food than she could have eaten in a week.

"Here," said Paul, breaking off a piece of toasted bread and handing it to her. Knife bit into it with relish, and was still chewing when he pulled out a book from the pocket on the side of his armrest and laid it open on the desk nearby.

"I found this in the other room," he said. "I thought you might like to see it."

"What is it?" asked Knife.

"It's about Alfred Wrenfield, a famous painter who used to live right around here—oh, must be over a hundred and fifty years ago now." Paul began turning pages. "At first he just painted landscapes and the occasional portrait. But later on he suddenly became obsessed with faeries and refused to paint anything else."

"Faeries?" said Knife, taken aback. "You mean . . . he saw them?"

"I didn't used to think so," said Paul. "But now that I look at you, I'm not so sure anymore. Alfred Wrenfield

116

wasn't the only artist who painted faeries, but he's the only one I know of who painted ones that look like you—not all plump and babyish or skinny and wrinkled like gnomes, but sort of wild and strange and . . ."

"And what?" prompted Knife.

But Paul only coughed, and turned the page. "Anyway, here's one of his early pieces, called *The Faeries' Dance*. What do you think?"

Knife stood up, took one look at the picture—and burst into laughter.

"What?" asked Paul, frowning. "You don't think they look like you?"

"Oh, the ones on the left aren't bad," said Knife, wiping away a tear of mirth, "but what on earth are those *things* lined up on the right?"

"Well, it's a dance," said Paul slowly, "so those must be the male faeries, right?"

"Male faeries," echoed Knife, and broke into chortles again.

"You mean . . . you've never seen a male faery? Ever?"

Paul sounded so puzzled, and so serious about it, that Knife's amusement faded. "Well, of course not," she said. "There aren't any."

"But there must be."

"We aren't *animals*," Knife explained patiently. "We don't need to rush about finding mates and having young. We live for three hundred years or more, barring accidents, and when we die, we just replace ourselves."

"Replace yourselves? With what?"

"Another faery, of course." He must be tired, she thought, to be this stupid.

"You mean—like a clone?"

Knife had no idea what that word meant, but she could tell that he had misunderstood her. "A new faery," she said. "Different from the one who died."

"Full grown?"

"No, of course not. The eggs are too small for that."

Paul's face took on an expression of disbelief. "You *lay eggs*?"

"No! Can you imagine—I mean, how ridiculous!" Knife nearly choked on her toast. "The egg just appears, when the old faery disappears. It's magic."

His eyes narrowed. "You told me you didn't have magic."

"We *are* magic, we just don't have very much power these days, and what's left we can't control. We don't will the eggs to appear, they just . . . do."

"All right, but one thing still doesn't make sense to me," said Paul. "I mean, I'm no scientist, and I'm no expert on magic either. But if there aren't any male faeries and never have been, why do you look so . . . well, *female*?"

Knife opened her mouth to argue—then shut it again with a snap as she realized he was right. Why should faeries who would never give birth to children or nurse them be shaped almost exactly like human women who did?

"Thank God," said Paul as he caught sight of Knife's stunned expression. "I thought I was going to have to get out the anatomy textbook. So do you understand now? I didn't mean to offend you by talking about male faeries—it was an honest mistake."

Knife folded back into her seat beside the plate, her mind churning. Could it be that long ago, the Oakenfolk had mated and born children as other creatures did? Perhaps something had happened to the male faeries, so the abandoned females had been forced to create their own eggs with magic—and after a while they forgot that there had ever been another way?

Heather's diary might be able to tell her. But it was back in her room at the Oak. Why did the answers Knife needed always seem to be just out of reach?

"I'm going to take a bath," said Paul, breaking the uneasy silence. "If I leave you here, will you still be here when I get back?"

It was a gesture of trust, Knife realized: He was asking her to stay, no longer behaving as though she had no choice. And though she did want to get back to Heather's diary and the mystery of the Oakenfolk's past, she also wanted to learn more about art—and this might well be her only chance.

"Yes," she said. "I'll be here."

Nine

"I've found you a better box," said Paul when he returned from his bath, damp-haired and freshly clothed. "And my mother's gone out to the garden, so we don't need to worry about her hearing us talk." He dropped the box onto the desk and pulled open the drawer. "Now where did I put my knife?"

Knife swallowed her last mouthful of toast. "Your . . . what?"

"Agh," said Paul in disgust. "My father must have poached it again." He shoved the drawer shut. "I bought him a proper letter opener two Christmases ago, but somehow my craft knife keeps on ending up in his study." He opened his hand to reveal a small, transparent canister balanced on his palm. "All I have are the blades, and they're

120

not much good without—"

"*Oh*," said Knife, eyes fixed on the sealed tube in his hand. There had to be at least five shards of metal in there, identical to the one she had stolen. Surely he could spare her one, if only she could think of something to offer him in return?

"What?"

"It's just . . . you have so many of them."

He looked at the canister dubiously. "Well, I suppose there are quite a few in there, but it's not like they're worth much."

Not valuable? Knife could hardly believe it. But if the blades were truly unimportant to him, then perhaps it wouldn't be so hard to strike a bargain for one—if only he didn't ask too many questions about why she wanted it. . . .

The longing must have been clear on her face, for Paul gave her a swift glance and then thumbed the tube open, scattering blades onto the desk. "Help yourself," he said.

Eagerly Knife stooped to snatch one up—yet even as her fingers closed around it, she realized what a fool she was being. "I can't," she said, feeling as though she had a nut wedged at the back of her throat. "I haven't got anything to offer you in return."

"So?" said Paul. "It's nothing to me. Like you said, I've got plenty."

All at once his kindness, and her guilt, were more than

Knife could bear. "But I stole from you," she stammered. "My first knife, the one I lost—I took it from your father's study. And I can't even pay for it." She looked down at the blade shining in her hand. "Or for this one either."

"You're really stuck on this idea of payment, aren't you?" said Paul. He sounded perplexed but, to Knife's relief, not angry. "Don't faeries ever just give things to one another?"

"The Queen gives out a few presents every year, at the Midwinter Feast," said Knife. "But that's only for faeries who have earned it."

"I'm not talking about rewards," said Paul, leaning forward. "I'm talking about gifts. This"—he touched the tip of the blade lightly with one finger—"is a gift, from me to you. You don't owe me anything for it, now or ever. All you have to do is take it. All right?"

"I—yes," said Knife.

"Good." He sat back in the chair. "Then it's settled."

"But I still stole the first—"

"So you said," said Paul. "But if you want me to get worked up about it, next time try stealing something that's actually valuable."

He was teasing her, Knife realized, but somehow she didn't mind. "I'll remember that," she said, and slid her new weapon—her *gift*—into its sheath.

Sometime later Knife sat cross-legged on the desk, studying the book laid open in front of her. Paul was right about

Alfred Wrenfield's paintings: The faeries in them looked quite a bit like the Oakenfolk, or at least the female ones did. But as she went further in the book the paintings became strange and confused, the faeries growing wilder and more cruel-looking as they increased in number, until Knife could hardly stand to look at them.

"What happened to him?" she said.

"Well, he did all right at first," Paul replied from his seat behind her, "because there was a bit of a craze for faery paintings at the time. But after a while his work became so weird that nobody wanted to buy it, and he went downhill pretty quickly after that. In the end even his family disowned him, and he died from an overdose of—"

"Paul, dear," came Beatrice's muffled voice from the other side of the door, "could you turn down the radio a moment? I need to talk to you."

Knife ducked behind a pile of books as Paul rolled out from behind the desk and went to answer. By the time he opened the door to his mother his face was a mask of indifference, and not for the first time, Knife felt sorry for the woman.

"I've just had a call from your father," said Beatrice, wiping her hands on her apron. "There's been a problem with his train—an accident on the line, they're not sure how long it will take to clear—and he asked if I might drive into the city and pick him up. I've made you up a cold dinner, and put the number for the home care service by the phone, just in case you need help—"

Paul said nothing. His mother cleared her throat nervously and went on:

"We'll be back as soon as we can. You'll . . . be all right?"

Paul gave a slight shrug, which seemed to be all the answer Beatrice needed. Stooping, she brushed her lips against his cheek, then hurried away down the corridor; in a moment Knife heard the front door open and shut, and the House settled back into silence.

"Looks like we have the place to ourselves tonight," Paul said as he wheeled the chair around to face Knife again. "What would you say to a cup of tea?"

The cup was a china thimble, and the tea was dark and bitter, but it made Knife feel like an honored guest to sit beside Paul in the House's opulent front parlor, sipping it. As she drank she studied the portraits hanging on the opposite wall: George and Beatrice on their wedding day, looking shy and very young; Paul as a boy, with shaggy hair and a gap-toothed smile; and a more recent one of the family together, Beatrice seated with her husband behind her and Paul leaning casually back against her knees. His face glowed with confidence, and as Knife noticed the lighted tree in the background she realized that the picture must have been done at Midwinter, only a few months ago.

"Who painted those?" she asked Paul. "They look so real."

"The photographs, you mean? They aren't paintings, they're . . . well, they're a sort of image made with light. You look through a box with a lens in it, and you press a button, and it makes a picture of what you're seeing. More or less."

It sounded like magic to Knife. "Do you have any more?" she asked.

"I suppose, but they're pretty dull if you're not in the family." He wheeled his chair over to the cabinet, returning a moment later with a thick, ring-bound volume. As he opened it, Knife jumped onto the arm of the chair and climbed up to his shoulder, leaning forward for a better view of the pages spread out below.

"Stupid baby pictures," said Paul, flipping briskly past the first section. "This is me on the first day of school. And here I am painting a mustache on Geoffrey Fisher—he was my best friend at the time."

"What's a *best friend*?" asked Knife.

Paul turned sharply to look at her. "You don't know?"

"Well," said Knife, defensive, "my people don't really do that kind of thing."

"What do you do, then?"

"We work together when we have to, and we give each other instructions and such. But when the work's done, and there's nothing more to be said . . ." She gave an indifferent shrug. "What would be the point?"

"The point is," said Paul quietly, "that a best friend is someone you *like* to be with. Someone you can talk to about anything, and count on to help you whenever you need it. You really don't have anyone like that?"

"No," said Knife. And neither did he, she suspected—or at least, not anymore. If he had friends, best or otherwise, he wouldn't be holed up alone in his room, hiding from his parents and the world.

"None of your people do?"

"No." Though perhaps it hadn't always been that way—but she would need to read more of Heather's diary to be sure.

Paul shook his head, and turned another page.

"What's that?" said Knife, pointing to a photograph of a much younger Paul standing beside a picture of a winter landscape.

"Oh, that," said Paul. "That's the painting I entered in a competition, when I was nine. It won first prize."

"Have you always been good at art?" asked Knife.

"Not at first. I mean, I always liked to draw, but they were just kid's scribbles mostly. But when I was about eight years old, I suddenly started sketching everything in sight. My parents didn't know what to make of it, but my teachers got all excited. I think they were hoping I'd be the next Alfred Wrenfield—only without the going mad part. And

I wanted to be a great painter back then, as much as I'd ever wanted anything."

He spoke distantly, as if it were some childish dream he'd since given up, and Knife frowned. He was still drawing, wasn't he?

"Anyway," said Paul, "back to the pictures—"

He stopped, and Knife felt his muscles tense. "What is it?" she asked.

He did not reply. At the bottom of the page a pale-haired boy sat in a narrow rowboat, teeth bared and arms flung skyward in exultation. But she had barely glimpsed the image before Paul's hand slapped down upon it and ripped it away.

Instinctively Knife flinched back, overbalanced, and toppled off Paul's shoulder. With a strangled cry she fell through the air, bounced off the corner of the sofa, and crashed to the carpet below.

For one dizzy moment she lay there, too stunned to move. Far above, Paul's fist closed around the photograph as he stared into the distance. He did not seem to notice that she had fallen, and she gulped a breath like a sob before calling out to him, "Paul!"

His face crumpled into rage. With a swift blow he knocked the book of pictures from his lap, and Knife threw her arms over her head as it crashed onto the floor beside her, scattering pages and photographs everywhere.

By the time she dared to look up, Paul was gone, but she could still feel the weight of the book's cover against her throbbing ankle. *It hit me,* she thought numbly, and then with dawning outrage, *He hit me.*

With or without magic to enforce it, the rules of a faery bargain were clear: If either party struck the other, even by accident, all obligations between them were canceled. Until now Knife had been in Paul's debt, no matter what he might say about *gifts*; but now, she owed him nothing.

Anger flooded through her, renewing her strength. Knife crawled out from the wreckage of the photo album and began limping across the carpet toward the hallway.

"There are no scissors!" shouted Paul from the kitchen, as cupboards banged and drawers slammed. "No knives, no matches—nothing!" Then came silence, and at last in a voice soft but deadly: "Oh, look. How sweet. She put all the hurty things up where her little crippled boy couldn't reach them."

Knife clenched her teeth and kept walking. All the windows at this end of the house were shut, so she quickened her pace, hurrying down the corridor to the sitting room as the crashing noises resumed. She glanced around, but the din made it impossible to think, and at last she shouted into the kitchen, "Stop it!"

A saucepan belled out as Paul flung it across the tile. "Shut up!" he spat back at her.

Knife ran to the sitting room doors and tugged, then with grim purpose took hold of the sheer curtain and began swinging herself up hand over hand. She had almost reached the latch when she heard Paul's voice behind her:

"What are you doing?"

Knife kicked herself upward, grabbed the latch with both hands, and hung there. "I'm trying—to open—the door."

"It's locked."

"Fine." She slid back down the curtain, turned to face him. "Then I'll find another way to get out."

Paul looked down at her, his expression bleak but no longer angry. "Look, I'm sorry if I frightened you," he said. "I'd just . . . I'd forgotten that picture was in there."

"I don't care! I don't want to hear about it! Just let me go!" She ran past him and jumped into the air, wings fluttering wildly as she tried to reach the window above the kitchen sink. Out of the corner of her eye she saw Vermeer slink into the room and crouch down, watching her; but still she continued leaping and dropping back to the floor, until she was almost sobbing with frustration.

"Knife," said Paul. "Knife, don't."

"I thought I could trust you." The words burst out of her, and only as she spoke them did she realize that they were true. She had stopped being afraid of Paul, stopped thinking of herself as his prisoner, stopped even trying to escape—what madness had possessed her, to make her think that she could be *friends* with a human?

Well, she knew better now.

"You can trust me," Paul was pleading. "I know I frightened you, but I never meant—"

"You nearly killed me!"

His face paled. "But you—you were on my shoulder. You jumped off—"

"I *fell* off. And then you threw that book on top of me!"

Paul's face went slack with despair. At last he said, "You're right. I'll let you go. Tomorrow."

She lifted her chin in defiance. "Tonight."

"No. It's almost dark, it's not safe. Just stay until morning. Please."

"I'm not going to change my mind, if that's what you're thinking."

"I know."

"And I'm not going to talk to you either. Not even about art."

"I know." His eyes begged hers, and finally she gave in. "Oh, all right," she said.

Paul let out his breath. "Thank you."

"Don't you dare!" she snapped at him, furious all over again. After what he'd done already—how could he cheapen something so precious, speak those sacred words as though they meant nothing?

"What?"

Too disgusted to answer, Knife stalked past him into the

130

corridor. She could feel his eyes on her, but she refused to look back until she was nearly to the bedroom, and by then he had turned away.

When she did look back, she saw Paul bow his head, then slowly unfold his hand to reveal the photograph he had torn from the album. With surprising gentleness he smoothed it out upon his lap and gazed down at his younger self, while Knife watched, her anger melting into perplexity. Why that picture, she wondered, of all the pictures they had seen?

No. She was not going to think about this—about him— anymore. Tomorrow she would return to the Oak, resign as Hunter, and throw herself into whatever other work the Queen might give her, until she had no energy left to even think about humans.

And maybe then she would stop feeling Paul McCormick's pain.

Ten

"All right," said Knife, "I've finished breakfast—now will you let me go?"

"Not yet," said Paul, pulling the curtains aside to let in the dim morning light. "This is my mother's shopping day. We'll need to wait until she leaves."

"I don't see why. You could just let me out right now."

"I know, but I'd prefer to go with you a little way at least. Make sure you get back home all right."

Knife blew out her breath in exasperation; for all his politeness, this human was as stubborn as Thorn. "I don't want to wait any longer. I have things to do."

"It won't be much longer."

Restless, Knife paced around the breakfast tray, flexing her injured wing. She could still feel its ragged edge, but it no longer hurt every time she moved. Which was a mercy, because it was bad enough being grounded without having to live with constant pain as well. . . .

Then a thought occurred to her: Was Paul in pain? Not that it made a difference—he had struck her, and deserved none of her pity. But his face looked especially drawn this morning, his skin sallow and his forehead beaded with sweat. Perhaps she had judged him too harshly.

"You should lie down," she said in a matter-of-fact tone, not wanting him to think she was softening.

He wiped his brow on his sleeve, and as his hand fell she saw that it was shaking. "I just need some fresh air," he said. "I haven't been outside for two days."

"Paul!" came Beatrice's voice from the other side of the door.

Paul opened his mouth to reply, then looked startled and shut it again.

"She almost had you there," murmured Knife.

"I'm just going into town, dear. I'll be back by lunchtime." She paused, waiting for a reply she must have known by now not to expect. "I'll bring you back something to read. Good-bye," she said, and the sound of her footsteps receded.

"I thought humans were supposed to be kind to their mothers," said Knife to Paul, who pretended not to hear. He opened the window and stuck his head out.

"Right, she's gone," he said a few moments later, wheeling around. "Let's go."

Knife jumped onto the seat beside him, looping her arm around a steel post for support. Paul barely gave her time to sit down before he began to move again, steering the chair across the room and out into the hallway.

Opening the front door was simple enough, but they had to take two runs at the frame before they cleared it. Then as Paul's chair bumped down the wooden ramp and onto the gravel drive, Knife thought her teeth would rattle out of her head. Even when they reached the smoother paving of the road, her jaw still ached.

"May I go now?" she asked, a little peevishly.

"Yes," said Paul, gliding to a stop. "You can go. Sorry to have kept you."

Knife hesitated. There was an artificial calm about his manner she did not trust. "Where are you going?" she asked, sliding off the seat and leaping to the ground beside the chair.

"Not far. Just up the road." He forced a smile. "I could use the exercise."

"Oh," said Knife.

"Well, I'm glad to have met you, if only for a little while. Can you get home all right from here?"

Knife curled her fingers about the unfinished hilt of her dagger, feeling the metal's hardness against her palm. "I'll be fine."

"Right, then," said Paul, too cheerfully. "I'll just go ahead."

His hands stroked the wheels, and the chair rocked into motion, picking up speed as it rolled down the lane. "Goodbye, Knife," he called back over his shoulder.

She had thought she would be glad to see him go. But the farther away Paul went the more Knife's uneasiness grew. She debated a moment, then decided that she would follow him a little way and see where he was going. Not for his sake, of course; just for her own curiosity.

Instinctively she spread her wings, then grimaced and folded them again. No chance of following him that way. She would just have to run, and hope he did not get too far ahead of her. Knife broke into a trot, then threw caution aside and began sprinting after him.

She had followed Paul only a short way down the road when he surprised her by turning the chair away from the pavement, bumping down a grassy incline toward the nearby wood. A path led into the trees, but it was rocky and overgrown, barely wide enough for Paul's chair. Still, he forced his way onward with such determination that Knife had to scurry to keep up with him.

Eventually the forest thinned, and they entered a clearing where a weed-ringed pool lay at the bottom of a slope, half hidden by stooping elms. Knife looked about, frowning. Why had he come here?

"I've always loved this wood," Paul said aloud, startling her. "It was my favorite place as a kid. I tried to build a house in that tree." He pointed to the stoutest of the elms.

"You knew I was here?" said Knife.

His mouth bent wryly. "I guessed you might come along. But you're going to be disappointed. There's really nothing here to see."

"Then why did you come?"

He shrugged, his eyes sliding away from hers. "Just a whim. I wanted to look at the old place again."

Knife nodded distractedly. She walked to the top of the slope, damp earth squashing between her toes. If Paul was telling the truth, then humans were even stranger and more impractical than she'd thought. He'd had enough of a struggle just getting down the hill—how did he think he was going to get back up?

"Knife?" said Paul. "It's all right, you can go." Then, with a hint of desperation: "Just—go now. Please."

Knife did not look back; her eyes were fixed on the pool. It was perhaps thirty crow-lengths wide, and so murky that her eyes could not penetrate its surface.

"I used to swim here when I was young," said Paul, rolling up behind her. He sounded resigned; he seemed to have realized that she had no intention of leaving. "It wasn't half so muddy then—or perhaps I just didn't care how muddy it was." He gave the wheels another push, and the silver throne lurched past her.

"Paul," said Knife sharply. "You're too close!"

For the rest of her life she would never forget the look he

gave her then. There was pity in it, and a touch of regret; but on the whole it was a look of terrifying serenity. "Yes," he said, and with a powerful thrust of both arms he propelled himself straight down the slope.

His wheels hit the mud at the pool's edge, slowed, stuck fast. Paul toppled out of the chair and hit the oily water with a splash. His legs were dead weight, and he made no effort to move his arms. He simply relaxed into the pool . . .

. . . and was gone.

Knife stared at the ripples spreading outward across the gloomy water, the last flurry of bubbles as Paul's bright hair sank beneath the surface. Her throat closed up, and a dull pain spread beneath her rib cage.

There was nothing she could do. With her crippled wing she couldn't fly for help, and she was far too tiny to rescue him by herself. . . .

Knife's shoulders slumped. She turned away, took one step—then spun around, hurtled down the slope, and dove straight into the pool.

Her hands swept circles through the grainy water, searching the spot where he had sunk, but touched nothing. She broke the surface for a gasping breath and dove deeper, flailing in all directions; but she snatched at emptiness, and when she came up again she found nothing but black water running from her hands.

One more time, she pledged silently. *Come on, go!* Again she dove, as deep as she could, kicking a little sideways this time. Her left arm sliced down through the water—

And her hand closed on something soft. Paul's shirt. She grabbed it with both hands and hauled, legs thrashing, every muscle strained to its limit. But even as she struggled, she knew it was hopeless: She could never hope to lift him so much as a beetle-length, let alone drag him to the surface. She had to let go, before she drowned as well.

Yet something in her refused to give up. She tugged again, fiercely, as her vision filled with sparkling lights. A million tiny moths fluttered beneath her skin, and she felt as though her lungs were bursting. Was this death?

Still clutching Paul's shirt, she gave one last kick— and shot upward, shattering the pool's surface. She flung her head back and gulped air, then scissored her legs, propelling herself and the limp body in her grip toward the shore.

Her feet touched bottom almost at once. She stood up and dragged Paul through the shallows to the edge of the pool. His face was spattered with mud, eyes closed and mouth hanging open. Pulling him as far as she could up the shore, she wrenched him onto his side and began to pound his back. He lay motionless as she thumped him, and she feared that she had reached him too late. Then suddenly he coughed, and water gushed from his mouth.

She waited until he had stopped coughing before rolling

him over again. His eyes remained closed, but when she laid a hand on his chest she could feel his breathing, ragged at first, but growing deeper. She slapped his cheeks. "Paul. Paul! Can you hear me?"

He did not respond. With her smallest finger she wiped the slime from his lashes, looking for some glimmer of consciousness beneath those lids. "Paul, please—"

His cheeks puffed out in a last, weak cough; he stirred, and opened his eyes.

"*Aaaah!*"

Alarmed, Knife snatched her hands away from his face. Only then did she realize what had made him cry out, and she stared at her filth-spattered palms in disbelief.

"You," croaked Paul. "You're—"

"I'm big," said Knife blankly.

"You're human," said Paul in a voice husky with wonder, and his cold fingers brushed her cheek.

Blood surged into her face; she jerked away from the touch. "I am not!"

"Your hair . . ." He lifted a strand. "It's blonde, instead of white. And your eyes look . . . lighter. Sort of gray."

"Stop it." She slapped his hand away. "I may be your size, but I am *not* human. It must be a trick of the light."

"Then where are your wings?"

Slowly Knife reached back and felt between her shoulders. "They'll come back," she said, fighting to keep the uncertainty from her voice. "As soon as this—whatever just happened—wears off."

Paul looked about to object, but was interrupted by another fit of coughing. "Magic," he said weakly when he had finished. "You know, that thing you aren't supposed to have?"

The reproach in his tone snapped her back to herself. "Paul McCormick," she exploded, "you are the most fly-brained, stone-stubborn, rabbit-witted—"

He gave a rasping laugh. "You dove in after me. What does that make you?" He moved to sit up, but she pressed his shoulders down with her hands.

"Don't you dare. You'll stay right here until we're both rested, and until I get your promise—no, your oath—that you'll never do anything like that again."

He glared up at her, rebellious; she stared down at him with equal determination. At last he turned his face aside. "Fine," he muttered.

She caught him by the jaw, forcing him to look back at her. "Swear," she said.

"I swear never to try and drown myself in front of you again."

"That isn't enough. You know what I want. Say it."

"That's all you'll get!" He struggled against her grasp, then fell back panting.

"Why did you do it in the first place?" demanded Knife.

"If you really wanted to die—"

"It's not my fault you wouldn't leave! Anyway, how was I to know you could change size? You lied to me!"

"I didn't lie," Knife said stiffly, letting him go. "I've never done magic before. I didn't know I had it in me." She stood up, wringing water from her sodden tunic. "And now I've probably used it all up, saving your miserable human neck."

Paul was silent.

"How much time do we have until your mother gets back?" Knife put a hand to her hair and let it drop, disgusted. "I can't believe you used to swim in that hole."

"Neither can I. And she won't be home for a couple of hours."

"Then we'll have enough time to get you back to the House. And if we're lucky, she'll never guess what you tried to do today."

"How long will you . . . stay like that?" Paul asked, raising himself up on his elbows with difficulty.

"I don't know. So we'd better hurry." She strode to the edge of the pool and yanked his wheelchair free of the mud. "Come on."

It was hard going back up the hill, though not as difficult as Knife had feared. She might be the size of a human, but Paul's shocked reaction when she picked him up and lifted him into the chair made plain that she was stronger than an ordinary human woman would be. So while she had to put all her weight behind the wheeled throne in order to push it up the slope, she did not worry that her strength would fail—only that her muddy feet might slip and send both her and Paul tumbling to the bottom again.

When they reached the crest, Knife paused to catch her breath, rubbing her aching palms against her thighs. All the way up the slope she had kept her head down, focused doggedly on the task at hand; now at last she could relax and see how far they had come.

"We made it," said Paul shakily.

Knife looked up, shielding her eyes against the sunlight. High overhead two crows were circling, but for the first time in her life, she could watch their flight without fear. A squirrel scampered across her path, all soft fur and bright eyes. Trees, grass, wildflowers—everything around her seemed lovelier and more meaningful than ever before, and it was hard for Knife not to wonder if this might be the way the world was *meant* to be seen. After all, it was a lot easier to appreciate a landscape when you weren't worried that something in it was going to kill you.

But there was no time for sightseeing; they had to get back to the House. She turned to Paul, only to find that he had already wheeled his chair back onto the road and was pushing it homeward with brisk, determined strokes. She had to run to catch up with him.

Once they reached the House, Knife fetched the garden hose from the side of the house and sprayed the chair, Paul, and herself until she had washed away all trace of mud. Then they went inside, where there were towels to fetch, laundry to gather, and wet floors to mop; and by the time Paul agreed they had done enough and took himself off to a hot bath, Knife was more than ready for one herself.

Yet even as she lay in the McCormicks' upstairs tub with the warm water lapping over her skin, Knife could not relax. The feeling of the porcelain against her shoulders reminded her of her missing wings, and all the worries she had tried to suppress bubbled back to the surface of her mind. She might not be the first faery since the Sundering to inadvertently cast a spell, but she was surely the first to turn herself human. What if she ended up stuck this way? Or worse, what if she shrank to her natural size, but her wings never came back?

Hastily Knife pulled the plug and stood up. Her tunic and breeches were still damp, but she wrung them out as best she could before wrestling herself into them. She might not know what would happen to her next, but when the magic wore off—if it wore off—at least she would not be caught unprepared.

By the time she made her way down the stairs, Paul was waiting at the bottom. "Sorry about all that," he said, not quite looking at her. "You can go now."

"Back to the Oak? Not at this size," she replied. "Besides, I'm not going anywhere until you—"

A tingling chill ran through her body as she spoke, and the room reeled around her. When her dizziness subsided she lifted her head, to see Paul staring down at her from a mountainous distance.

It's worn off, she thought, her relief oddly muted by disappointment. She struggled to her feet—and froze as something rustled behind her. Her wings lifted, spreading wide . . .

"Great Gardener," she whispered.

"Well," said Paul in a flat voice, "that solves one problem."

Excitement rippled through Knife, making her lighter than air. She leaped from the floor and soared toward the ceiling, ducking the light fixture as she swooped past Paul into the corridor. Rolling and twisting, she tested her wings from every angle, then turned a somersault and pulled herself up to a hovering stop, giddy with delight.

Then she caught sight of herself in the hallway mirror. Her wings might have returned to her whole, but they had also changed. They seemed paler now, more fragile; less like paper, and more like glass. And now that the first thrill of flight had passed, she could feel that her wing muscles were not as strong as they had been. Already her shoulders ached, and keeping herself suspended in the air was an effort.

But even so, she was flying. And that meant that she was still the Queen's Hunter, free to return to the Oak and take up her duties. It was more than she had dreamed possible, and as she spiraled down to land on the end of the banister, Knife smiled.

Paul smiled back, but his eyes remained somber, and Knife's happiness drained away as she realized how he must feel. What would it be like to be broken beyond hope of healing, and have to watch someone else celebrate being made whole?

"Tell me," she said quietly.

"Tell you what?" He swung the chair around and began rolling back toward his bedroom. Knife sprang into the air and followed.

"Back there," she persisted as she landed on the top of the wardrobe, "at the pool. Why did you try to kill yourself?"

"Isn't it obvious?"

"No," said Knife. "And there are a few other things I don't understand. Why won't you talk to your parents? Are you angry at—"

"No!" He spun the chair away from her. Knife launched herself from the wardrobe and bounced onto the corner of his bed.

"Look at me!" she insisted.

"I don't want to talk about this."

"Maybe not, but you will." She stalked to the edge of the mattress, as close to Paul as she could get without touching him. "I saved your life today. You owe me."

"Fine. What do you want? More knife blades?"

"No." Although the offer was tempting. "I want to understand."

"Why? What difference does it make to you?"

"I don't know!" Now it was her turn to shout, and Paul's to wince. "I don't know why I dove into that pool after you, or why I grew big, or why I lost my wings and got them back again. I don't know why I'm still sitting here talking to you when I should be on my way home—I don't know why I should even care!" She pressed her knuckles against her forehead in frustration, then added in a lower voice, "All I know is that I do."

For a moment Paul sat unmoving, his head bent. Then he said quietly, "All right. I'll tell you."

Eleven

Knife sat down cross-legged on the mattress, waiting for Paul's answer. He knotted his hands together, then cleared his throat and began to speak:

"I already told you that I started drawing when I was just a kid, and that I was good. Better than good, even—there were words like *genius* and *prodigy* being tossed around. But after a couple of years, my creativity just . . . dried up. I could still draw, but everything I did seemed ordinary. Lifeless, even. I wasn't special anymore.

"I was pretty unhappy, and my parents could tell, but I couldn't explain it to them. How could I, when I didn't even understand it myself? In the end they decided there must be something wrong with the art program at the local school, so they sent me to boarding school instead. Which was actually not bad, once I got used to it. My art didn't get any better, but I made some friends and they got me interested in something I'd never tried before—rowing."

"Rowing?" said Knife, but Paul did not seem to hear her.

"I'd never been much of an athlete, but once I felt those oars in my hands, I just knew. I dropped everything else and threw myself into training, and by the end of the year I was winning competitions." His face brightened with the memory. "I don't know if I can describe it to you—the feeling you get when you've just finished a race, when you're all out of breath and your nerves are shredded and every muscle in your body is screaming, but at the same time you feel so incredibly *alive*."

"Oh, yes," said Knife. That feeling, at least, she understood perfectly.

"Once I started winning, I couldn't get enough of it. I'd failed as an artist, but as a rower I just kept getting better, and after a while sculling was the only thing I cared about anymore. I had so many plans—I was going to qualify for the World Championships, maybe even the Olympic team. But then—"

He hunched forward, his hands sliding up over his face. "It was a Friday night," he went on thickly, "and I'd gone out with some friends to watch a football game, but I stayed too late. . . . I could see the school gates closing ahead of me, so I started to run. The light hadn't changed, but the road looked clear, and I was halfway across when this car came around the corner, I didn't even see it until it hit me, and I felt my spine just *snap*—"

Knife bit her lips, appalled. There was a long silence.

"And now," said Paul in a whisper, "I'm paralyzed from the waist down. I can't walk, I can't row, I can't even—" He gave a humorless laugh. "Believe me, you don't want to know about some of the things I can't do. I'll never qualify for the Olympics, never row properly again. All my dreams—gone. Just like that."

"And that's why . . . ?" asked Knife, still uncertain. She could imagine how devastated Paul had been: She had felt the same helpless misery when she'd thought she would never fly again. But to give up on life completely . . . that part she couldn't understand.

"No," said Paul, sounding tired. "I mean, yes, but that's not the only reason. After the accident, none of my friends knew what to say to me anymore. Oh, they came, and they tried, but it was just pathetic all around, and in the end, nobody came to see me except my parents.

"My parents," he repeated bitterly, "didn't give up, but after a while I wished they had. When they told me they'd fixed up the house for me, and that they were taking me home . . . it was like the last few years had just been erased from my life. As though I'd never gone away to school, never grown up at all. I'd stopped being the son who was going to make them proud, and had become this sad, crippled little boy."

"I thought you said you weren't angry with them," said Knife.

"I wasn't, not exactly. I knew it wasn't their fault. It was more like—" He rubbed a hand across his brow. "I didn't want them to make any more sacrifices for me. I didn't want them to care. I wanted to stop being their son, and become a thing in a chair that they would get tired of. So when I finally got the chance to kill myself, it'd be a relief for them, too."

"So," Knife said slowly, "you stopped talking to everyone. Except me. Why?"

"You were different."

"I don't understand."

"You should." He let his hand drop, and Knife flinched at the anguish in his eyes. "I never expected to meet you again," he said. "After so many years, I'd given up believing you were real. But there you were, standing by the hedge, looking at me. It took me a long time to get my mind around that. And then, just as I'd almost convinced myself I'd been dreaming, you fell out of the sky and landed in my lap.

"When I saw you lying there, with that ripped wing, I—I wanted you to live. I wanted to see if you could still fly, or what you would do if you couldn't. But then you woke up, and you talked to me. Without gentleness, without pity. As if I were—whole."

Apprehension prickled up Knife's spine. She opened her mouth to tell him that he'd said enough, but it was too late. Paul squeezed his eyes shut, and an unfamiliar ache grew inside her as she realized that he was crying.

"Then you let me sketch you, and it turned out—it was perfect. The best thing I'd done in years. And when we were talking about art, you were so interested in everything I said, it made me think that maybe—"

"Stop," pleaded Knife. "You don't have to go on, I understand." And she did, for the rest of the story was painfully clear. He had come to think of her as a friend, but then he had lost his temper and frightened her away. The one good thing that had happened to him since his accident, spoiled—and it was his fault. No wonder he had decided to give up.

Paul gave a shaky laugh and wiped his face on his sleeve. "Spreading it a bit thick, I know. Sorry."

"No," said Knife, "I'm sorry. I shouldn't have asked, I was being . . ." She hesitated. Had she ever used this word before in her life? But it was the truth. "Selfish."

"You're a faery," said Paul. "Of course you don't think like a human would. I don't blame you."

Knife looked down at her feet. "I should go. My people—they'll be wondering where I am."

151

Paul reached up, unlocking the window and sliding it open. "I know it's not much, considering you saved my life," he said. "But if you ever want to come and talk about art, or look at my books, or anything . . . I'll be here. All right?"

"All right," said Knife, a little dazed by the generous offer. With a flick of her wings she leaped to the sill, then paused and looked back at him. "I'll come," she said. "I'm not sure when, but—I'll try."

He smiled. "Good."

Knife turned and stepped straight out into the air. Wings thrumming, she dropped lightly to land on the old stone path, half buried in mosses and grass. Sunlight warmed her back, and she heard lark song in the distance. She was free.

"Good-bye, Knife," said Paul's voice from above, and she heard his chair creak as he rolled away. Knife stood still, looking up at the empty window. Then she shook herself, squared her shoulders, and set off down the path into the Oakenwyld.

Skirting the edge of the garden, Knife slipped from shadow to shadow as she made her way back toward the Oak. Halfway through the journey she paused by one of the flower beds, plunged her hands deep into the moist earth, and rubbed them over her face and arms, leaving muddy streaks everywhere. With her fingers she raked her hair into a tangle, crumbling in bits of bark and dead leaves for good measure. Then she wiped her palms on her breeches and continued on.

She had barely set foot inside the Oak before she ran into one of the Gatherers, who turned white and stumbled off down the corridor toward the kitchen, yelling. Within moments Knife found herself at the center of a commotion, goggle-eyed Oakenfolk all quarreling and pushing to get a look at their Hunter, seemingly returned from the grave.

It was Thorn who finally broke through the crowd and addressed Knife, her scowl doing nothing to hide her obvious relief. "Well," she said, "you may look like you've crawled through a molehill and been worried by a fox, but you seem to be in one piece."

Of course she was glad, thought Knife: She must have been dreading the thought of having to become Queen's Hunter again. "What happened to Linden and Tansy?" she asked. "Did they get back all right?"

"Linden died soon after she was brought to me." The quiet response came from above, and Knife looked up to see Valerian rounding the last bend of the Spiral Stair. "But Tansy was unharmed, and we were able to save Linden's egg. Are you hurt?"

"I'm fine," said Knife.

"But I saw you fall." The quavering voice was Tansy's. "I thought the crow had got you for sure, or that human—"

"If he had, would she be here?" Thorn interrupted scornfully before Knife could reply. "Don't talk nonsense. She only dove, to throw the crow off her track—it's an old Hunter's trick."

"That's as it may be," said Mallow's harsh tones from the back of the crowd. "But if there's nothing wrong with her, where's she been? We've had no meat in two days."

"What you mean is, you've had no chance to gorge yourself on scraps," retorted Thorn, "and I don't see why anyone should shed a tear over that." She caught Knife by the elbow, steering her through the crowd. "Besides, it's the Queen's privilege to talk to Knife before any of you lot, so clear off."

Grumbling, the rest of the Oakenfolk dispersed. Thorn let go of Knife and said in a low voice, "But if I were you, I'd have a long soak and a spot of hard scrubbing before you report to the Queen. You stink."

"She is certainly dirty," agreed Valerian mildly from beside them, "although I hadn't noticed the smell. Come, Knife. I can look you over while you're having your bath, to save time. We shouldn't keep Her Majesty waiting."

"I believed we had lost you," said Queen Amaryllis. "For all our sakes, I am glad that I was mistaken. Are you well?"

"Yes, Your Majesty," said Knife.

"And yet"—the Queen's eyes narrowed as they swept

over Knife—"you appear . . . changed."

My wings, thought Knife with a flash of panic. *She's noticed my wings. What do I tell her?*

"Bluebell, bring our visitor a chair," ordered the Queen, and her attendant hurried to obey. Knife did not feel much like sitting, especially with the Queen looking down at her, but when Bluebell nudged the chair against the backs of her knees, she had no choice.

"Tell me, then," continued Amaryllis when Knife was seated. "What became of you, after you fought the crow? I sent Thorn out to search for you, but she could find no trace."

Was this a trap, or genuine concern? It was impossible to tell. Knife decided to keep her story as close to the truth as she could. "I was flying ahead of Old Wormwood, trying to lead him away from Linden and Tansy," she began, "when he struck at me and ripped my wing. I fell to the ground unconscious, and when I woke I found myself lying in a dark place, where the crow couldn't reach me.

"At first I was weak, and needed to rest. After a while I found food and water, and my strength began to return, but I was still a long way from the Oak. I couldn't fly, so I started out on foot, but then I met a cat. It could have killed me, but . . ."

This was it, the giant leap. She could only pray that the Queen didn't guess how much of the story she was leaving out. "At the last moment I managed to make myself bigger— even bigger than the cat. I didn't know how I'd done it, but I knew it had to be magic." Forcing herself to be bold, she looked straight up at the Queen. "How could that be?"

"It has happened before," said Amaryllis. "But rarely, and only at times of great need. The Great Gardener was merciful."

Knife nodded. "Anyway, it saved me. When the spell wore off I tried my injured wing again, and it worked—the magic had healed it somehow. So I flew back to the Oak, and here I am."

The Queen regarded Knife, one finger crooked thoughtfully against her chin. Then she said, "I confess I am relieved to hear your story. Tansy's report led me to believe that you had fallen into the garden, not far from the Oak. When Thorn could not find you, I feared that you had been taken by the humans, and that we might all be in danger."

An icy hand closed around Knife's throat. The Queen's guess had come so perilously close to the truth—did she sense, even now, that Knife was deceiving her? Perhaps it was a test, and this was Knife's last chance to prove herself a loyal subject. Perhaps she should throw herself on the Queen's mercy, and tell her everything.

And yet Knife was no longer sure she could trust Amaryllis. If the Queen had been willing to burn a shelf's worth of precious books just to keep her people from taking too much interest in humans, what would she do if she found out her Hunter had actually befriended one? Of course she could hardly execute Knife for treason, not with so few faeries left in the Oak. But she might harm Paul, if her magic could reach him—and Knife didn't like that thought at all.

"In any case," the Queen went on in a brisker tone, "you showed great courage in rescuing Linden from the crow, especially at such risk to yourself. It is evident that you have been through a grave ordeal, and it is to your credit that you returned to the Oak as quickly as you did. Valerian, you have examined her and found her well?"

"Yes, Your Majesty," came a quiet voice from the back of the room, and Knife started. She had forgotten the Healer was there. "All she needs is a chance to rest."

"Then I relieve you of your duties until tomorrow," said the Queen to Knife. "You are dismissed."

Knife stumbled into her room and threw herself down on the sofa, exhausted. After her interview with the Queen she felt as though all her bones had been taken out one by one and examined, but she seemed to have made it through all right.

So why did she still have the disquieting feeling that Amaryllis had not believed her?

She swung her legs around and sat up. After spending

so long in the House, her room now seemed more cramped than ever, with naked walls and furnishings so crude it hurt to look at them. She longed for a few pictures to brighten up the place—but no, that was impossible. Nearly everything beautiful the Oak had to offer had been sent to the archives; even the Queen's walls were bare. Art was too rare and precious now to be entrusted to a single person.

But why should it be that way? Before the Sundering the Oak had been full of artists and writers and craftswomen of all kinds. What had happened to their creativity? And was there any way of getting it back?

She might find some clues in Heather's diary, if it had not gone missing in her absence—ah, there it was. Knife lit a candle, sat down on the bed, and eased the book open at the place she had last marked.

Jasmine's temper has improved greatly since the others stopped slighting her, and I am glad to see that my words on her behalf did not go unheeded. She has certainly begun to greet me with more warmth, especially once she saw the work I did on her gown, which I flatter myself was as subtle a mending as I have ever effected. One would hardly know that it had arrived in such poor state, and she looks very well in it. . . .

Several entries of little interest followed, but a few pages later Knife found this:

If my own dear friend Lavender had not brought me the news herself, I should hardly have believed it: The Queen has appointed Jasmine to her Council! It is a great honor, to be sure, and for Jasmine's sake I am glad. Still, I cannot be fully at ease about the Queen's decision. I have no doubt of Jasmine's cleverness, but she has a passionate nature, and is sometimes too quick to act when wiser heads would urge caution.

Which was all very well if you were interested in politics, thought Knife, but she was tired of hearing about life in the Oak. When would Heather stop talking about Jasmine and tell her something that really mattered? Impatient, she began flipping pages, until finally—

I was taking tea with Lavender this morning when the news came that Queen Snowdrop wished me to attend her. With so many other able faeries in the Oak, I scarcely dared hope that she would choose me; but my prayers were not in vain, Great Gardener be blest. In six months' time I shall pass the title of Seamstress to my apprentice, Bryony, and take up a greater commission.

I must prepare myself carefully for the task ahead, and I know it will not be easy, for I still have much to learn. Yet at this moment I can find no room in my heart for worry, or dread, or anything but glorious anticipation—I shall go Outside, among the wondrous folk of humanity!

Knife started, and the book tumbled from her fingers to land facedown upon the floor. She picked it up and smoothed out the crumpled pages, reading the last line of Heather's entry again, and again, and again, while the bedside candle sputtered in its puddle of wax.

Twelve

Outside Knife's window the stars were beginning to fade, the first light of dawn creeping up over the horizon; the table beside her was littered with candle stubs, and scribbled notes lay everywhere. She had been reading all night, and her eyes were so blurred with exhaustion that she could hardly see the page—but still she could not bring herself to put Heather's diary down.

> . . . I have chosen the name of Miss Harriet Oakwood, a young
> woman lately arrived from the Continent, which I hope shall
> help to explain any oddities in my speech and manner. I shall be
> attended on my journey by Lily, a faery of maturity and good
> sense, who is to accompany me in the guise of a spinster aunt, and
> act as my chaperone. She knows much of the human world, and

I will be glad of her guidance.

Still, I could wish that Lavender might come with me as well; it pains us both to part, knowing that it may be years before we meet again. Nevertheless, she is too loyal a friend to grieve me by begging me to stay. I only wish I could say as much for Jasmine. . . .

Knife rubbed her temples, trying to silence her nagging headache. *Just a few more pages,* she told herself.

. . . I had thought at first that she would be pleased with my good fortune, but her own sad experience Outside (of which I still know little) had filled her with misgivings, and she all but pleaded with me not to go. "You are already skilled at your craft," she said, "and have no need to learn another. Why venture among the humans, when you might serve the Oak as well by remaining here?" and with many other such flattering words she sought to persuade me.

She spoke earnestly, and I knew that her concern for my welfare was sincere; yet to follow such counsel would be madness, and I fear I was quite short with her in making my excuses. Since then she has been cool toward me, and it seems that our friendship, such as it was, has come to an end.

As has this, the first of what I hope shall be many diaries; I shall leave it behind with the other relics of my life in the Oak, and begin a new volume when I reach my destination. Till then, dear reader, farewell!

That's all? thought Knife in disbelief as she turned the final page and found it empty. Heather had spent months taking lessons on every aspect of human life imaginable. She'd written freely about the struggles of learning to pass herself off as human, and how anxious she was to succeed. All that work, all that anticipation, until finally she was ready to go out into the human world—and yet she hadn't even explained what the Queen wanted her to do there, or why it was so important!

On the other hand, it didn't seem as though Heather was deliberately trying to hide the truth about her mission; it was more like she'd assumed her readers already knew the answer, so there was no need to tell them. Knife closed the book and propped her chin on her hand, thinking. What had she read elsewhere in the diary that might help her understand why Heather had to leave the Oak?

Then she remembered Jasmine's words: *You are already skilled at your craft, and have no need to learn another.* . . .

So Heather was going out to learn a new skill. Something she couldn't learn by staying in the Oak. . . .

Galvanized by a new idea, Knife snatched up her notes and began leafing through them for confirmation. What if the Oakenfolk hadn't lost their creativity along with their magic, as she had assumed? What if they'd never been creative to begin with, and all their inspiration had come from the human world they called Outside?

Of course! Knife had seen for herself that humans were

gifted with amazing powers of invention. They always seemed to be moving forward, discovering new things—unlike the Oak, where everything stayed the same, or even went backward if the faeries weren't careful. So that must be why the Oakenfolk had needed people like Heather, willing to go out and learn new skills and ideas from the humans, and bring that information back to the Oak.

And yet, Knife realized as her excitement began to subside, the theory didn't explain everything. Why had Heather said that her mission might take years to complete? Why had Jasmine's return to the Oak caused such a scandal, even though she'd learned how to draw while she was away and was willing to share her knowledge with the others?

I need to find the rest of Heather's diaries, thought Knife as she slid the book under her mattress and lay down. *But where do I start, when I don't even know who gave me this one?*

"Wake up, you lazy—" Mallow's heavy fist pounded on Knife's door. "Do you hear me? Get up at once!"

Knife rolled over, groaning, and winced as the morning light struck her face. How long had she been asleep? All she knew was that it hadn't been nearly long enough. "All right, I'm coming," she mumbled as she dragged herself out of bed.

Mallow stood on the landing, arms folded and legs braced wide. "Do you know how late it is? While you've been lolling about, the rest of us are starving—or soon will be, if you don't get yourself downstairs and do your duty!"

"Downstairs?" Knife regarded her blearily. "What for?"

"To guard the Gatherers, of course! After what happened to Linden, they won't set foot out of the Oak without you, and they've been waiting since dawn—so you'd best hurry up, or I'll report you to Her Majesty!"

That was the beginning of a long and unpleasant day. Exhausted as she was, Knife soon found that her weakened wings slowed her down even more. It was a struggle just leading the Gatherers across the field, and they had barely reached the wood when she had to sit down and rest. After a little while she mustered enough strength to try hunting, but her hands shook on the bow, and she wasted several arrows before bringing down her only prey of the morning—a scrawny young robin.

"A fine catch," sneered Mallow when Knife brought the half-plucked carcass to the kitchen. "And I see you haven't wasted any of your precious time dressing it either. Well, my proud lady, you'd best take out that fancy knife of yours and finish what you started, because it's certainly not my business to do your work for you!"

Knife had no strength to argue, much less obey. Without a word she walked out, knowing that the other workers would be perfectly willing to clean and cut up the robin even if Mallow was not. But the Chief Cook had no intention of letting Knife escape so easily. She followed her all the way down the corridor and up the Spiral Stair, cursing her laziness and incompetence in tones loud enough to be heard all over the Oak. Not until they were nearly at Knife's door did she run out of insults and huff back down to the kitchen again.

When she had gone Knife stopped and leaned against the wall, breathing heavily. It would have been so easy to turn around and hit Mallow right in her smug face—but what good would that have done?

She tried to take another step, but her legs wobbled, and she had to sit down.

"Knife."

She turned to see Valerian standing a couple of stairs above her, holding out a hand. Too tired to protest, she took it and let the Healer pull her to her feet.

"You need to rest," said Valerian, and then to Knife's surprise she added, "If Mallow should bring her complaint to the Queen, I will intercede for you."

"It's not your quarrel," said Knife.

"No, but neither is it yours, for all that Mallow tries to make it so." Valerian walked with her up the last few stairs and around the curve of the landing, until they stopped at Knife's own door. "She will never be content until you are as unhappy as she is."

"Unhappy! She's in her glory down there in the kitchen,

ordering everyone about, making them all frightened of her. Why should she care about me?"

"She hates you," said Valerian calmly, "because you make her feel unimportant. Though she could force your obedience, she could never bully you into fearing her. You have a strength and a confidence that she lacks, and though deep down she knows you have done nothing to deserve her hatred, that only makes her hate you all the more."

Knife frowned at the older faery. She could sense truth in what Valerian was saying—but how did the Healer know? She had never heard anyone in the Oak talk like this before, explaining someone else's thoughts and feelings. If she hadn't known it was impossible, she might have thought Valerian had been spending time with the humans.

"Go and rest," said Valerian. "I should not have told the Queen you were fit to return to duty. You are far more weary than I thought."

Knife felt a prick of guilt—she would have been well enough if she hadn't stayed up all night. But how could she explain that to Valerian without telling her about Heather's diary? So she gave the Healer a subdued nod, then went into her room, fell on her cot, and within moments was deeply asleep.

Late in the afternoon she woke again, her stomach snarling with hunger; but when she arrived at the Dining Hall, she received only glares and a plate of limp greens. Furious all over again, Knife stalked back up the Stair to her room, wolfed down a handful of dried berries, and sat by the window, chewing.

I should have stayed in the House, she thought mutinously. *It would serve them all right if I left the Oak this minute, and never brought them so much as a road-flattened hedgehog again.*

Swallowing her meager supper, she spread her notes across the table and began to review them—but it was no use. In the fevered concentration of last night her jottings had made perfect sense, but now she could barely read her own handwriting, let alone recall what all those hasty abbreviations meant.

Sighing, Knife pulled over a fresh page and let her charcoal pencil wander across it. It was no use being angry at Mallow: If Valerian was right, there was nothing Knife could do to change her mind, anyway. But she could at least prove that she had not forgotten her duty.

Her wrist relaxed and her fingers moved of their own accord, sending black lines looping across the paper. She'd get up early tomorrow, before anyone else, and hunt until she'd found some prey worth having. It wouldn't take much, if she were lucky: all she really needed was one good-sized . . .

Knife bolted upright, staring at the page. Instead of random scribbles, the lines she had drawn formed a single, coherent shape: the plump body and upraised listening ears of a rabbit.

No, it couldn't be. She must have imagined it. She snatched

up her drawing and held it closer to the light. But however she turned the paper, it still looked like a rabbit. With no magic, no training, and hardly any effort, she had done what no faery had done for over a century: She had created art.

Unthinkable, impossible—yet it was real, it was *hers*. With almost reverent care, Knife laid the drawing aside, then grabbed another sheet and bent over it, scratching furiously. Please the Gardener it hadn't just been an accident!

When she straightened up again Old Wormwood glared back at her from the page, wings spread and claws outstretched to strike. Not a crude likeness this time but an exact one, right down to the mad glint in his eyes; it made her wing ache to look at it.

Instinct told her that the drawing was good, even brilliant. Yet part of her still refused to accept that this talent could be real. She needed a second opinion—but whom could she trust with a secret as enormous as this?

There was only one answer to that, and she knew it without thinking: *Paul.*

By the time it was dark enough to leave the Oak, Knife was fidgeting with impatience. She rolled up the picture of Old Wormwood and slipped it down the bodice of her tunic, then climbed through the window and launched herself headlong into the night.

She had to rap at Paul's window several times before he answered. "I knew something was out there," he said as he slid it open. "But I didn't think you'd be back so soon—come in, quick."

Knife ducked under the window and sat down on the inside of the sill. "I have something to show you. I need to know what you think," she said, and she pulled the drawing out and gave it to him.

Paul squinted at it. "It's too small. Just a minute." He rolled to his desk, rummaged through the drawer, and returned with a large round lens, which he held up between himself and the page. "It's . . . a crow," he said blankly.

"Is it good?" asked Knife, her heart skittering. "I mean, it isn't just a sort of crow-shaped scribble?"

"It's very good," Paul confirmed in distracted tones, his lens hovering over the sketch. "What is it, charcoal? The stick must have been tiny—" He lowered the glass to stare at her. "You mean *you* did this?"

Knife nodded.

"I had no idea. Why didn't you tell me you were an artist?"

"Because I'm not," she said. "Or at least, I wasn't, until . . ." *Until I met you.*

"That's ridiculous," Paul said impatiently. "You must have had training, or at least plenty of practice. Nobody develops this kind of eye for detail overnight."

"I know," said Knife. "That's why I didn't think it could really be any good—but if it is, then . . ."

Then perhaps the Oakenfolk of Heather's day hadn't just borrowed creative ideas from the humans they met Outside; they'd absorbed their creative abilities as well. *I have gained some little skill as an artist,* Jasmine had told Heather, *since I went away . . .*

"I don't understand," Paul said.

Knife hesitated, wondering how much to tell him. Then she got to her feet and jumped off the sill, landing lightly on the end of Paul's bed. She walked up to the pillow and sat down, tucking her feet beneath her.

"What are you doing?" asked Paul.

"Making myself comfortable," she said. "Do you have anything to eat? Because I think this story is going to take a while."

"I had no idea," said Paul slowly, when she was done. "I knew something must have gone wrong when you said you couldn't do magic, but this . . ."

Knife swallowed her last bite of biscuit, brushing the crumbs from her fingers. "I know," she said. "It's big."

She had said little about the Oakenfolk's past connection to the human world; she was still trying to understand that aspect of the problem herself. But she had told him about the Sundering, how their population had dwindled and their culture decayed rapidly in its wake; and finally she had explained about her people's lack of creativity, and why she had been so surprised to find herself able to draw.

"And now you're trying to find out how this Sundering thing happened?" said Paul. "So then you'll know how to get your magic back—and maybe your art, too?"

"That's part of it," she said. "I have a lot more questions, but I have a feeling they're all connected somehow."

Paul drummed his fingers on the arm of his chair, his gaze abstracted. "What about your Queen?" he asked.

"What about her?"

"Well, she must know about your people's past—she lived through it, after all. Why isn't she telling you what you need to know?"

"I've wondered about that myself."

"Stop me if I'm going too far," said Paul, "but it's pretty strange that she was the only one who wasn't in the Oak when the Sundering happened. Do you think she might be the one who did it?"

"I . . . don't know what to think," said Knife. "In some ways it makes sense, but in others, it doesn't. She might have become Queen that way, but what did she really gain? There are so few of us now, and we have so little."

"Hmm," said Paul.

Knife jumped up from the bed and brushed at her skin waistcoat and breeches, dusting off the last remnants of biscuit. "I should go. It's late. No, keep it," she said as Paul offered her back her picture. "I've got no use for it, anyway. But I am grateful—"

"I've noticed," Paul interrupted, "you never say 'thank you.'"

She tensed. "No."

"Why not?"

"Because it means something to us that it doesn't to you. We don't say it lightly." *Or ever.*

He gave her a quizzical look. "So . . . what does it mean to you, then?"

Knife tilted her head back, searching for words. "It means," she said, "that the one you . . . *thank* . . . has done something so enormous for you that you could never begin to repay them. And that no matter how long you live, you'll always be in their debt."

"Can you give me an example? Do you know anyone who—"

"Not in my lifetime. It's that rare."

Paul's brows rose. "No wonder you don't like to hear me say it," he said. "All right, then: I'm *grateful* you stopped by tonight. Is that better?"

"Much," said Knife.

With Heather's diary finished and nothing more to read, Knife found herself increasingly restless. She could not resist the urge to draw, and night by night the pile of sketches hidden beneath her mattress grew. But what was the use of making art that no one but herself would ever see?

The faery in her warned that she must not take advantage of Paul's generosity, or she would end up indebted to him again. Besides, he had begun speaking to his parents now, so he might not even need to talk to her anymore. But when for the next three nights Paul's room remained lit long after the rest of the House had gone dark, it was too clear an invitation for Knife to refuse. Soon she was tapping on his window again.

On her first few visits she was all business, showing him her latest drawings and asking his advice. But eventually she dropped even that pretense and came by simply to see him. By the time the Oak's leaves turned to autumn gold, she was visiting the House every night.

Now at last she understood why humans liked to talk to each other so much, for even if Paul could not solve her difficulties, it eased her spirit just to tell him about them. He seemed fascinated by her accounts of daily life in the Oak, even finding humor in people and situations that Knife found merely exasperating. Before long it was all she could do not to smile at Mallow's blustering or Bluebell's fussy ways, just imagining how funny Paul would think them.

Meanwhile Paul himself seemed to be growing healthier, and taking more interest in the world around him. He had even pulled out his box of art supplies and begun painting. His days were mostly spent on schoolwork, and mealtimes with his parents; but the evenings he kept for art—and Knife.

She had never felt so content, and yet deep down she knew that this happiness could never last. More than once when leaving the Oak at night she had the crawling sensation of being watched, and she knew that if she kept on seeing Paul this way, it would only be a matter of time before she was caught.

The wisest thing would be to stop visiting the House, at least for a while. She had managed by herself before; surely she could do so again. But staying away from Paul proved harder than she had expected. Her research into the Oaken-folk's past had come to a standstill; there was no sign of Old Wormwood and little else worth hunting; and Mallow's latest amusement was to ruin Knife's meals whenever she could, giving her the stalest knobs of bread and lacing her stew with bits of bone and gristle. Knife tried to take all these frustrations calmly, but it was not long before she felt she would burst if she didn't talk to *someone*—so she went winging off to Paul again.

Soon the last ragged leaves of autumn fell, and the Oakenwyld lay dank and lifeless beneath the shrouded sky. Knife was coming back from a successful hunt, her pack heavy with meat, when a cry rang out from the roots of the Oak: "Knife! Come inside! Hurry!"

"What is it?" asked Knife. She dropped her pack in front of the root-sheltered door and peered into the darkness, but could not see who had spoken. Knife knocked the mud off her boots and ducked in, only to be swept up in an unexpected tide of Oakenfolk rushing through the corridor.

"What's going on?" she shouted to the faery beside her, who turned out to be a rather red-faced Dandelion.

"Linden's egg is hatching," came the breathless reply.

"Oh," said Knife.

The heat in the Hatching Room was oppressive, and Knife slipped off her cloak, careful not to let it brush the lighted brazier behind her. Of course, if everyone didn't stop pushing her back in their eagerness to see the egg, she'd end up burning herself anyway. She turned out her elbows and shoved until she had bought herself some more space. Now if only the lot of them would stop squeaking and chattering like so many squirrels—

Amaryllis, draped in crimson and crowned with holly, stepped to the head of the room and lifted one hand for silence. Immediately the clamor ceased, and the only sound was the shuffling of restless feet.

"We have gathered here," the Queen's clear voice rang out, "to witness a miracle, the beginning of a new life. Now let us watch and wonder, for behold"—she flung out one arm toward the table, light scattering from her fingertips and splashing against the egg—"the moment has come!"

The egg quivered, and scarlet streaks swam and writhed across its surface. All the Oakenfolk held their breath as the shell began to dissolve in a hissing shower of sparks. A shout went up from the crowd as a curly head appeared. White, dimpled arms emerged, hands clasped beneath the lowered chin; two plump legs shone through the swirling light, and the child fell wailing onto the cushions as the last of the eggshell sparkled into dust.

"Her name is Linden," announced Amaryllis, "in honor of the one who went before her."

"Her name is Linden," echoed the Oakenfolk.

"Every child must be Mothered," the Queen continued, her gaze sweeping the crowd. "This is a task that requires courage, determination, and tireless vigilance. It is a work of paramount importance to our survival, and cannot be taken lightly. . . ."

She went on for some time in this manner, indifferent to the child's piercing cries, while Knife shifted her weight from one foot to the other and tried not to yawn. Why did the Queen have to choose this time to make a speech? Especially when it was so hot. Great Gardener, you could roast nuts in here. . . .

"Knife."

"What?" she said automatically, before she realized who had spoken.

"Step forward," said Queen Amaryllis, a dangerous edge in her voice. "Now."

All the Oakenfolk were staring at her. Wondering what she had missed, Knife began to walk slowly toward the Queen as the crowd parted with disapproving murmurs to let her pass.

Amaryllis strode to the table and swept up the naked, squirming Linden. Then she turned and thrust her into Knife's arms.

"By the Oak and by the Great Gardener, I charge you," she said. "Take this child, for you are now her Mother."

Thirteen

Knife stared down at the wriggling, red-faced baby. "What?" she said. Then the full meaning of the Queen's words sank in, and panic swarmed through her. "I can't!"

The Oakenfolk's whispers turned into gasps. *"Refuse the Queen?"*

"Treason," said Mallow in a satisfied voice, and Knife rounded on her. "You! If you had something to do with this, I swear I'll—"

"Silence!" snapped the Queen. She stalked back to the head of the chamber, then turned to glare at Knife. "You will accept this task," she said, "for it is sacred, and cannot be refused. But do not think that I am relieving you of your position as Queen's Hunter. That duty will also remain yours—unless you prove unable to fulfill it."

Knife knew she ought to be relieved: Even a little freedom was better than none. But it would be impossible to hunt and carry Linden at the same time—how was she to manage? Trying to keep her voice steady, she said, "Your Majesty, may I speak with you in private?"

"You may," said Amaryllis. She turned to the crowd. "You are dismissed."

Muttering, the Oakenfolk filed out, while Knife whipped one of the moleskins off the table and bundled the shrilling baby up in it. "I don't understand," she said to Amaryllis when the room was empty. "Why this? Why *me*?"

"Because," said the Queen coolly, "it has become clear to me that your present responsibilities are not enough to occupy you. And since you appear to have an interest in helpless things . . ." She turned to leave.

"But I can't," protested Knife. "How can I hunt and look after a child at the same time? And you need me to hunt even more than you need . . . this." She looked down at Linden, who had stopped crying and begun sucking noisily on her shoulder.

"You have always proven yourself resourceful at getting what you want, Knife," said Amaryllis. "If you wish to continue as my Hunter, I am sure that you will find a way. And if you find yourself with no time for any of your . . . *other* interests, then you have only your own folly to blame."

And with that, she swept out.

Knife closed her eyes, feeling sick. So that was the answer: She had been found out, and the Queen was punishing her for it. What was she going to do?

Numbly she pulled another moleskin off the table and wrapped it around her new foster daughter. Then with dragging feet she left the Hatching Room, and began the long climb up the Spiral Stair.

Knife groaned and pulled the pillow over her head as Linden woke for the third time that night, her sleepy whimpers rising rapidly into a full-throated scream. The first time Linden had been wet, and after Knife had changed her it took a small eternity of bouncing and rocking to get her back to sleep. The next she had been thirsty, and spent a long time sucking at her bottle while Knife stared bleary-eyed into the darkness. Knife had only just got her settled, and here she was up again—what now?

Knife stumbled out of bed and over to the cushions where Linden lay, screeching as though she'd fallen into a nest of hornets. "Shush," she mumbled, picking up the child and rocking her back and forth. "None of that." A brief check confirmed that the diaper was still dry, and an offer of the bottle met with head-turning refusal. Knife began to walk about the room in circles, bouncing the baby as she went, but Linden's screams never abated.

Minute after minute crept by, while Knife rocked and swayed and made shushing noises until her throat was sore, but to no avail. She wiped her brow with her forearm. This was torture. She wasn't meant for this. She'd never get it right, never, and she felt hopeless and angry and frustrated nearly to the point of tears, and still the baby wouldn't stop—

Knife snatched up a blanket and threw it over her shoulder, muffling Linden's cries. Then, still clutching the baby, she flung herself out the door and down two flights of the Spiral Stair. Racing around the landing, she hammered at one of the doors until it creaked open and a tousled red head poked out.

"What?" said Wink, in a voice thick with sleep.

"Please," Knife panted. "I've got plenty of furs and skins, you can have your pick, or I'll give you anything else you want. But you have to help me. She won't stop, she just keeps crying, I don't know what's wrong, I don't know how to make her—"

Without another word Wink held out her arms, and Knife thrust the struggling, howling Linden into them. The instant the baby was out of her grasp she felt as though a colossal weight had been lifted, and she sagged against the door frame in relief.

"Oh, the poor little thing, she's in pain," said Wink, unwrapping the child. "Did you check her diaper? There could be a pin sticking into her."

"I looked," said Knife wearily. "I couldn't see anything."

Wink lifted the baby to her shoulder. "Then it's probably just gas in her stomach. You had it when you first hatched, too. Never mind, I'll look after her. You go and sleep."

Knife stared. "You—are you sure?"

"Of course I'm sure," said Wink with unusual firmness. "You're in no shape to deal with this: You look like you've spent the night with a badger. Off to bed, and don't come back until morning. *Late* morning. We'll talk more then. Good night." She gave Knife a light push back into the corridor.

"Wait," said Knife, "don't you want to barg—"

The door slammed in her face.

Back in her own room, Knife shut the door and leaned back against it. She slid downward and landed on the mat with a thump, dropping her forehead against her knees. She had feared it, but now she was certain: Her friendship with Paul McCormick was over. It would be years before Linden no longer needed her constant attention, and by then Paul would have forgotten all about her. The Queen had done her work well.

An icy dampness crawled around the edges of the shutters and crept across the floor. Stiffly Knife rose and walked to her cot, dragging the smoldering brazier a little closer to the bed. The straw mattress crunched when she sat down, and Knife's eyes stung as she thought of the sketches tucked away so carefully beneath it—worthless now, because Paul would never see them. And all her notes on Heather's diary, too—what use were they, except to remind her that her quest to learn the truth about the Oakenfolk's past had failed?

In a burst of angry misery Knife flipped the mattress aside, snatched up the papers, and threw them on the brazier. The coals smoked, then shot out crackling tongues of flame, licking the pages to red-gold tatters before swallowing them whole. When nothing was left but a drift of blackened ash, Knife dragged the mattress back into place and lay down, hugging the furs about her and shivering until she finally fell asleep.

But even without the baby's cries to wake her, Knife could find no rest. In her dreams Paul McCormick sank deeper and deeper into the black water, hands outstretched in mute desperation, while she stood on the bank holding Linden and pretending not to see him. After he drowned, she walked back to the Oak and found nothing but a blackened stump and a sky full of circling crows.

"I told you to sleep in," Wink chided when she found Knife at her door early the next morning. "Don't you listen to *anyone?*"

Knife ignored the rebuke, slipping past her and looking around the room. The hanging lamp was lit, washing the room in yellow light, but she could not see the baby anywhere.

"Here," said Wink, pointing beneath her sewing table. There in a cradle of branches and woven grass lay Linden, eyes closed and small mouth blissfully slack. "She's been asleep for . . . oh, about five hours."

Knife stared. "How did you . . ."

"I wrapped her up tight, then I rocked her and hummed in her ear, and off she went. Poor little thing, I think she was just overwhelmed."

"I've been a fool," said Knife weakly. "I should have come to you right away."

"Yes," said Wink, "you should have. Couldn't you see me trying to catch your eye at the Hatching, and then later in the Dining Hall? I did everything short of dancing to get your attention, but you looked right past me. I know I'm not very big, but *really*."

Knife flushed. "I'm sorry. I just didn't think . . ."

"Well, never mind that," said Wink. She stooped and slid the cradle out onto the floor. "You can take this with you, if you like; I can always ask Thorn to make me another one."

"Another? Why?"

"For when Linden stays here, silly. You do want me to look after her while you hunt, don't you?" She must have seen the flare of hope in Knife's eyes, for she went on briskly: "Of course you do. Well, then, just bring her to me whenever you need to go out, and I'll keep her until you come back."

"What . . . would you have me give you in return?" asked Knife, forcing the words past the tightness in her throat.

"Oh, I'll think of something," replied the little redhead. "But don't worry, it won't be too much." She looked down at the slumbering Linden and smiled. "I've rather missed having a baby to look after."

Over the next few days, Knife's confidence as a Mother rose. Linden slept longer between feedings, and fussed less afterward. With Wink's help Knife was able to make a couple of hunting trips, and by the end of the week had supplied the kitchens with enough meat to silence even Mallow's complaints.

Still, Knife dreaded what Amaryllis would say when she found out. Would she accuse Knife of shirking her duty, and force her to keep Linden with her all the time? Wink dismissed her worries, insisting that the Queen would never be so unfair; but after the things Amaryllis had said to her in the Hatching Room, Knife was far less certain.

Then one night her worst fears were realized when she answered a soft but persistent tapping at her door to find Queen Amaryllis standing there, demanding to see Linden at once.

"But . . . she's sleeping," said Knife. What could the

Queen be doing here so late, and unattended?

"Then wake her," said Amaryllis. "And wrap her well, for I must take her with me."

"That's not fair," Knife protested. "Wink and I struck a bargain, and anyway, it's only while I'm hunting—"

Amaryllis silenced her with a gesture. "You misunderstand me, Knife. I do not object to your arrangement with Periwinkle. And I have no intention of removing Linden from your care."

Strange, thought Knife, that she should feel relieved. "Then . . . what do you want with her?"

The Queen strode to the corner, bent, and lifted Linden from the cradle. "You never cease to ask questions," she said. "But there are times when you must learn to restrain your curiosity, Knife, and simply obey." She pulled one of the furs from Knife's cot and wrapped Linden up in it until only her small face was visible. "I will return her to you shortly, when I am done." And with that she swept out, taking the baby with her.

Knife stood beside the empty cradle, listening to the Queen's footsteps fade away. Then she stalked across the room and flung open the clothespress, reaching for her boots and cloak.

Crouched at the mouth of the secret tunnel, invisible amid the shadows of the hedge, Knife watched as the East Root

187

door cracked open and the Queen slipped out, moving lightly as a spider. The dry grass whispered beneath her boots as she crossed the lawn and paused, glancing up at the generous moon. Then she crouched down, laid Linden upon the ground, and began to unwrap her.

She moved quickly, peeling back layer after layer until the baby was almost naked. Linden wailed piteously as the wind swirled around her, and it was all Knife could do not to rush out from her hiding place at once—but she forced herself to remain still, and wait.

The Queen reached out, laying one white hand upon Linden's brow and the other upon her belly. She remained there unmoving, head bent, while the child writhed and sobbed upon the cold ground. Knife's indignation flamed up again, and she was just about to step forward when she saw the Queen's hands begin to glow, magic fanning outward from her fingers and rippling like moonlit water. It swirled about the baby, enfolding her in a chrysalis of light, and as Linden's cries melted into happy gurgles, Knife sat back on her heels. A spell of blessing, perhaps, or protection. Whatever it was, it didn't seem to be doing the child any harm—

All at once Amaryllis clenched her hands. The magical cocoon pulsed, and Linden began to scream.

Knife could bear it no longer. She burst out of her hiding place and plunged across the lawn, knocking the Queen aside and snatching Linden up in her arms. For an instant she felt a wrenching pain deep in her belly, but she did not even have time to gasp before it stopped. The bubble of light burst, and Linden's shrieks turned to sobs as Knife cradled her close and wrapped the cloak around her.

"Stop it!" she shouted at Amaryllis, too angry and frightened for courtesy. "You're hurting her!"

"I must finish the spell!" The Queen struggled to her feet, hands outstretched. "Quickly, give her back to me, before—"

Knife held the baby closer and took a step back. "Leave her alone!"

"Foolish girl," said Amaryllis between her teeth, "you have no idea—" Then she stopped, staring at something over Knife's shoulder.

Knife turned to see a fox slip out from the shadows and pad across the lawn toward them, tongue lolling with hunger. Her mouth went dry.

"Why didn't you scent it?" demanded the Queen.

"Because we were upwind," said Knife shortly, never taking her eyes off the fox. "How do you think it scented us?"

"Can we outrun it?"

"Are you joking?"

Amaryllis whipped off her cloak and flung it on the ground. Wings spread, she leaped into the air—and a gust of wind caught her, tossed her like a dry leaf, and flung her down again.

"The air currents are wild out here," Knife shouted to

her. "It's no use—even if we could stay aloft, we'd never get anywhere against this wind!"

The fox stepped closer, steam threading from its mouth. Knife backed away, stripping off her own cloak as she went and bundling Linden up in it. "Take her!" she said, thrusting her at Amaryllis, who had struggled to her feet. "Get back to the Oak!"

The Queen reached out and took the child, but it was only to lay her down upon the frosty ground again. "Not without you," she said.

"Take her!" roared Knife. She waved her arms, willing the fox to focus its attention on her, to ignore Amaryllis and the child. "Get away while you have the chance!"

"And what will you do?" retorted the Queen. "Die?"

Knife drew her dagger. The fox lunged; she ducked away from its snapping jaws. "Not if I can help it," she panted. "But I don't have time to argue, Amaryllis—just go!"

"I have seen too many of my people die," said the Queen grimly. "Knife, stand aside."

Knife scarcely heard her, intent on the circling fox. The icy wind bit through her tunic, needling into her skin; already her muscles felt stiff, and she knew she could not dodge the vixen long. But if she could distract it for another few seconds . . .

"I said, stand aside!" thundered Amaryllis, and an invisible hand plucked Knife off her feet, tossing her back across the lawn. Then the Queen's wings burst into shimmering light as she raised both hands, palms outward, and directed a beam of blinding radiance at the fox.

It yelped and leaped backward, head tossing and paws scrabbling at the snow. "Begone!" commanded the Queen in a ringing voice, and the fox turned tail and dashed away.

Still glowing, Amaryllis stood erect until the fox squirmed through the hedge and vanished in the darkness beyond. Then she turned toward Knife, her face drained of color, and collapsed.

Knife stumbled across the lawn and dropped to her knees. She rubbed Linden's face until the baby whined in protest; then she tucked her into the crook of one arm and reached for Amaryllis with the other. "Your Majesty," she pleaded, "wake up!" But the Queen did not stir.

Gritting her teeth, Knife hefted Amaryllis by the waist and began dragging her toward the hedge. But her legs were made of stone, and even breathing was an effort. A curious warmth enfolded her, tempting her to lie down; the ground looked so soft, so welcoming. . . .

Panting silver clouds into the air, Knife lurched across the lawn, muscles screaming as she hauled her double burden. Her breeches were stiff with ice, and she could no longer feel her hands. She plunged forward another step, and another, until her foot kicked something warm and she fell, nearly crushing Linden beneath her. Struggling to her feet again, she turned to see Amaryllis lying on the ground; she had dropped the Queen without realizing it. Wearily she bent, slung Amaryllis's arm about her shoulders, and hauled her a few more steps into the tangled shadow of the hedge.

As she stooped into the secret tunnel, Knife began to shout for help. Shuffling along, feeling Linden and Amaryllis grow heavier with every step, she called out until her throat was hoarse, but no one answered. She had almost given up hope when she saw light glimmer at the other end of the tunnel, and a stocky figure hurried toward her with lantern in hand.

"Thorn," rasped Knife. "Take Linden, quickly. And the Queen—" Then her knees buckled, the floor rushed up to meet her, and she knew no more.

Fourteen

"Knife, oh, Knife, wake up, please—"

Her eyes cracked open to see a white blob that gradually resolved itself into Wink's face. "Oh, merciful Gardener," the other faery breathed, "drink this," and she tipped something into Knife's mouth.

Knife spluttered but forced herself to swallow. "What does Valerian put in that stuff?" she gasped as the medicine seared its way down her throat. "Pine needles and fish oil?"

"Probably," said Wink, wavering between laughter and tears. "Oh, Knife, I'm so glad you're all right. For a little while, I thought—"

"Linden," said Knife, struggling to sit up. "Where is she? And the Queen?"

"Sleeping. Both of them. Valerian says they'll be fine— Knife, do lie down, you're making me nervous."

Reluctantly Knife lay back as Wink plumped her pillow and pulled the blankets up about her shoulders. "You do know you aren't my Mother anymore?" she said.

She had meant it as a joke, but Wink's face fell. "No one ever asked me if I was ready to stop being your Mother," she said. "I just woke up, and they'd taken you away from me, and there was nothing I could do about it. So . . . no." She lifted her head, eyes brimming. "No, I don't know that. I don't think I ever will."

Knife felt as though a tree branch had clubbed her in the stomach. "I didn't know," she said lamely.

"Oh, I don't blame you," sniffled Wink. "You were only a child. You probably thought they were punishing *you*."

This was true, but Knife had also assumed that Wink had been glad to see her go. She had never imagined that Wink had actually *missed* her—why would she, when Knife had never given her anything but trouble?

"Anyway," Wink went on, taking out a handkerchief and blowing her nose, "none of that matters now. What I want to know is what you and Linden and the Queen were doing out there in the first place."

"I'm not sure," said Knife slowly. "The Queen took Linden into the moonlight and started casting some kind of spell. I managed to stop her, but—"

Wink's mouth fell open. "You *stopped* the Queen?"

"She was hurting Linden. What else could I do?"

"Oh," said Wink, looking stricken. "Oh, dear. So that was why the Queen wouldn't let me come with her, the night she took you."

"Took me?" Knife sat up again, ignoring the pounding in her head. "When?"

"You can't have been much older than Linden is now. The Queen just turned up at my door one night and took you away for a while. She never would tell me why, but you seemed to be all right when she brought you back, so . . ." Her voice faltered. "I'm sorry, Knife."

"It's all right, I don't remember it," Knife said, but her hand slid to her belly as she spoke, and for a moment she felt an echo of last night's brief, wrenching pain. "Is Linden here?"

"Knife, you can't just—oh, do get back in bed!" Wink fluttered about her, trying to drape the blanket around her shoulders, but she was too short to reach. "It's too cold, it's too soon, Valerian said you weren't to get up until tomorrow—"

"I'm fine," said Knife shortly. In truth she felt as though she had fallen down all nine flights of the Spiral Stair, but she managed to shuffle over to Linden's cradle.

Studying the baby's face, Knife had to admit that she appeared none the worse for her ordeal. Her cheeks looked redder than usual, the points of her ears chapped and flaking, but otherwise—Knife folded back the blankets to be sure—there was not a mark on her.

"You don't see anything, do you?" said Wink.

"No," said Knife. "But I know the Queen did something to her." *And whatever it was,* she finished silently, *I'm going to find out.*

After a day's rest and two more doses of Valerian's noxious medicine, Knife felt almost well again. It helped, of course, that Wink stayed with her the whole time, keeping her and Linden warm, fed, and mostly undisturbed.

The exception was Thorn, who showed up in the middle of the day to give Knife a hard, questioning look and mutter a few words to Wink before leaving again with ill-concealed impatience. Wink, surprisingly, seemed to take this in stride, and when Knife asked her what was going on, she only shook her head and said that it would wait until Knife was better.

Then came Midwinter's Day, and the Oak itself seemed to vibrate with excitement as faeries rushed up and down the Spiral Stair, preparing for the Feast. Some dashed about the corridors hanging garlands of beads and dried berries, while others lit the brass lamps and set them in place. Campion and her helpers draped the Dining Hall with tapestries and linens from the archives. At Amaryllis's command Wink opened the wardrobes where the prettiest gowns from the Days of Magic were kept, and began helping the eager Oakenfolk into them.

Knife, however, spent most of the day in her room, distracting Linden as best she could while she leafed through a book called *On the Nature and Uses of Magical Power*. She had found it in the library—albeit with no help from Campion, who had made a point of ignoring her—and though she could not say exactly what kind of spell the Queen had been trying to cast on Linden, she was learning more about magic than she ever knew before.

Late in the afternoon Wink burst in breathless and triumphant, her arms full of yellow silk. "I've been wanting to try this one for years!" she announced, shaking out the gown and holding it up to her shoulders. "Do you think it will look well on me?"

"I suppose," said Knife, without much interest.

"It's such a shame." Wink sighed. "Everyone tries to take good care of these gowns, but they can't last forever. And when they're gone, no one will even remember what they looked like." She folded the dress over her arm. "What are you going to wear to the Feast, then? The same thing as last year?"

"Of course." Knife had grown even taller since she was first presented to the Queen, and nothing in the old wardrobes would fit her. Besides, she found her own simple tunic and skirt more comfortable than corsets and layers of petticoats. "But never mind that," she said, "listen to this: 'The light magics or glamours may be wrought at any time; but to effect a permanent alteration requires great power, and is best done by moonlight.' "

"Moonlight?" said Wink. "You mean that's why the Queen had to take Linden out of the Oak to cast her spell? But that would mean—"

"A permanent change," Knife finished for her. "The only question is, what?" *And what will it mean for Linden, that I stopped it?*

Wink draped the gown over the table and hurried over. "What else does the book say?"

"There are two kinds of magic," said Knife. "The first kind is light magic or glamour, which is easy to do but doesn't last—growing or shrinking, turning invisible, that kind of thing. The second kind is deep magic, which takes more effort but is permanent: You can use it to turn wood to metal, or change a crow into a mouse. You can even use it to heal wounds and such—but if you want to work deep magic on another person, you've got to get their permission first."

"Why?" asked Wink.

"I'm not sure," said Knife, turning pages. "Maybe it just makes the spell easier, or . . . no, I've found it." She bent over the book, her finger running down the paragraphs. "Because," she said slowly, "if you use deep magic on someone against their will, it becomes dark magic. Which the book describes as . . ." She paused, then read out in a low voice, "'. . . forbidden by the Great Gardener's decree, an evil of which it is better not to speak.'"

Wink let out a little gasp. "You mean—you think the Queen was doing *that* to Linden?"

"Maybe," said Knife. "Maybe that's why she had to do it now, before Linden was old enough to refuse."

"But that's horrible!" Wink jumped to her feet. "No, I can't believe it. I know the Queen can be cold sometimes, but she isn't *evil*."

For a moment Knife had been tempted to tell Wink everything she had learned—about Heather, about Jasmine, even about the humans. But hearing Wink defend the Queen in spite of all the suspicious things she had done, Knife realized what a mistake confiding in her might be.

"No," she said, "you're right. There must be some other explanation." She closed the book and put it aside. "Anyway, it's nearly time for the Feast. Do you need me to help you get dressed?"

The clack of goblets meeting in toast resounded through the Dining Hall, and drops of berry wine darkened the tablecloths as the Midwinter Feast began. Knife watched Amaryllis closely as she swept up the aisle to her seat, and thought that the Queen still looked a little pale. But her poise never faltered, and she wore her elaborate gown as though it were weightless—which, since it looked too new to be anything but a glamour, it probably was.

Knife stood at the head of her table, slicing the roast hare and passing platters to the faeries waiting at the other end. Plates rattled, cutlery scraped, and hands reached for bowls heaped high with roots, nuts, and berries.

"Do you want me to hold Linden while you eat?" asked Wink, at Knife's elbow.

"No," said Knife, "I'll take her." She laid down the carving knife and sat. "I'm not especially hungry."

Wink handed Linden over, and Knife settled the baby on her knee. Now that she was used to it, she rather liked holding Linden; touch was rare among the Oakenfolk, and there was a simple honesty in that little form nestled against her that Knife found comforting. Linden had not learned to bargain or scheme, and her wants were easily satisfied. And that, thought Knife wryly, probably made her a better person than anyone else in the Oak.

Meanwhile the faeries at her table seemed bent on proving her right, shoveling food into their mouths with greedy abandon. Now and then they paused to finger the embroidered tablecloth, or admire the reflection of the torchlight on their silver cutlery. But they paid no attention to each other's finery, only to their own; and they made no conversation, except to demand more food and drink. If each of them had been alone at her own private feast it would hardly have made a difference.

Inwardly, Knife sighed. Already she longed for the Feast to be over—but that would take hours. After the meal there would be more toasts; then they would play some silly games, leading to the inevitable quarrels about who should get the prizes; the Queen would make a speech about duty and cooperation while everyone else tried not to fall asleep, and then—

She stood up, her fork clattering onto her plate. "I have to go," she said to Wink. "Would you keep Linden for me?"

"But Knife, you can't! The Queen—"

"Tell the Queen," said Knife, "that I am unwell." She held the baby out, and reluctantly Wink took her.

"Perhaps you'll feel better if you lie down?" she said.

Knife gave a halfhearted nod. Ignoring the disapproving glances of the Oakenfolk around her, she threaded her way between the tables and hurried out into the corridor, heading for the Spiral Stair.

Later, her formal skirt traded for breeches and her hands clasped around a steaming mug of chamomile tea, Knife sat beside her bedroom window and gazed at the distant House. From here she could see the humans only as shadows. But as she watched, two of those dark shapes rose and moved about, while the third never stirred from his chair.

"Merry Midwinter, Paul McCormick," she murmured.

Their gathering looked so peaceful, just father and mother and son. Now and then Paul gestured as though he was talking, and the familiarity of the motion made her ache; she wished she could be there to hear him and share his company.

"Why?" she demanded of the silence. "Why do we have to be so ignorant and petty and—and selfish? Why can't we be more like them?" She set her mug down with a thump.

"Like whom?" said a familiar voice.

Knife froze. Behind her the door clicked shut, and measured footsteps approached. "You left the door open," said her visitor. "And you were shouting."

Knife spun around. "Thorn, what are you doing here?"

"The Queen sent me."

"Why?"

"Another *why*. You're full of them, aren't you?"

Knife stared into the older faery's face, trying to read the expressionless features.

"As it happens," said Thorn, "Her Majesty asks that you return to the Feast as soon as you are able, because she has need of you."

"Oh," said Knife, and there was a long pause.

"So," Thorn said, "you're asking questions."

"No harm in that, surely?" Knife tried to keep her voice light, but she did not like the look in Thorn's eye.

"Well," Thorn said, "it depends on the questions, doesn't it?"

Several heartbeats passed while the two faeries eyed each other. Then Thorn threw up her hands and said, "I can't stand all this dancing around the toadstool. Listen, midge-wit—you're not the only one who wonders what's wrong with us. I've been wondering for years. But as for whether the humans are better off than we are, you'd know more about that than anyone, wouldn't you?"

Knife ran her tongue around the inside of her mouth, unsure of whether it still worked. "What do you mean?"

"Oh, stop pretending you don't know," said Thorn crossly. She walked to the far side of the room and plopped onto a chair. "The Queen summoned me a few days after you got back from your *ordeal* in the *woods*"—she gave the words a sarcastic twist—"and told me she'd noticed you sneaking out of the Oak at night. She asked me to keep an eye on you, find out what you were up to."

"And did you?"

Thorn rolled her eyes. "Well, since you'd been stupid enough to let her see you in the first place, I couldn't very well say no, could I?"

Knife's lips flattened. "So," she said. "That's why she punished me by making me Linden's Mother—because of what you told her."

"I could have told her a lot more!" snapped Thorn. "Yes, I told her I'd seen you hanging about the House, gawking in the windows. What I didn't tell her was that I'd seen you go inside it, and that a while later I'd seen a human open the window and *let you out again.*"

Knife's heart stuttered; she backed over to the sofa and sank down onto it, no longer trusting her legs to hold her up. "What do you want from me?" she said. "If you want me to bargain for your silence—"

Thorn snorted. "You think I'm going to report you unless you pay me off? I've already got more furs and skins than I can use in a lifetime." Her face sobered. "No, there's only one thing I need from you—and I don't think you'll refuse, once you know what I've got to offer in return."

"Oh? And what's that?"

"Heather's next two diaries."

Knife's breath clotted in her throat. Her unknown benefactor, so mysteriously aware of her interest in humans and her desire to learn more about the Oakenfolk's past—*Thorn?*

"I thought you'd be interested," said Thorn with satisfaction. "Wink wasn't sure at first, but—"

"Wink?" Knife exclaimed, feeling as though her head were about to burst like a seed pod. "Wink knows about all this?"

"Of course she does. She started it."

"*Wink?*"

"The little redheaded one with the attention span of a gnat? That would be Wink, yes." Thorn propped her feet up on the stool, clearly enjoying herself. "She found Heather's diaries hidden in the bottom of a sewing chest that old Bryony, your egg-mother, had given her. It took her a while to get around to reading the first one, but as soon as she did, she knew she'd found something important. So she came to me."

"When was this?" said Knife.

"Oh, a few years ago." Thorn crossed one leg over the other and leaned back. "Anyway, reading that first diary turned us both upside down, let me tell you. Wink wanted to go to the Queen with it and I convinced her to wait until we'd found out more. But the second diary was in a human place where neither of us could go, and we couldn't figure out how to open the third one. So we ended up just sitting about like a pair of broody pigeons, wondering if we'd ever find someone brave or mad enough to help us out."

"And all this time you've been waiting . . . for me?" said Knife.

"Not exactly. We knew you were brave—or mad—but after all I'd done to put you off humans myself, it didn't seem likely you'd be interested in helping us. Once you started flashing around that metal knife of yours, though, and I realized you must have gone right into the House to get it—well, I know a ripe berry when I see one."

"So . . . why didn't you come to me then?" asked Knife, her head swimming with all this new information.

"I wanted to, but Wink thought it was too soon. She

had some silly notion about how it ought to be your choice to get involved, not ours. So I had to wait, and I don't mind telling you I nearly chewed my leg off with impatience. But when that young human arrived with his fancy chair, and I heard the Gardeners wittering about how you'd walked right up to him and weren't afraid . . . well, even Wink had to agree you were ready."

It was finally starting to make sense, thought Knife. Thorn's short-tempered reaction when the other faeries complained about humans, the way Heather's diary had turned up at her door only a few hours after she'd met Paul in the garden . . .

"Wait," Knife said, sitting up. "When I came back to the Oak, after I'd been gone those two days . . . you convinced Tansy she was wrong about seeing me fall close to the House, and then you told me to take a bath."

"You reeked of human," said Thorn. "I was pretty sure nobody else would recognize the scent, but I thought it best not to take chances."

"So you knew, even then . . ."

"Well, I knew you'd been in the House, of course. But it wasn't until I saw you go back there that I realized you hadn't just been a prisoner—that you and that young one had struck some kind of bargain." Thorn tipped her head to one side, regarding her shrewdly. "What is all that about, anyway? Do you owe him, or does he owe you?"

"I'm not sure I know anymore," said Knife tiredly. "Does it matter?"

"It might," said Thorn. She picked up Knife's abandoned mug and sniffed at it. "I wouldn't say no to a cup myself, you know. I hear it's called *being hospitable.*"

Knife rose and put the kettle on. She was glad to have Thorn on her side, but she wished the other faery would not keep talking about Paul; every reminder of him smarted like a nettle sting. "Where is this second diary you couldn't get to, then?" she asked, to change the subject. "You said it was in a human place."

"That's right. Heather wrote her second diary while she was still Outside, and that's where she left it." Thorn glanced at the door, then lowered her voice and said, "We need you to get it back."

"But if you have the third one—"

"We do, but it's spell-bound, so it won't open without a password. Whatever's in there has to be either very private or very dangerous. Maybe both."

"You mean—it might tell how we lost our magic?"

Thorn nodded.

"And you think the password is somewhere in the second diary."

"We can hope," said Thorn.

"All right," said Knife. "Where is it?"

"It's far. Too far for you to go on your own."

"You mean you'd come with me?"

Thorn scowled at her. "Are you cracked? No, I mean you can't fly there without getting eaten or dropping dead of exhaustion. You'll need some kind of transportation."

"Like what?"

"I don't know, nab a passing owl!" barked Thorn. "The question is, if I tell you where to find Heather's second diary, *will you go?*"

Knife gazed down at the kettle, watching the steam coil and rise into the air. At last she said, "Yes."

Thorn relaxed. "Good. I'll give you the map tomorrow."

"But I can't do this alone," Knife warned her. "Wink will have to look after Linden, and you might need to hunt while I'm gone—"

"We've time enough to work all that out," said Thorn with a wave of her hand. "The weather's too cold and it's only going to get worse, so you won't be leaving for a couple of months at least. The important thing is that we're all agreed on what we're going to do, even if we don't know yet how we're going to do it."

"Don't you mean how *I'm* going to do it?" said Knife.

"I said *we*, and I meant it," Thorn retorted. "Do you really think you're the only one risking your neck here? Just because we don't all zoom about the countryside teasing crows and hobnobbing with humans doesn't mean we've got nothing to lose."

To hide her surprise, Knife busied herself with the teapot, filling Thorn's cup and handing it to her before refilling her own and sitting down again. It sounded as though Thorn did not trust Queen Amaryllis nearly as much as Wink did—but how much did she really suspect? For a moment they sipped in silence, until Knife said cautiously, "So you think the Queen will be angry if we're caught?"

"I don't know," said Thorn. "But I'm not in a hurry to find out. There's got to be a reason she hasn't told us about our past—and for all I know, she's right. Maybe, when we finally find out the truth, we'll wish we hadn't. But since we're halfway up that tree already, we may as well see what it's like at the top."

"And once we know, what then?" Knife laced her fingers around her teacup, holding in its warmth. "It can't be enough just to find out how we lost our magic; we need some way to get it back."

"True," said Thorn. "But you can't eat a walnut before you've cracked the shell. First things first, don't you think?" She rose, brushing irritably at the wrinkles in her velvety gown. "Stupid thing—I don't know why I let Wink talk me into it."

"The dress, or the conspiracy?" said Knife, and then as the other woman moved toward the door: "Are you leaving?"

"I should. I'll tell the Queen I delivered her message,

spent a while arguing with you—she'll have no trouble believing that—and that you'll be back at the Feast by midnight."

Knife set down her empty cup. "I'll do better than that," she said. "I'll come back with you."

Fifteen

"For her faithful care of the Oak's precious books and artifacts," said Queen Amaryllis in her clear voice, "I call Campion."

Applause rippled up and down the tables as the Librarian walked to the front of the Dining Hall to receive her gift from the Queen. She turned and held it up for the others to see: a heavy-looking volume bound in dark leather, its pages edged with gilt. Such a prize could only have come from the Queen's own private collection, and Campion ought to have been delighted. But her expression remained grim, and watching her, Knife felt a flicker of unease.

"For her prudence in ensuring the safety of her fellow Gatherers, I call Holly," said Amaryllis, and the dark-haired faery scrambled forward, nearly tripping over her skirts with excitement.

Knife helped herself to a slice of cold leveret and began cutting it up, too distracted to pay much attention to the ceremony. Incredible to think that she was not alone in her quest after all and that all along Wink and Thorn had been secretly on her side. When she was a child they had done everything they could to keep her away from the humans; now they seemed just as intent on pushing her toward them. Obviously Heather's diary had convinced them that humans were not monsters after all—yet they still had no idea of what the human world was really like. Should she try to explain it to them? Would they even be able to understand?

"And now," said the Queen, "I have a special gift to bestow. Knife, come forward."

Knife choked, and had to take a swig from her goblet. Hastily wiping her lips, she rose and began the long walk to the dais where the Queen awaited her.

"Over the past year," Amaryllis began, "Knife has proven herself remarkably courageous and resourceful for one so young. As Queen's Hunter she has not only kept the kitchens well supplied with meat, but acted far beyond her duty to ensure that the Oakenwyld remains secure and our people safe. Even the crows have learned to be wary of her presence, and for this we all owe her our thanks. But two nights ago she performed an even greater service to the Oak than this, when she saved my life."

Gasps and exclamations filled the hall, for this was the first time most of the Oakenfolk had heard the story. "On that night I went out into the garden alone," the Queen continued, "so that I might cast certain spells necessary to the Oak's survival. I believed that I could do my work quickly, and return without need of assistance. But the wind was against me, and when I turned back, I came face-to-face with a hungry fox."

She looked down at her audience, all leaning forward in their eagerness not to miss a word, and gave a twitch of a smile. "My magic proved sufficient to frighten the beast away," she told them, "but the effort of casting such a powerful spell weakened me, and I fainted. I might well have perished then, had Knife not come to help me. She ventured out in the icy wind and darkness, risking her own life, to find and carry me back to the Oak. Such loyalty has more than earned her this token of her Queen's gratitude."

She beckoned to Bluebell, who stepped forward carrying a small chest of polished yew. Opening it, the Queen took out a pendant like a drop of blood, suspended on a delicate gold chain. She held it high for the others to see.

"This jewel is the Queen's Heart, the highest accolade the Oak has to offer. From now until the next Midwinter's Day, Knife will wear this stone as a witness of my favor. Furthermore," she continued, raising her voice above the envious murmurs of the crowd, "the one who wears the Queen's Heart is entitled to a special privilege. At any time during the year to come, she may make of me one request, whatever her heart may desire. So long as it does not violate our Oak's sacred laws or imperil her fellow Oakenfolk, it shall be granted."

She paused as though expecting Knife to respond, but the young Hunter could only stand speechless, eyes fixed on the slowly twirling gem. Dazed, she bent her head to receive the gift, then curtsied and left the platform, the applause of her fellow Oakenfolk ringing in her ears.

"Oh, Knife, how wonderful!" said Wink as she sat back down. "What do you think you'll ask for?"

"I don't know yet," Knife said, fingering the crimson jewel. Linden, who had been nestling half asleep against Wink's shoulder, roused at the sight of the pretty thing and leaned toward it with one small hand outstretched. "But I'm sure I'll think of something."

"You'd almost think she was trying to help us, wouldn't you?" said Wink the next morning. "Now all you have to do is ask for a day or two off to go exploring, and she'll *have* to give it to you." Then, catching Knife's eye, she added hastily, "If you want to, that is. I mean, it's your Midwinter's Gift, so it's not really fair for us to—"

"No," said Knife, "you're right. It's the only way. But what if the Queen asks what I plan to do with my time? I'll need to have some excuse ready."

"I have one," said Thorn's voice unexpectedly, and Knife looked up to see her standing just inside the door, looking smug. Despite the way she usually clumped around, it seemed she had lost none of her old Hunter's skill of moving silently when she chose. "Tell her you're going to look for other faeries. It's even true—in a way."

"What other faeries?" said Knife.

"The ones the Queen herself has been looking for all these years. Only, she can't leave the Oak, and her magic can only reach so far—why do you think she spends so much time in her library, going over her books again and again? She's trying to find some clue to tell her where the rest of our people might be, the ones who still have all their magic."

"So that we can bargain with them to help us get ours back," said Knife, as comprehension dawned. Now she understood why Wink and Thorn trusted the Queen: In their minds, how could Amaryllis be responsible for the Sundering when she'd been working so hard to undo it?

Wink nodded. "But it's been terribly hard on her. I overheard Bluebell telling Valerian that the Queen spends all day and half the night studying, and that she'll never live to see three hundred and fifty at this rate. She sounded so worried—and she sees Her Majesty more than anyone, so she should know."

"I know what you're going to say," said Thorn before

Knife could speak. "You think the Queen might have had something to do with the Sundering, and now she's just trying to make amends. But before you say anything against her, you should have a look at this." She pulled a roll of parchment from her sleeve and held it out to Knife.

"What is this?" Knife asked as she took it.

"Just read," said Thorn shortly.

Gingerly Knife unrolled the note and laid it across her knee. In spidery, faded handwriting, it read:

For years now I have lived in forgetfulness and confusion, my mind wandering from one moment to another; like so many of my sisters, I have often counted myself grateful to remember my own true name. But the Silence in its cruelty has brought my lost youth back to me, and as my death approaches, I remember everything.

I remember a time when magic sang through my veins, when my mind was whole and my hands shaped things that were beautiful and new. I remember what it was to have purpose, to know that my existence was not in vain; I remember art, and friendship, and laughter—all the things that make a life worth living. But those things are lost to us now, perhaps forever, and the Oak I once loved has become less a home than a prison.

I surrender my body to the cold in a last act of service to my people, for if I delay any longer the Silence will consume me, and I will have nothing left of myself to give. May the Great

*Gardener have mercy upon my egg-daughter, if she survives; may
she be blessed with the courage I lack, and free our people from
their chains. To Wink, faithful apprentice and child of my heart, I
give my love; to Queen Amaryllis, who has done all she could to
help us, my respects; and to the rest of our people, who may never
know what they have lost, my everlasting pity. Farewell.*

The letters grew shakier and shakier as the letter went on,
and finally ended in an almost illegible scrawl. Still, Knife
was just able to make out the signature: *Bryony.*

"My egg-mother," she whispered in disbelief. "She took her
own life, to give me mine. And all this time, I thought . . ."

"That she was a silly old woman who'd lost her wits
and blundered out into the cold by accident?" said Thorn.
"That's what I thought, too, when Wink came to tell me
she'd gone missing. It was a foul night, too, I don't mind
telling you—I'd nearly given up when I tripped over the egg
with you in it. And then when I picked it up, I found this
letter underneath."

"That's really how it started," said Wink. "Thorn and me
wondering what had gone wrong with us, I mean. Because
I was there when she got back with your egg, and I saw the
letter, too, and, well—"

. . . *Queen Amaryllis,* Bryony's words repeated in Knife's
mind, *has done all she could to help us . . .*

"I understand," said Knife quietly.

Over the next few weeks the snow came and went, but the cold remained, and the earth lay lifeless beneath a shroud of dead grass. Prey became scarce, and hunting a dismal chore. Late one morning Knife was crouched at the foot of the humans' bird feeder, blowing on cold fingers and hoping for a sparrow to come by, when she heard the low growl of an approaching car.

At first she paid it little mind: A thick tangle of hedge stood between her and the road, and these metal wagons always moved too quickly for their drivers to notice her, in any case. But when the car slowed in front of the House and began to turn into the drive, she realized that this one was about to become a dangerous exception.

Pulling up the hood of her jacket, she crouched down and flattened her wings against her back, trying to look as much like a bird as possible. The car rumbled to a stop a few crow-lengths away, and when its doors opened, she was startled to see a stranger unfold himself from the passenger seat and reveal Paul sitting behind the wheel.

"Good driving," the man called as he rounded the car and pulled Paul's wheelchair out of the backseat. "A bit more practice with those hand controls, and you'll be ready for the motorway."

Knife caught her breath. For weeks now she had agonized over the map Thorn had given her, wondering how she could possibly get from the Oak to the place where

Heather's diary was hidden. But if Paul was learning how to drive . . .

I have to talk to him, thought Knife, watching Paul as he hauled himself into the chair and began wheeling toward the House. Seeing him after so long apart, she felt a desperate urge to fly to him at once; but the strange man stood in her way, and she dared not move.

"I'll manage the chair from now on, thanks," Paul said to the man. "See you next week."

"Right then," the stranger replied, hopped into the car, and drove away. As soon as he was gone, Knife leaped up and flew after Paul. If she could catch him before he reached the House—

"Wait!" she called, but Paul did not hear her. With a vigorous push he cleared the threshold, and Knife could only watch helplessly as the door swung shut in her face.

When Knife returned to the Oak she was cold, windblown, and empty-handed. She wrapped a rabbit-wool blanket about her shoulders and sat on the sofa shivering until Wink thrust a cup of hot chicory into her hands.

"I don't know what to do," Knife mumbled.

"Oh, I shouldn't worry," said Wink absently, tickling Linden with a strand of her hair until the baby chuckled. "We're not starving yet, and you can always hunt again tomorrow."

Knife was tempted to correct her, but then she realized

that she might be better to let the misunderstanding pass. If Wink did not know that Knife planned to see Paul again, then she would not be blamed even if Knife were caught.

And yet, was it really fair not to tell her?

Knife sipped the chicory until its hot bitterness revived her, then set the mug down and held out her hands for Linden. "I'll take her now," she said, but Wink's face was averted, and she did not respond.

"What is it?" Knife asked.

Wink lowered her head, her cheeks coloring. "It's just . . . I know it can't be very nice being a Hunter, and I really wouldn't want to do it myself. But you can go out whenever you like, and even if it's cold and miserable you at least get to see and do new things every day, and, well . . ." She picked a loose thread from Linden's smock and rolled it distractedly between her fingers. "I've spent my whole life in this room sewing the same patterns over and over, and sometimes I envy you, just a little."

Knife watched her for a moment in silence. Then she set down her cup and rose to fetch a stick of charcoal and a piece of paper. "What are you doing?" asked Wink, but Knife only shook her head, sat down at the table, and began to draw.

She meant to sketch some of the clothing she had seen the humans wear, much as Jasmine had done for Heather. But though she concentrated with all her might, the figure she traced was a crude one, barely recognizable as human. She was attempting to clothe it in one of Mrs. McCormick's pleated skirts when the charcoal broke in her hand; she threw it down and crumpled up the paper in frustration.

"Knife," Wink said in a hushed tone, "was that really . . . a picture? But where did you learn—"

"From Paul," said Knife, too miserable to guard her tongue anymore. "But I haven't talked to him in so long, and I'm starting to forget everything he taught me." She slumped forward. "I miss him, Wink."

Wink untangled Linden from her curls and put the baby down hastily. "A human," she breathed. "Thorn said you'd been to the House, but I never guessed you'd been *that* close."

Knife sat up, the color easing back into her face. "I'm sorry. I shouldn't have mentioned it. If the Queen finds out that you know, we'll both be in trouble—"

"It doesn't matter," said Wink quickly. "Just tell me. Tell me everything."

When Knife had finished, Wink did not move for a long time. Then she raised her head, her face white except for two spots of color on her cheeks, and said, "You have to go back."

"Back?" said Knife.

"To the House. To him—that Paul." She clasped her

hands against her heart. "I can *feel* it's important, this connection you have with him. And if you wait much longer, you might lose it completely—Knife, we can't let that happen."

"We?" said Knife. "Wink, I already told you, the Queen—"

"The Queen is wrong!" Wink burst out, with a passion that startled them both. She flushed and glanced nervously at the door before continuing in a lower voice, "Wrong about this, I mean. And you're wrong, too, to try to protect me from her. I know I'm not strong like you, or clever like Thorn, but I want to help—so for the Gardener's sake, let me do what I can!"

"You do help," said Knife, and all at once it seemed natural to put her hand on Wink's shoulder. "You've done so much already, I didn't dare to ask for more. Are you really sure about this?"

Wink sniffed, then nodded. "I'll look after Linden whenever you need me to, day or night, and I won't tell the Queen or anybody."

"Then I'll go," said Knife quietly. "Tonight."

"Knife!"

Paul slid up the window so quickly that Knife nearly fell off the ledge. Recovering her balance, she hurried forward, into the House's warm embrace.

"I was beginning to think you were out," she said, shaking the sleet from her cloak. "I knocked and knocked—"

"I thought it was hail," Paul said. "God knows I didn't think there was a chance of it being anything else." His mouth flattened. "Where have you been?"

He had missed her, too, Knife realized with a flare of happiness. "I'm sorry," she said. "The Queen gave me a . . . new responsibility, so I couldn't leave the Oak at night. I've only just been able to get away."

"You could have left a note," said Paul.

"You thought I'd forgotten you?" She spoke lightly, hoping to wipe the shadows from his face, but they only deepened.

"I thought you were dead," he said.

Knife sat down hard on the windowsill. "Oh," she said.

Paul passed a hand over his eyes. When he took it away, the anger had vanished, leaving only weariness. "Well, never mind that. You're here now. So . . . how have you been?"

Confused. Frustrated. Lonely. "I'm all right," she said. "But—" She looked up into his face. "I need your help."

Quickly she explained about Heather's diaries, and what she had learned about the Oakenfolk's past interest in humans. "I know it sounds strange," she finished, "but it's important. There's a connection between your people and mine—and that diary may be the only way to find out what it is."

"And you think this could help you get your magic back?" said Paul.

"I don't know. Maybe."

"So where do I fit in?"

Knife bit her lip. "I have to get to a place called Waverley Hall. And this morning, I saw you driving a car . . ."

"You want me to take you there?" He looked surprised, but not displeased. "Well, I probably could—just not right away. I've still got six lessons left, and then I have to pass the road test."

Relief washed over Knife. "I can wait that long," she said.

Sixteen

"He's really going to take you there?" exclaimed Wink. "Knife, that's wonderful! When do you leave?"

"It'll be a few weeks yet," Knife said, pulling off her cloak and hanging it up to dry. "Paul needs time to prepare, but he's promised to give me a signal when he's ready."

"You mean . . . you're not going to see him until then? But—"

"It's all right," Knife reassured her. "We talked about it, and we both understand that it's for the best." Tempting as it was to take full advantage of Wink's offer to help, she knew it would be unwise to try and see Paul any more than necessary. The Queen had already caught her sneaking out at night once; she might easily do so again, and then their whole plan would be ruined.

"I know," said Wink dolefully. "But if you don't see him, then you won't be able to draw—and I really wanted to see that picture."

Knife let out a disbelieving laugh. "Is that all?" she said. "Well, give me some paper and I'll see what I can do."

This time the lines flowed smoothly, and soon she had completed three sketches: not only the skirt she had failed to draw before, but a blouse and tailored jacket to go with it. "Here," she said, handing them to Wink.

The Seamstress gazed at the drawings, oblivious to Linden's attempt to climb up her skirts. Then her eyes welled up and she let the pages fall back to the table. "They're so beautiful," she said in a quavering voice. "And I would love to sew them, if I could only figure out how . . . but then I couldn't wear them, or everyone would want to know where I'd got the ideas from. And what's the good of making something beautiful that nobody else will ever see?"

"I know," said Knife. "It's hard. But I promise you, Wink, it won't be this way forever. Once I get Heather's second diary, and once we know the truth—" She clenched her fist around the charcoal, feeling it crumble against her palm. "Things in the Oak are going to change."

"This is your request?" asked Amaryllis incredulously, looking down at Knife from the height of her carved throne. "Three days away from your duties, nothing more?"

It had been Thorn's idea that Knife should ask the Queen for three full days, to make the claim that she was going out to look for other faeries more plausible. "I'd like to do some more exploring," Knife said, trying to keep her voice casual. "Not now, of course, but once the ground's thawed and the crows stop flocking . . ."

The Queen's brows rose. "Exploring, you say. What do you hope to find?"

Here it comes, thought Knife. *Please the Gardener she doesn't use the Sight on me—and that I'm not as obvious a liar as Paul thinks.* Aloud she said, "When I was gone for those two days last summer, I came across a place that reminded me of a Wyld. I didn't see any faeries there, but it made me think that if I looked around a little more, I might find some—or at least a clue to help us figure out where they went."

Amaryllis's lips parted, but she did not reply, and as the silence deepened, Knife's temptation to fidget became an even stronger impulse to bolt. Had the Queen seen through her request? But finally, Amaryllis spoke:

"I have long yearned to send out an emissary to search for other Wylds," she said. "Yet in a hundred years and more I have found no one fit for such a task, let alone willing. That you have come to this of your own free will, and would ask it of me as a boon—it is more than I dared hope."

She spoke quietly, without a trace of her usual imperious

manner, and Knife's stomach twisted with guilt. "It's not too much," she said. "I'd be glad to help." After all, she told herself, just because she was going to find Heather's second diary didn't mean she couldn't keep her eyes open for other Wylds on the way. And there would always be time to make a proper survey later.

"Then I would be pleased to grant your petition," said the Queen, and for the first time Knife saw her smile. "But you need not spend your Midwinter Gift on this. Save your request until you have thought of something that you, and you alone, desire. Whatever you ask, I swear it shall be yours."

"Aren't you afraid I'll ask for half the kingdom?" Knife said, shaken.

"I know you do not want it. And that is well, for I would not wish such a burden on anyone." She smiled again, but thinly. "You may go. Come again when you are ready to leave—or when you know what you truly want."

"I will," said Knife.

As she walked back down the Spiral Stair, the Queen's words reverberated in her mind: *Whatever you ask, I swear it shall be yours.* How much did she mean what she had said? Amaryllis was not given to making promises she did not plan to keep. But then, she did not know how close her Hunter had already come to betraying her.

Or did she?

Soon winter began to lose its grip on the Oakenwyld, finger by icy finger; frost melted into dew, and rain coaxed life from the frozen ground. Crocuses exploded into bloom at the foot of the Oak, and new grass dappled the lawn.

For Knife, however, spring that year was marked by a different sign entirely—a piece of yellow paper stuck to Paul McCormick's bedroom window, announcing in bold letters:

I PASSED!

When she caught sight of the note, Knife was just returning from her morning's hunt. She knew she ought to wait for nightfall to respond—but that was hours away. Did she dare to visit him now? She cast a furtive glance at the Oak, then shoved her pack beneath the hedge and doubled back around the front of the House.

He was still in his room, as she had hoped. The curtains were open, a shaft of sunshine slanting into the room and making the dust motes dance. And in that beam of golden light sat Paul, half dressed and with his hair still tousled from sleep, lifting weights.

One hand gripped the heavy barbell, the other the wheel of his chair; his clenched fist lifted and curled toward his shoulder, the lean muscles of his arm flexing. His hair stuck damply to his brow, and beads of perspiration slipped down his back. *Helpless*, the Queen had called him, but looking at Paul now, Knife could see nothing but strength.

She had missed him more than ever these past few weeks, seen his face a hundred times in her dreams. And yet she was suddenly struck by how beautiful he was, in a way she had never noticed before. Her heart bounded giddily at the sight of him, as though he were some marvelous work of art the Gardener had created just for her. Paul. Her human. Her friend.

She raised her fist eagerly and rapped upon the glass.

Paul stopped exercising at once, snatching up a shirt from the bureau and pulling it on before skimming across the room to meet her. He flung up the window, and she stepped through onto his outstretched palms.

"You got my message," he said with a flash of a smile.

"I did," said Knife. "And I was so glad, I couldn't wait to talk to you. Can we go, then? Soon?"

"I don't see why not. For a while I wasn't sure we'd be able to get in, but then I looked up this Waverley Hall place in a guidebook and it turns out they give tours, so that's all right. When it comes to stealing the diary, though . . ."

"It isn't *stealing*," protested Knife. "It's got no value to them, and anyway, how can they miss it when they don't even know it's there?"

"They won't," said Paul, "unless they catch us with it."

He spoke solemnly, but there was a spark in his eye she had not seen before; he seemed to be looking forward to the adventure, and Knife felt her own spirits lifting in return.

"They won't catch us," she said confidently. "How soon can we leave?"

By the time Knife returned to the Oak, she was glowing with satisfaction. Everything seemed to be coming together perfectly: Paul had permission to use his parents' car, he'd called ahead to make sure that Waverley Hall would be open for them to visit, and barring some unforeseen disaster, they'd be leaving tomorrow.

Tomorrow! It felt so unreal to think of getting into that strange metal wagon with Paul and speeding off to a place she'd never visited before, so far away that she couldn't even see it from the top of the Oak. To him the journey was nothing; he didn't even think it would take long to get there. But to Knife it was as exciting—and daunting—as a trip across the world.

She had just dragged her meat-heavy pack into the cold room and was about to unload it when she heard a thump from the corridor outside, followed by a muttered curse. It sounded like . . . Campion? Frowning, Knife looked out and saw the Librarian staggering past with a teetering armload of volumes, one of which had just fallen onto the floor.

"I'll get it," said Knife, stooping to collect the book.

But its spine had cracked, and the pages came loose in her hand.

"You've ruined it!" screamed Campion. She dropped the rest of the stack and launched herself at Knife, who barely had time to throw up her hands before the other faery barreled into her. Together they tumbled to the floor, and it was all Knife could do to hold Campion at bay: Fingers stiffened into claws, she seemed determined to scratch Knife's eyes out.

"I was only trying to help!" Knife shouted at her. "I didn't mean any—Campion, stop!"

"I know what you're up to! You want to destroy them, and leave me with nothing!"

"What are you talking about?" panted Knife, grabbing the other faery's wrists as she glanced down at the pages scattered over the floor. Could it be that Campion had found some more books about humans? But no, the damaged volume was just a simple herbal, and the rest looked just as ordinary.

"I'm taking them away," Campion spat at her. "Where they'll be safe. You'll never find them—and *she* won't either—"

"Campion, nobody wants to take your books! Will you just listen to me?"

The other faery stopped fighting, and looked confused. Then the wildness came back into her face and she shrieked,

"You're trying to trick me!" as she flung her weight against Knife again.

First you become fretful and short-tempered, said Thorn's voice in her memory. *Sometimes even violent . . .*

Horror shivered through Knife, and she stumbled back. "No," she breathed. "Oh, no."

At that moment the kitchen door flew open and Mallow marched out. "Well, I must say this is a fine way to behave!" she exclaimed. "What would Her Majesty say if she could see the two of you brawling in the corridor like a pair of cats?"

"Call Valerian," Knife gasped at her, still wrestling with the furious Campion. "Get the Healer—hurry!"

Campion writhed free of Knife's grip, leaped up, and lunged at Mallow. "You!" she spat. "You greedy, selfish, miserable *thief!* I know what you took from the archives, when you thought I wasn't looking—"

Mallow's ruddy cheeks turned pale as dough. She stumbled backward, then turned and rushed away. Taking advantage of the distraction, Knife pulled Campion's feet out from under her and brought her crashing to the floor, then leaped onto her back and sat there while she rifled through her belt pouch for something to tie her up with.

Campion struggled mightily, but she was smaller than Knife and much less fit; it was not long before she collapsed, her frenzied energy spent. Knife bound her wrists and ankles together with twine, and was just about to heave the other faery onto her shoulders when she saw Valerian hurrying toward them.

"There you are!" said Knife, climbing off Campion's back and stepping aside to let the Healer take over. "She just flew at me—" But Valerian held up a hand.

"Let me look at her first," she said, slipping an arm around Campion and rolling her over onto her back. The Librarian immediately began to thrash about again, hissing into her face, "I know what you are! I've seen the records. You're not one of us, Motherless—*changeling!*"

Valerian went very still. Then she said quietly to Knife, "You were right to call me." She reached into the pocket of her apron and took out a small bottle, which she pressed against Campion's lips. The Librarian spluttered and tossed her head, but in a moment her eyes glazed over and she went limp.

"Now," said Valerian, "we can carry her back to her room."

"I had thought—I had hoped," said the Healer as they laid Campion down upon her cot, "that we were done with this." She brushed back the hair from the Librarian's forehead, letting her hand rest there. "No fever yet, but it will come."

"It's the Silence," said Knife. "Isn't it?"

Valerian walked to the window, opening the shutters

to let in the afternoon air. Without turning back she said, "Yes."

"And if Campion could get it, then . . ." Knife closed her eyes, chilled with dread. "It doesn't just take the old ones after all. None of us are safe."

Valerian did not answer.

"There has to be something we can do. I know there's no cure, but there must be a way to slow it down, or—"

"The first faery taken by the Silence," said Valerian, "was my own foster mother, Lavender. The Queen and I did everything we could think of to save her—teas and potions, poultices and liniments, healing spells by moonlight. But in the end she died, just the same."

"Lavender?" asked Knife. "But if she raised you, then . . . what was Campion talking about when she called you Motherless?"

Valerian's face was unreadable. "It has long been the Healer's duty," she said, "to make a note of every death among the Oakenfolk, along with the circumstances of that death. But nowhere is there mention of a faery named Valerian. It seems as though I am the first to bear that name in all the Oak's history—as though my egg-mother never existed."

Changeling. "You came from Outside," breathed Knife, suddenly comprehending. A human child, stolen and transformed into a faery to increase the Oak's population; it was the only explanation that made sense.

Valerian nodded. "I believe so. And I was not the first."

Knife sank down on the end of Campion's bed. Could this be the reason Heather and others like her had gone out into the human world? It made a terrible kind of sense, for unless the Oakenfolk found some way to add new faeries to their number, their population would eventually die out. Perhaps that was why Jasmine's return to the Oak had been such a disappointment: They had sent her to steal a human child, but she had failed. . . .

And yet it seemed so wrong, so unfair. Borrowing ideas and inspiration from the humans was one thing; but taking their children? What could any faery give to a human family that would make up for such a loss? And how could the gentle, kind-hearted Heather have looked forward to her mission so eagerly, if all the while she knew this was how it would end?

"Burned . . ." came a husky whisper from behind her, and Knife turned around to see Campion's eyes fluttering open. But there was no anger in the Librarian's face now, only unhappiness. "I tried to stop it . . . but I couldn't."

"I know," said Knife, shifting closer and taking Campion's limp hand in hers. Valerian's brows rose, but she did not interrupt as Knife went on quietly, "I'm sorry, Campion. You were right—it was my fault the Queen burned them. I don't blame you for hating me."

Campion shook her head, eyes closing as though even that slight movement exhausted her. "Not hate," she murmured. "I just . . . once you'd read those books, I wanted to talk to you about them so badly, but I could never find the nerve. I kept hoping you would bring it up, give me some sign to let me know . . ." Her words trailed off in a sigh.

"Let you know," said Knife, leaning forward in an effort to hear. "Know what?"

"That you saw the same things in them that I did. That you understood . . . how important they were." Campion opened her eyes again, staring blindly at the ceiling. "But then the Queen had them burned, and you disappeared, and when you came back . . . you didn't seem to miss them anymore. You asked me for books about other things instead . . . I knew then that I'd been foolish to hope, that nobody . . ." Her throat moved in a convulsive swallow. "That nobody believed in the humans, nobody cared about them, except me."

Knife sat back, stricken. She had been afraid to trust Campion with the things she had learned about humans, unwilling to take the risk that the Librarian might misunderstand or betray her. Now she understood how wrong she had been not to be honest with her from the start—but now it was too late.

Still, she could at least talk to Campion, in these few moments before the Silence stole her wits completely. She owed the Librarian that much, and perhaps it would bring her some comfort. "Valerian," she said over her shoulder, "would you do me a favor? Go up to my room and ask Wink if she can look after Linden a little while longer."

It was, she realized belatedly, a very human sort of request: She had not even made the traditional offer to bargain. But Valerian did not reproach her, or even look surprised. Instead, she walked straight past Knife and out into the corridor, closing the door gently in her wake.

Knife turned back to Campion. "Listen," she said in a low voice. "I have a story to tell you, about an old diary, and a Seamstress named Heather. . . ."

Seventeen

"And that's where Heather's first diary ended," said Knife to the motionless Campion, leaning close to make sure the Librarian did not miss a word. "But there's another one, and as soon as I've read it, I'll come back and tell you all about—"

She stopped, her throat tightening. Campion's mouth hung slack, and her eyes had closed. Her hand slid from Knife's and fell to the mattress, limp as a dead bird.

"She can't hear you now," Valerian said quietly. She drew the covers up around Campion's shoulders. "Let me look after her. You've done all you could."

Knife felt a dull pain beneath her ribs, as though she had swallowed a bone. "But not enough," she said bitterly, and turned away.

＊ ＊ ＊

"Valerian was a *what?*" asked Wink.

"A changeling," said Knife wearily, taking Linden from her and sitting down on the sofa. "Born human, then stolen and turned into a faery. Or at least that's what we both think."

Wink sank down beside her. "And Campion has the Silence. . . . I can't believe it. She isn't even the oldest of us; she's younger than Thorn. How could this happen?"

There was no answer to that, and Knife did not try to give one. They sat together without speaking for a long time. Finally Wink said in a soft voice, "Well, I hope you find Heather's diary tomorrow. But even if you don't, I'll be glad if you just come back safe." She looked away, as though embarrassed. "I know you're used to taking risks, but . . . I worry about you."

Looking at Wink's small, forlorn figure, Knife felt as though someone had taken hold of her heart and squeezed it. "You needn't worry," she said gently. "I'll be careful. I promise."

As Knife headed out the Queen's Gate the next morning, the sky hung gray and lowering, and cold mist blanketed the ground. Rain seemed inevitable, so she set off across the Oakenwyld at her briskest pace, consoling herself that if she got soaked at least Paul's car would be dry.

When she reached the stone bridge where they had

agreed to meet she was apprehensive at first, for she had never ridden in a car before. But the longer she waited the more restless she became, and by the time the berry-colored wagon finally rumbled over the bridge and crunched to a stop beside her, Knife leaped up and ran toward it without hesitation. Surely this was how Heather must have felt on the day she left the Oak, after all those months of planning and waiting. . . .

"Knife?" said Paul's voice as the door cracked open.

"I'm here," she said. One fluttering leap took her to the floor of the car, another to the seat. It smelled strange—of dirt and metal, and a sour tang she did not recognize. But it also smelled like Paul, and that was reassuring.

Paul frowned at the map in his hand. "Just a minute, while I check . . . right, I've got it." He folded the page and tucked it away, then leaned past her to yank the passenger door shut. "You'd better sit down," he said.

Knife dropped to her knees, curling her legs beneath her. Unable to see out the window high above, she concentrated on the brisk movements of Paul's hands as he jolted the car into motion and steered it down the narrow lane. The growl of the engine changed its timbre, an invisible hand pressed her back against the upholstery; then Paul swung the wheel and she tumbled over, skidding across the seat with a cry.

"Sorry," said Paul. "I should have buckled you in—or maybe you'd be better off in my pocket?"

"I think so," she gasped.

"Here, then." He slowed the car and brought it to a stop. Picking herself up, Knife hurried across the seat and climbed into the inside pocket of Paul's jacket. It was too shallow for her to stand in comfortably, but there was just enough room to sit.

"All right?" asked Paul.

"Yes," she said, and the car picked up speed again.

Cradled in a hammock of soft fabric, Knife could finally relax. She leaned against the comforting warmth of Paul's side and closed her eyes.

"Knife."

She stirred, dimly aware that the car had stopped moving again. "Mmm?"

"We're here. No," he cautioned as she began to clamber out of his pocket, "you'd better stay where you are. Can you see?"

"Not much." The jacket draped across her view on one side, and his body all but blocked the other; it was like peering out through the flap of a very tall and narrow tent.

"Well, then, I'll give a signal when it's time for you to come out. Like this." He nudged her lightly with his elbow. "All right?"

"All right," said Knife, sinking down into the pocket again.

"Hang on, I'm going to open the doors." A creaking

noise followed, and a rain-scented breeze flowed into the car. "Just have to pull my wheelchair out of the backseat and set it up . . . and now I'm ready to transfer out. Here goes."

The pocket swung outward at an alarming angle, then bumped back into place. Gravel crackled as the chair rolled backward; then the doors slammed shut. Knife raised herself up on her knees, bracing herself with a hand against Paul's side, and leaned forward to see where they were going.

She had expected that Waverley Hall would be little different from the House, but now she knew she might as well have compared a sapling to the Oak itself. It towered above them, morning sunlight flashing on its tall windows and setting its russet brick aglow. *This* was where Heather had left her diary?

"Three cheers for wheelchair accessibility," Paul muttered, pushing his chair up a slight ramp and pressing a button on the wall. With a low hum the door swung inward, and Knife ducked back inside Paul's jacket as they entered Waverley Hall.

Inside, the air was cool and smelled faintly of roses. She heard whispers and giggles around them; it seemed that she and Paul were not the only ones touring the estate that morning. Money changed hands, guidebooks were handed out, and in a few moments a bright female voice hushed all the others into silence:

"Welcome to Waverley Hall, built by Sir John Waverley in 1683 and still owned by his descendants today. The family is glad to welcome you to their estate, but before we begin our tour we'll need to go over a few simple rules. . . ."

The young woman went on to explain that they must stay with the group at all times, respect the privacy of the owners, and above all *not touch anything*. Knife grimaced. With several other people on the tour and the guide watching them all closely, how could she hope to slip out of Paul's pocket without being seen?

"We'll begin our tour here in the main hall," the guide said, her footsteps receding, and Knife clung to Paul as his chair rolled forward. "This is where the Waverley family portraits are kept: Over the fireplace you can see Sir John, and on the far side his wife, Prudence, and their firstborn son, James. Several generations of the family are represented here, all painted by leading artists of the day. . . ."

As they wound their way through the room, Knife felt Paul's ribs expand with his sudden intake of breath. "That's a Wrenfield," he murmured to her. "Can you see it?"

She peered cautiously out of his jacket and looked up to see a painting of a man with reddish hair and sober gray eyes. His lips were curved a little upward, but one could see at a glance that the smile was false, a brave attempt at hiding some secret pain. "Who was he?" she whispered back.

"Philip Waverley," Paul said behind his hand. "Born 1798, died in 1832. Some sort of poet, I think. But never mind that. Look at the background."

Knife obeyed, but saw nothing out of the ordinary. She was about to ask Paul what he meant when her eye fell upon it, almost invisible among the shadows: a dark, slender figure . . . with wings.

"That's the first faery Wrenfield ever painted," Paul went on softly. "But this portrait was the last time he ever painted anything else."

"Now that we've met the family," said the young woman leading the tour, "I'd like you to follow me into the drawing room. . . ."

The group moved on, and Knife waited with growing impatience as the guide led them from one room to another, chattering on about the history of the estate, the development of its architecture and décor, and other unimportant matters. She was beginning to wonder if she would have better luck searching the house on her own when she heard the guide say, ". . . and now let's move on to the library."

Knife grabbed a double handful of Paul's shirt and swung herself free of his inside pocket, crouching just inside the front of his coat as the group slowly circled the room. As they drifted out again Paul hung back, leaning to one side while he pretended to adjust his wheel brake. "Go," he whispered, and Knife slithered down his hip, swung off the frame of the chair, and dropped to the carpet by his side. Paul gave her a quick crossed-finger gesture, then pushed himself out into the corridor, leaving Knife alone.

Knife straightened up and looked around to find herself in a fresh, well-lighted room lined with shelves and cabinets. An exotic rug covered the floor, flanked by leather furniture, while in the middle of the room an oval table squatted under the weight of an enormous porcelain vase. Somewhere in all this opulence, Knife knew, she would find Heather's second diary—but where?

The bookcases seemed the most logical place to start. She flew to the top of the first shelf and began running her hands along the spines, reading each one as quickly as she could. *I'm here,* she pleaded silently. *Heather sent me. Where are you?*

Every creaking footstep, every distant voice, made her heart jerk; every few seconds she glanced at the door, ready to dive into hiding the moment anyone should appear. Flitting from row to row, she had touched all the books in three full cases and was just beginning the fourth when a burning pain shot through her fingertips. With a cry she jumped back—and plunged off the edge of the shelf.

Her wings caught her before she had fallen more than a sparrow-length, and she bit off her scream almost at once; but the commotion had not gone unheard. A rapid clicking sounded in the hallway, and a squat, wrinkle-faced dog ambled in. Hovering in midair, Knife held as still as she could as the animal padded toward her, and a questioning noise rumbled in its throat.

"Good dog," whispered Knife—but that was a mistake. The air erupted with hoarse barking as the little dog bounced up and down in a futile attempt to reach her. Knife clapped her hands over her ears and leaped to the top of the bookshelf, getting as far away from the noisy animal as she could.

"Yahtzee, hush!" said a woman's reproachful voice from the corridor, and Knife glanced about in panic for a place to hide. The shelves were all full, the cabinets sealed; the furniture stood too high and the porcelain vase too low—

"Silly creature, what are you fussing about?" chided the human as she bustled in, bending to seize the agitated dog by the collar. She was a small woman with upswept hair and beautifully made clothes. Knife's heart sank as she realized that this must be the owner of the house.

The woman tried to coax the dog back toward the door, but still it strained toward Knife's hiding place, yelping. With a frown the woman picked it up and stepped forward, so close now that Knife could smell her perfume. She glanced out the window at the lawn; then her face cleared and she held the dog up in front of her, crooning, "Naughty squirrels! You'd like to teach them a lesson, wouldn't you? But not today, so come along and behave." Tucking her pet tenderly into the crook of her arm, she carried it out and shut the doors behind her.

Knife let go of the curtain and collapsed to the window-sill, head tipped back against the cool glass. When her heart stopped pounding she clambered to her feet again and flew back up to the bookcase.

She could see the diary tucked away at the far end of the shelf: an ordinary-looking little book, except for the faint glow emanating from its spine. Gingerly she reached out, bracing herself for another shock—but even as she touched it the light died away, and she was able to put her hand upon it. Heather's second diary was hers at last.

There was only one problem, and she cursed herself for not having anticipated it: The diary was human-sized. How could she possibly get it off the shelf, let alone sneak it out of the building, when it was bigger than she was?

Knife glanced from the shelf to the window and back again. Perhaps she could open the window and push the diary out for Paul to retrieve later? It was not a very good plan, but it was better than no plan at all, so she decided to try it.

Her fingers dug into the leather, tugging hard. The diary shifted grudgingly forward. Knife's wings blurred into action as she stepped backward into the air, and for one excited moment she believed her plan would work. But then the book's full weight toppled onto her, crushing the wind from her lungs, and in an instant the whole library spun upside down and she was falling—

She thumped down between the sofa and the table, the diary clutched in her sweat-slick palm. The vase wobbled dangerously, then began to tip toward her; she flung out a hand and caught it just in time. *Oh no*, thought Knife as she looked at her human-sized fingers spread out against the porcelain, *I've done it again.*

Her head swam and her muscles felt like bags of wet sand, but Knife dared not stop to rest, or even think: She had to get out of the library at once. Shoving the book down the front of her tunic, she hauled open the window and scrambled through it, landing painfully on the gravel drive. Quickly she leaped up and dragged the window shut again, then crawled behind the shrubbery and crouched there, rigid with fear. Surely Mrs. Waverley had heard her fall and was coming to investigate; any moment she would hear her cry, "Thief!"

But the only noise Knife heard was the song of a distant thrush, and through the branches she glimpsed nothing but an empty stretch of gravel. Awkwardly she rose, one hand clasping the diary against her chest, and slipped out of the cover of the shrubbery. She hurried along the back of the house and around the corner to Paul's car.

But the door was locked, and Paul had the keys. She would just have to brazen it out, and pretend to be an ordinary visitor—albeit a strangely dressed one—while she waited for Paul to finish the tour.

Knife brushed the gravel from her knees, combed her hair with her fingers, and took Heather's diary out of the bottom of her tunic. Then with all the casualness she could muster she walked to the nearest bench, sat down, and began to read.

"*Knife?*"

Paul didn't just sound surprised; he sounded thunderstruck. Caught off guard, Knife leaped to her feet and blurted the first thing that came into her head: "I'm sorry."

"But . . . how did you do it?" he asked. "I thought you'd used up all your magic."

"So did I. But I was trying to get the diary and it just"— she waved a hand at herself—"happened."

Paul's eyes traveled down her body to the book in her hand. "Well, you've got what you came for, at least," he said. "Did you find out anything useful?"

"Not yet," Knife admitted, watching him unlock the car and begin transferring himself and his wheelchair inside. "So far she's just been meeting people and going to balls and such. What about you?"

"They had a terrific collection of Dutch masters," said Paul with enthusiasm as she climbed in beside him. "And a couple more Wrenfield paintings, including a portrait of a woman named Jane Nesmith. The guide was telling us—" He glanced at Knife, who had opened the diary again. "Well, never mind. You want to read."

"It's all right," said Knife, leafing through the pages to find where she had left off. "What were you saying?"

"About this woman Jane. Seems that Wrenfield caught sight of her on the street and decided he *had* to paint her, and soon she became his favorite model and eventually his mistress. She was with him for three years, and during that time he turned out more and better paintings than ever before. But when she left, he fell apart."

"Why did she leave?" asked Knife.

"Nobody knows." He turned the key, and began backing out of the parking space onto the drive. "Some historians believe that Wrenfield was unfaithful, or that Jane herself found another lover. Others think he beat her—his temper was legendary. There's even a theory that he'd started taking laudanum already, was useless half the time, and that his most successful paintings were actually finished by Jane." He gave a flickering grin. "I like that one, though I'm not sure I believe it. But there's no doubt that after she disappeared, Wrenfield was never the same again."

"I see," said Knife absently, and turned another page.

"The one thing nobody has been able to figure out, though," Paul went on as they headed down the tree-lined lane, "is why he started painting faeries—"

"*Oh!*" said Knife.

"What is it?"

Knife lowered the book, staring out the car's front window at the distant roadway. "She's just met Philip Waverley."

"Really," said Paul. "What does she say about him?"

Everyone speaks well of him; his manner is most pleasant, and he shows not the least inclination to melancholy or ill-temper; I would scarcely have known him for a poet, but in truth he is a very fine one. He gave me a copy of his Sonnets on an English Garden, *and I have been carrying it about with me ever since. . . .*

"She likes his poetry," Knife replied in a distracted tone, finding it difficult to read and talk at the same time, "and she hopes they'll meet again so they can talk about it." She was silent then, absorbed in her reading, until Paul said, "And did she?"

"What? Oh—yes. Quite a few times, actually." She read a few more paragraphs, then added slowly, "It looks like they've become . . . friends."

"You sound surprised," said Paul.

Knife gave a wan smile. "I suppose I am." She had thought that her friendship with Paul was something special, perhaps even unique in the Oak's history. But if Heather had been able to talk to Philip in a similar way, then perhaps humans and faeries were more alike than she had supposed . . . and she wasn't quite sure how she felt about that.

I am overwhelmed with roses—Lily declares that she has never seen such handsome ones, and their fragrance lingers about me as I write. They were brought to my door this morning by a little messenger boy, bright as a robin, who bowed prettily and presented me with a card:

Receive this gift, O gentle Muse,
And Heaven's poetry peruse;
For mortal tongue can ne'er compose
A sonnet sweeter than a rose.

Which is not perhaps quite up to Mr. Waverley's usual standard, but I am very well pleased, nonetheless.

"So what's happening now?" prompted Paul.

"She's . . . started writing poems," said Knife, looking at the next page, which was full of crossed-out lines and lists of rhyming words. "Her own, I mean, not his."

"So you were right," Paul said, nudging her with an elbow. "About your people borrowing creativity from us, I mean."

"Yes, but . . ." Knife edged away from him, unaccountably flustered. "I'm still not sure why she's there, or how what she's doing is supposed to help the Oak. I mean, writing poetry is all very well, but what use is it?"

"You could say the same thing about art," said Paul.

"I know," said Knife, "but that's not what I meant, not exactly—" Her eyes traveled down the page as she spoke, and all at once she broke off, fingers clenching around the diary. "No," she breathed. "No, no, no . . ."

"What?" asked Paul sharply, but Knife could not bring herself to answer.

For all my hopes and ambitions, my eagerness to be of service to the Oak, I never thought it should come to this: Philip Waverley has asked me to become his wife. And I . . .

This was madness. It was a mistake. It simply couldn't *be*. And yet even before she turned the page, Knife knew what she would find there:

. . . I have accepted him.

Eighteen

Knife's cheeks flamed, and her hands shook beneath the diary's slight weight. More than anything she wanted to slap the book shut and fling it away from her, but it was too late: Heather's words had seared into her mind, and nothing could make her forget them.

Was this really how the Oakenfolk of Heather's day had repaid their human benefactors—by pledging their own bodies and souls to them in marriage? But Philip Waverley had not known himself to be marrying a faery; he thought Heather was a woman of his own kind. Had Heather been prepared to spend a human lifetime keeping up that illusion? Did she really think the gift of poetry that Philip had given her, or even the pleasure of his friendship, was worth so great a sacrifice?

It was no use speculating. She had to know. Shutting out Paul's curious look, the drone of the engine and the tree-dotted hillsides flashing by, Knife hunched over the diary and began turning pages as quickly as she could read them.

Heather was true to her word: She soon married Philip, and came to live with him at Waverley Hall. With her by his side his poetic gift flourished, and near the end of their first year together, Heather wrote:

> *I dared not speak of it until I was certain, but now there can be no doubt. I am with child: a human child, a son. How delighted Philip will be!*

Knife put a hand to her temple, feeling her pulse drumming against her fingertips. That a faery might conceive a human's child, carry it in her own body, and give birth to it without dying—she had never even imagined such a thing could be possible. Yet Heather seemed to think it perfectly natural, and in all this time, she had never once mentioned eggs. . . .

Feverishly Knife leafed through the second half of the diary, skimming over the birth of Heather's son, James, and several months of motherly anecdotes, until she came to this:

> *I have done a thing I believed I should never do; yet in my heart I knew it was right, indeed that it was meant to be so. Tonight I*

have cast myself upon Philip's mercy, and told him everything.

He knows now that his beloved wife and Muse is in truth a faery; he knows that his daughter, also faery, grows within me unseen; and he also knows that I must return to the Oak before she is born, for no infant with wings and magic can thrive apart from the protection and guidance of her own kind—things that I in my human guise cannot give her.

My dear Philip bore all this in silence, though I could see that he was shaken to his very marrow. It was not that he could not believe me, for I took pains to be sure that he did; yet even my promise to return to Waverley once our daughter was safely delivered seemed to bring him little comfort.

At length I ended my confession, and cast myself in tears upon his feet. I feared that he might disown me then, and banish me from his presence; yet by the Gardener's mercy he did not hesitate to lift me up and enfold me in his arms. I knew then that despite all, my husband had not ceased to love me; and that such faithfulness must not go unrewarded. . . .

"I think," said Paul to the air at large, "that I ought to get some sort of medal for patience."

All at once the car seemed far too small, and Knife could not bear to look at him. She leaned against the passenger door, pressing her forehead to the sun-warmed glass. "I'm sorry," she said. "It's too much. I can't talk about it. I can't."

Silence. She glanced back, saw the rigid set of his jaw and

the way his hands had tightened on the wheel, and knew that she had hurt him.

"It's not you," she added hastily. "I trust you. It's just—"

Just that everything she had believed about faeries and humans, even about Paul and herself, was wrong. She had thought that they could comfortably go on being friends forever. But now that she knew what might have been, what *should* have been if not for the Sundering, how could she ever be at ease with him again?

Paul sighed. "Look, it's all right. It's only curiosity; I'm not going to die of it. And it's really nothing to do with me, anyway."

He shrugged as he spoke, and the realization that he was trying to spare *her* feelings was more than Knife could bear.

"I don't know what to do," she burst out, clutching her elbows and rocking miserably. "The Sundering changed my people so much, I can't see how we can ever make things right. All the things we've been missing, that we'd forgotten— there's no way for us to get them back, not when we've so little magic left. And now Campion's got the Silence, and we're all going to die of it, me and Linden and Wink and Thorn and all of us—"

Paul's hand dropped from the wheel to the lever below; the car angled away from the road and bumped to a stop by its edge. Another car flashed past as he turned to her and said fiercely, "No."

Knife cringed, but he took her by the shoulders and went on: "I don't know what you read in that diary, but it doesn't matter. Even if you can't go back to the way you used to be, why should that mean there's no hope? Look at yourself, Knife! Look at all the things you've done, even without magic. And ask yourself: How many people would be dead right now if not for you?" He lowered his voice and added, "Including me."

"But the Silence—"

"—is there, yes, and I'm sorry to hear about Campion. But she's not dead yet, and there's still a chance that you or someone else will find a cure." He brushed a strand of hair back from her forehead. "You're a fighter, Knife. Don't stop fighting now."

Knife gave a reluctant nod. Paul tugged her toward him, and she closed her eyes and laid her head against his chest, listening to the strange, slow beat of his heart. She knew it was unwise to get so close to him, and all her instincts told her to pull away—and yet she wanted to savor this moment, because once she went back to her own size no one would ever hold her like this again.

"All right," she murmured.

"Look," said Paul. "We're almost home."

There in the distance lay the familiar S-bend of the road, with the wood on one side and the arch of the stone bridge beyond. Knife could just make out the topmost branches of the Oak rising above the fringe of lesser trees, and a pang went through her as she realized that her time with Paul, and the magic that had made it possible, was about to end.

"Stop the car," she said. "Please. I need to tell you something."

Paul glanced over his shoulder, then pulled the car over onto the verge. Loose stones rattled against the wheels before fading into a soft hiss of grass, and the sunlight around them dimmed to shadow as he brought them to a stop. "All right," he said, slinging one elbow over the top of the steering wheel and turning toward her. "What is it?"

Knife looked down at the diary in her lap. Now that the first shock of discovering that faeries used to marry humans and even have children with them had subsided, she felt strangely calm: She knew what she had to do, for both their sakes. "I know we talked about spending the next two days together, but I can't. I have to go back to the Oak and tell them what I've found."

"Is that all?" He sounded relieved. "Well, that's no problem. Just let me know when—"

"No." Her voice was quiet, but resolute. "You've given me so much, Paul, and I'll never forget what you've done for me today. But I can't keep meeting with you like this. The Queen's already caught me once—the next time she won't be so forgiving. Besides, I belong with my own people. And so do you."

Paul looked at her in disbelief. "You mean . . . that's it? We're never going to see each other again?"

Knife closed her eyes. If only she didn't have to look at him, hear the pain in his voice; this would be so much easier, if only she could pretend he wasn't there. "Yes," she said. "That's what I mean."

"I thought we were friends." The words were edged with anger. "After everything that's happened, everything we've done for each other—none of that matters?"

"Of course it matters!" She gripped the diary hard with both hands, wishing once more that she had never seen it, never learned the secrets it contained. "And yes, you are my friend." Her voice lowered. "My best friend."

"Really?" The bitterness left his tone. "But then . . ."

"Don't you see? That's just why! This isn't right, Paul, it doesn't make any sense. You're human, and I'm a faery—" *And once this magic wears off, I'll be seven inches tall.*

"I know," he said. "But there's something else I know, too." He shifted closer to her, intent. "There's a reason I told you that story about Alfred Wrenfield. What Jane gave to him—that inspiration, that genius even—that's what you've given me. When you're around, I can draw, I can paint, I can capture the images in my head and put them on paper in a way I haven't done for years. And if you leave—"

"Don't!" She jerked away from him. "Don't make this any harder for me, Paul. I have a child to look after back at the Oak, and friends who need my help. The Queen's depending on me to help her find more faeries, because she believes that's our only hope for our people to survive—and now I know she's right." Knife pushed her hands up into her hair, clenched them. "I love your art, and I . . . I wish I could help you. But they need me more."

"All right," said Paul, with surprising calm.

Caught off guard, she dropped her hands, and found his face close to hers. "I'll let you go," he continued, "and I won't ask for anything more. Except . . ."

"Yes?" said Knife faintly. Her heart felt as if it were trying to beat sideways, and her lungs seemed to have shrunk to faery size.

"This." And with that his hand slipped around the back of her neck, and his mouth pressed down on hers.

She had read about kissing in the books that Amaryllis had burned; a strange human custom, she had thought. But as Paul's lips moved against her own, it suddenly seemed the most natural thing in the world. His arms locked around her, strong as oak and warm as fire; she melted into the embrace, her fingers curling against his cheek. This, she realized with her last flicker of conscious thought, was what had drawn Heather to Philip Waverley; not obligation or even friendship, but—

No!

Knife stiffened, then writhed free of Paul's grasp. One hand flew to her burning face; the other flailed wildly at the door handle.

"Knife? What's the—"

"I can't!" she shouted, throwing her weight against the door. It popped open, and she half leaped, half fell out onto the grass. Her foot turned over, and pain shot up her ankle, but she paid it no heed; she dragged herself away from the car and began struggling toward the Oakenwyld.

"Knife!"

The door slammed behind her; the engine woke with a groan. Knife limped deeper into the grass as Paul backed the car onto the road. "I was going to say I was sorry," he called out the window. "But that would be lying, so I'd better just say—good-bye."

Knife stood still while he drove past, watching the vehicle pick up speed as it vanished into the distance. Distracted, she walked forward—and put her foot straight into a hole. Fresh agony tore through her muscles as she stumbled, and flung out both hands to catch herself.

It was then that she realized something was missing. Aghast, she looked down at her empty, mud-smeared palms.

"Oh, for Garden's sake!" she screamed at the sky. "I've left the diary in his blighted crow-eaten car!"

No sooner were the words out of her mouth than her body tingled, and the world overwhelmed her with its enormity. For a moment she stood swaying, dizzy with the cruel abruptness of the change; then she sank to her knees, dropped her face against her hands, and wept.

Nineteen

Swiping the tears from her eyes, Knife forced herself back to her feet. Her ankle throbbed, but she gritted her teeth and started back up the slope toward the road. Only after several painful steps did she remember that she was a faery again, and there was no need for her to walk unless she wanted to.

Knife flexed her shoulders. She could feel her wings, but only just; they were mere ghosts of themselves now, light as dry leaves and almost as brittle. She had to concentrate hard to lift herself off the ground, and once in the air she could only glide a short distance before dropping back to her feet again. In accidentally making herself human for the second time, she had used up nearly all the magic that made her a faery.

She settled for walking again, with a few intermittent

leaps, until she reached the road. But she had only gone a little way along it when she saw an enormous dead crow splayed across the pavement, no doubt struck by some passing car. Wrinkling her nose in distaste, Knife began to limp past—then stopped.

This was not just any crow. This was Old Wormwood.

She ought to have been glad to see him dead. But instead she felt disappointed, even a little sorry. She had imagined meeting him in one last battle, all her wits and skill concentrated into giving him the death he deserved. But that could never happen now, because the humans had killed him first—and not even on purpose.

One of the crow's breast feathers lay at her feet. Knife picked it up and tucked it into her belt. Then she spread her wings again and continued her awkward journey home.

"Oh!" gasped Wink, dropping her sewing as Knife climbed through her window. "What are you doing here? You're not supposed to be back until—" She stopped, her brows crooking together. "Knife . . . you look awful."

Knife glanced about the room, rubbing her cold arms. Linden appeared to be comfortably asleep in her cradle, but she stooped to drape another blanket over the child just in case. "Do you know where Thorn is?" she said.

"She's in her room, I think—but what happened to you? What's wrong?"

Knife dropped into the nearest chair and sagged forward,

leaning heavily on her knees. "I don't have the diary," she said to the floor. "I'm sorry."

Wood scraped as Wink pulled up another chair beside her, and she felt a small hand warm her shoulder. "You did your best," the other faery said. "Don't blame yourself."

"Oh, Wink. I only wish it were that easy."

"What do you mean?"

In halting words Knife told her story. By the time she finished, her cheeks were burning, and she did not dare to look at her foster mother's face for fear of what she might see there. But Wink only said, in an almost wistful tone, "Was it nice?"

Knife blinked at her. "You mean . . . Waverley Hall?"

"No, I mean what Paul did. Did you like it?"

Knife choked back a laugh. "Wink, you are the strangest—after all the things I've just told you, how can you even think about that?"

Wink only looked at her, but it was enough. Knife's shoulders slumped. "It's not about how I feel," she said. "It's about what's possible. And this . . . isn't."

"Why not?"

"Because I'm too small!" Knife almost shouted. "And I don't have enough magic to make myself human again, even if I knew how. So how could I bear to keep seeing him, talking to him, when I can never—"

"You mean . . . you're *in love* with him? Like Heather and Philip?"

"I don't know," said Knife wretchedly. "I'm not even

sure I know what love is."

"Yes, you do," said Wink with surprising confidence. "For a while I wasn't sure, but . . . you do care, Knife. Not just about Paul, but about Linden, me, even Thorn. You just aren't good at admitting it."

Knife groaned and put her head in her hands. "But I don't *want* feelings, Wink."

Wink put an arm around her shoulders. "I know. They can be awful at times. But I think you're much nicer with them, myself."

For a moment Knife sat stiffly, resisting the embrace; then she sighed and dropped her head against Wink's. "I'm sorry," she said. "All my life you've been kind to me, and I haven't always appreciated that the way I should."

"It's all right." Wink gave her a little squeeze before letting her go. "But Knife . . . this is serious, about losing Heather's diary. I believe what you've told me, even if it scares me a little. But if we can't find another way to prove that our people used to mate with humans, and that all our new ideas used to come from the humans as well—"

Knife's gaze slid to the open window and the distant House. "I know," she said. "It's going to be hard to make people believe. Maybe the Queen was right not to tell us, especially since it seems there's nothing we can do to fix it."

"Thorn isn't going to like that *at all*," said Wink. "She'll—"

A rap at the door interrupted her, and she jumped up to

answer it. Valerian stood on the landing, her Healer's kit in hand. "There you are," she said to Knife. "They told me you'd gone, but then I heard your voice . . . Campion's asking for you."

"Asking?" said Knife, startled. "But I thought the Silence had taken her."

"Yes, so did I," said Valerian. "But she only slept through the night, and when I visited her this morning, I found that she could still hear and speak. She's been holding on, waiting for you to come back and tell her more . . . I've never seen anything like it."

Knife turned quickly to Wink. "Can you find Thorn, and tell her where I am? Tell her I need Heather's third diary right away—not for me, but for Campion."

"I will," said Wink. "But Campion needs you. Go!"

Campion's cheeks were sunken, and her hair lay lank and dull upon the pillow. But when she caught sight of Knife her face brightened, and her hand fluttered toward the bedside chair, beckoning.

"I'm here," said Knife, limping over and sitting down. "But—" She glanced back at Valerian uncertainly.

"I cannot claim to be deaf," said Valerian, "but I can at least pledge to be discreet. Whatever you say here will remain here." She opened her Healer's bag and took out a roll of bandages. "Now, will you lift that injured ankle so I can bind it up while you talk?"

Still Knife hesitated, but only for a moment. Campion was surely dying anyway, and would take these secrets to her grave; and Valerian was the Oak's only Healer, so she could not be punished too severely even if the Queen found out. Turning to Campion, Knife took the Librarian's hand as she had done the night before and began to tell her what she had learned from Heather's second diary.

It did not take long for Valerian to bind Knife's ankle, and after it was done she put her Healer's kit aside and sat down on the end of the bed, listening. As the story drew to its close, with Heather preparing to return to the Oak and give birth to her daughter there, Knife saw Valerian's expression become troubled; but Campion simply absorbed the words, like a parched root drinking water.

"Is that . . . all?" she said when Knife had finished.

"No," said Knife. "There's a third diary—but it won't unlock without a password, and I'll need time to read it before I can tell you the rest of the story."

Campion nodded, her eyelids drooping shut again. Valerian rose swiftly and laid her hand on the Librarian's brow; then she motioned Knife to follow her to the other side of the room so that they could speak in private.

"This is remarkable," she said, glancing back at Campion. "She should have passed into the next stage of the Silence hours ago. Yet she seems no weaker than when you first spoke to her last night, and the delirium has passed. Perhaps I am seeing only what I hope to see, but . . ."

"You're not imagining it," said Knife. "She actually gripped my hand, near the end. But what's going to happen when there's no more story to tell?"

Valerian was silent for a long time, looking down at her folded arms. "This Heather you spoke of," she said at last. "The one who married the human. She was Lavender's friend, correct?"

"Yes."

"Then do you think perhaps . . ." But she had no time to finish the sentence before the door scraped open and Thorn pushed herself through, disheveled and breathless.

"I've got it," she said, waving the book in her hand, then stopped short at the sight of Valerian. "Oh, blight."

"Make that blessing," said Knife, steering her toward the Healer. "She'll tell you what was in the second diary while I read the third one; it'll be quicker that way."

"Are you cracked?" demanded Thorn. "Bringing her into this, when we don't know we can trust her?" But Knife had already pulled the diary from her hand and raised it to her lips.

"Philip," she whispered to it, and it opened.

I have missed the Oak, and part of me is glad to return; yet I long for my husband and my little James, and even these few days without them seem like an eternity. I could not bear to think of

271

leaving my daughter here, were it not for the hope of seeing her again one day, and if not for my confidence that dear Lavender will care for her more tenderly than any human nurse—indeed, perhaps more so than I could do myself.

Yet it has troubled me to find the Oak so altered from when I left it. Snowdrop is dead, and Jasmine has become Queen in her place; my sisters seem content enough to accept the change, but my heart is filled with foreboding. Jasmine— though I suppose I must say Her Majesty, now—welcomed me and received my report with all courtesy, and yet the cool- ness of her gaze made me shiver. If I had not pledged long ago to put the needs of the Oak above my own, I should gladly have returned to Waverley Hall at once; but I have sacrificed much to come this far, and I dare not leave before my daughter is born.

Lavender has done much to reassure me about Jasmine, say- ing that she rules the Oak justly and well, and that I am wrong to fear her. Still, I think that I shall set a password upon this diary, just in case. . . .

"*What?*" yelped Thorn from the other side of the room, where Valerian was explaining what Knife had found in the second diary. "The bit about Heather marrying a human was bad enough, but now you expect me to believe she had a baby, too?"

"You should believe her, if you believe anyone," interrupted

Knife, putting her book down. "She's Heather and Philip's daughter."

Valerian turned sharply. "It's true, then? I was right?"

"I'm sure of it," said Knife.

"But that's ridiculous," Thorn objected. "All right, we had magic back then and we weren't frightened of the humans, but why go to all this trouble and nonsense to have children with them? There were still plenty of Oakenfolk alive in Heather's day without having to make more, and if it weren't for the Sundering and then the Silence, there still would be. Why fuss about with humans when you can make a perfectly good egg on your own?"

Knife and Valerian exchanged glances. "I cannot tell you that," the Healer said at last, "and clearly Knife is not yet sure of the answer herself. But I am not certain that leaving eggs behind when we die is as natural to us faeries as you think. In fact, since no other creatures do like-wise, one might well call our method of doing things . . . *un*natural."

"Speaking of strange things," said Knife, waving the diary in her hand, "did either of you know about Jasmine becoming Queen, when Snowdrop died? I knew I'd heard her name somewhere before, but I'd thought the throne passed straight from Snowdrop to Amaryllis."

"I . . . know," said Campion's weak voice from the bed, and they all turned to look at her. She gave a thin smile and went on, "Finally . . . reading all that history . . . worth something."

"What can you tell us?" asked Knife.

"Can't prove it, but . . . now I know more about Jasmine, I think . . . maybe Snowdrop's death wasn't . . . an accident."

"But the South Root tunnel collapsed on top of her," said Valerian. "I read of it in the death records—three other faeries perished the same way. What else could it be?"

"You're forgetting," said Thorn, with sudden grimness. "Our people had magic then. All of them."

Campion nodded. "By then . . . Jasmine had . . . already made herself popular at Court," she said. "She was . . . next in line . . . for the throne. And she was there . . . when the roof fell in."

"But there must have been witnesses," Knife said. "If she'd used magic, they would have noticed—"

"No," said Campion. "Kitchen workers . . . heard a rumble, went to see what was going on . . . found Jasmine scrabbling in the dirt . . . trying to get to the Queen."

"As any loyal subject would do," said Valerian.

"Or any murderer who wanted to *look* like a loyal subject," retorted Thorn. "I know it's a thin twig for such a heavy acorn. But my gut tells me Campion's right."

"So does mine," admitted Knife. "But if it's true that Jasmine murdered Snowdrop—what does that say about Amaryllis? Surely, if Jasmine was that powerful and that determined, she'd never have given up the throne except by force?"

The faeries all looked at one another, but no one spoke.

"Let me finish this diary," said Knife, sitting down by Campion's bedside and opening it up again. "Then maybe we'll know."

My time is near now, I can feel it; I am glad that Lavender has prepared herself to attend me, so that I shall not have to labor alone. Such a dear and faithful friend—whatever should I do without her?

The next entry read:

The ordeal is past, and my daughter safely born. I wish that Philip could see her, with her gray eyes so like his. She is perfect, a faery to make the Oak proud: I have nursed her and laid her down to sleep, but I find it hard not to steal glances at her even as I write. Already it breaks my heart to think of leaving her, and I cannot help wishing that there were another way. . . .

But Heather's delight in her new daughter was soon shadowed by uneasiness as she learned more about the situation in the Oak. It disturbed her particularly to learn that she was not the only one who had lately returned from Outside; apparently Queen Jasmine had sent word that all the Oakenfolk must attend her to swear fealty, and three other faeries had already left their missions in order to do so.

Why this made Heather so anxious, Knife was not sure, but it was not long before she found out. Only two entries later the Oak's uneasy peace was shattered forever.

I can scarcely write these words for weeping, and the pain within me is so great that I fear my heart must burst rather than contain it. Jasmine—I will not call her Queen now, for she is no liege of mine—has betrayed us all. Great Gardener, have mercy upon us!

With pounding heart Knife read through the few pages of the diary that remained. She had already begun to suspect Jasmine of having a hand in the Sundering, but even her darkest imaginings had not prepared her for Heather's final entry:

Lavender is lost to me, her reason and her memory overthrown; she babbles nonsense, and whenever I speak of humans she claps her hands to her ears and screams. The whole Oak is in chaos, faeries milling and bleating like sheep; they hear only Jasmine's voice, not mine, no matter how I plead. The horror is unbearable—I cannot leave my daughter here—I must escape. Yet how can I return to Waverley, trapped in this small body and robbed of all my magic? Even if by some miracle I could survive the journey, how could I endure the sight of Philip's face when he learns that he has lost not only his daughter, but his beloved Muse as well?

Yet I have no choice. It will not be long before Jasmine discovers that my mind remains unclouded, and that I cannot submit to her schemes. I must leave tonight, with the moon to light my path and my little Valerian in my arms; for even if we perish, it will be a better fate than the one Jasmine offers us.

I shall put this diary away in a secret place, with a prayer that someday it may be found by those with the wits to comprehend it, and the courage to bring the truth to light again. Forgive me that I can do no more. Farewell.

Numbly Knife let the diary fall. "Jasmine," she whispered. "She cast the Sundering—but why? *Why?*"

She glanced over at Campion, but the Librarian's eyes had closed again. Across the room, Thorn was still arguing with Valerian about the practical merits of eggs as opposed to children, and neither of them seemed to have noticed Knife's distress.

Not that it mattered. She was grateful for their help, and Wink's, too, but they had risked enough for her already. This riddle she would solve alone, even if she had to demand the truth from Queen Amaryllis herself.

And yet something nagged at her mind, a sense that she had the answer already but had somehow failed to see it. She

thought back on all she had learned about Jasmine, frag-
ments of Heather's diaries floating through her mind:

> *A gown in need of mending . . . the bodice was badly torn and*
> *one sleeve ripped . . .*
>
> *"I have gained some little skill as an artist since I went*
> *away." She smiled, but her eyes remained bitter. . . .*
>
> *I had thought she would be pleased with my good fortune,*
> *but her own sad experience had filled her with misgivings, and*
> *she all but pleaded with me not to go. . . .*

His temper was legendary, added Paul's voice unexpectedly, and
just like that, Knife knew. Jane Nesmith, the beautiful, the
mysterious; the woman who had vanished, and left Alfred
Wrenfield madly painting faeries. . . .

Jasmine.

Slowly Knife bent and picked up Heather's last diary
from the floor. She laid it on the bedside table and said in
her calmest voice, "I'm just going upstairs for a bit." Then
without waiting to hear what Valerian or Thorn would say,
she slipped out.

Queen Amaryllis sat at her writing desk, her back to the
door. She was dressed in a faded blue tunic and skirt that
spoke less of elegance than comfort, her only mark of office
a slim circlet about her brow. "What is it, Bluebell?" she

said, but then her head came up like a fox on the scent and her body went very still, as though she had already realized her mistake.

"Your Majesty," said Knife, "we need to talk."

Twenty

"Have you returned already?" asked Queen Amaryllis, turning in her seat. Then her gaze fell to Knife's bandaged ankle, and she exclaimed, "You are hurt!"

She sounded concerned, and Knife felt an unexpected stab of guilt. "It's not serious," she said. "I mean, it'll take a few days to heal, but . . . that's not what I came to tell you."

Amaryllis's brows rose. "Very well: Speak."

Knife stood up straighter, gathering courage. "I didn't go looking for other faeries today."

"So you lied to me." The Queen's face darkened. "Why?"

Quickly Knife explained about Heather's diaries and what she had learned from them, taking care not to mention Wink and Thorn, but to make it sound as though she had made all these discoveries alone.

"And once I knew Heather's story," she continued, "I was able to piece together Jasmine's as well. She too had loved a human, an artist named Alfred Wrenfield—but one day he became angry and struck her, betraying her trust and shattering the bond between them. She left him and returned to the Oak, but all the while her bitterness grew, until she had convinced herself that all humans were just as brutal and unworthy as her lover had been. She tried to persuade the other faeries to stop going Outside, telling them they should be content with the skills and knowledge they already had. But no one listened to her, and in the end she decided the only way to free the Oakenfolk from their dependence on humans was by force.

"She murdered Snowdrop and took her place as Queen, then ordered all the faeries who had gone Outside to return to the Oak. They obeyed her without question, and once Heather's child was born, she had only to wait for the next full moon to carry out her plan.

"On that night Jasmine stepped out of the Oak and cast a terrible dark magic spell, tapping into the power of all the other Oakenfolk and twisting it against them. First she changed their bodies, so that they could replace themselves with eggs instead of needing human mates. Then she confused their memories, so that they wouldn't be able to remember what the Outside world was like; and finally she planted in them a powerful fear of humans, so that they would never be tempted to go near one again. The Sundering used up nearly all the power the Oakenfolk had, but Jasmine believed her actions would be worth the cost, for now her people would be free of human influence forever.

"Since then Jasmine and nearly all the faeries she changed have disappeared or died out," Knife finished. "The new generation of Oakenfolk aren't confused like the old ones were, and we're not as frightened either. But still the belief that humans are monsters lives on—and now I know it's killing us."

Throughout this speech, Amaryllis had kept her eyes lowered and her face impassive. Now her head snapped up, and her voice took on a cutting edge as she replied:

"*That* is killing us, you say? The simple belief that humans are a threat to our people? How can they be anything less, when they are so large and powerful, and we have so little magic with which to defend ourselves? And what of the other dangers that have claimed so many lives—the crows, the foxes, the electrical wires? What of the Silence, which has been responsible for nearly every death among us since the Sundering?"

The Queen rose from her chair, her face stony. "Have a care, Knife. You may well take pride in your own cleverness for discovering the truth—and yes, it is the truth, I do not deny it. But if you mean to tell me that after a few nights of skulking at windows and reading books you have learned more about humans than I knew after eighty years of living in their midst . . ."

"Eighty years?" said Knife, taken aback.

"A 'scholarly venture,' the historians called it," said Amaryllis, her lips pursing with contempt. "In those days students of humanity such as myself were often overlooked, our work taken for granted. But without the information we passed back to the Oak, faeries like Heather would have been ill-prepared for their missions; they would have been unlikely even to meet gifted humans such as Alfred Wrenfield and Philip Waverley, let alone have opportunity to bond with them."

Knife blinked at this, and the Queen's mouth curled in a mirthless smile. "You look surprised: Did you think that all faeries who left the Oak were seeking human mates? No doubt Heather and Jasmine's stories made you think so, but in truth such unions were rare. The rest of us made acquaintances among humans both male and female, but seldom became their close friends; in this way we could spread our influence more widely among them, and encourage them to greater creativity even if we could not inspire them to genius."

"But . . . we couldn't make eggs before Jasmine changed us," said Knife slowly. "So if only a few faeries ever married humans, and only their daughters came back to the Oak . . . shouldn't we have died out long before the Sundering?"

"In times of need," said Amaryllis, "there were other ways of finding children. The stories about changelings are not wholly fables; though in truth it was not loved and wanted children that we took from the humans, but the orphaned, abused, and neglected. Jasmine herself was one such, though she would have scorned to admit it."

"All right," said Knife. "That makes sense—but there's still something I don't understand. If Jasmine cast her spell on everyone in the Oak, how did you escape?"

"I ignored her summons," the Queen replied. "I was busy at the time, and it seemed unreasonable that I should return to the Oak on such short notice. Besides, the news of the call had come to me secondhand, so I had reason to believe that Jasmine had forgotten my existence—I told you already that scholars of my kind were often over-looked."

"But you came back anyway, in the end," said Knife. "Why?"

"The night Jasmine cast her spell, I dreamed of faery voices crying out for help, and knew that something was wrong. I cast off my human guise and returned to the Oak; but I was too late to undo what Jasmine had done.

"I could not even save Heather," she went on bitterly, "for Jasmine had already caught her and two others trying to escape, and pronounced them traitors. Whether she was enraged by their disobedience or merely her own failure to bend them to her will, I do not know; but she lost no time in carrying out the execution, and by the time I reached the throne room, there was nothing left of them but eggs." Her face contorted with disgust. "By the Gardener, how I loathed those eggs when I first saw them—"

"Was it then that you challenged her?" Knife asked.

"It was. Though I feared to lose," said Amaryllis, "for her magic had always been the stronger. But the effort of casting the Sundering had weakened her, and in the end I was victorious. I stripped her of her remaining powers, and executed the most fitting punishment I could devise." She gave a tight smile. "I transformed her into a human and banished her from the Oak forever."

Knife stared at her, appalled.

"And yet the shadow she had cast over the Oak remained, for all I sought to dispel it. I could not persuade the faeries she had altered to look favorably on humans again, and once I saw how weak and vulnerable they had become, I realized that it would be dangerous to try. And when the first eggs hatched, I found to my dismay that the new faeries had no magic at all—so I was forced to make them capable of creating eggs as well, for I could see no other way to prevent our people from dying out."

"So that's what you were doing to Linden," said Knife. "And I stopped you."

"Yes," said the Queen. "But understand that I only altered the new faeries' bodies; I did not touch their minds. And before all else, I gave back to each of them a small portion of the magic I had taken from Jasmine." She looked down at her hands. "Small recompense for a great wrong, I know; but it was all the power I could spare without putting the Oak itself in jeopardy."

Now at last Knife understood what old Bryony had meant in her letter: *To Queen Amaryllis, who has done all she could* . . . "Your Majesty," Knife said, "I misjudged you. I apologize."

"And well you might," said Amaryllis with sudden harshness, "for you have done me a great wrong." She walked toward Knife and looked up into her face. "When you saved me from the fox even after seeing me cast my spell on Linden, I believed that your loyalty had proven stronger than your doubts, and that I could trust you. And when you told me of your plan to leave the Oak and search for other faeries, I rejoiced to think that my confidence in you had been so well repaid . . . but I see now that this was nothing but deceit."

She seized Knife's chin in her hand, forcing her not to look away. "Do you think I cannot tell that you have been with a human? The scent of him is all over you. And did you think I had not noticed the state of your wings?" Her eyes bored into Knife's, accusing. "You have not only endangered yourself and the Oak, you have made yourself useless as my Hunter. For the sake of your own selfish curiosity you have rebelled against my commands, you have deceived me at every turn, and now you have robbed me of the last hope I had for saving our people—how dare you come here and boast of your discoveries, when it is I and your sisters who must pay the price?"

"Your Majesty," said Knife in desperation, "you don't understand—"

Her words ended in a gasp as Amaryllis brought both hands down in a sweeping gesture and a sheet of white flame sprang up around their feet. "I have given you the truth," said the Queen coldly, the pale fire reflected in her eyes. "Now it is time for you to repay in kind."

Knife struggled, but her feet were fastened to the floor, her hands too heavy to move. "You don't need to do this!" she pleaded with the Queen. "I'll answer your questions—just ask!"

"I cannot trust your words," Amaryllis said. "And I am weary of talking. The choice is yours, Knife. If you willingly recall for me your dealings with the humans, I will look at those memories and nothing else; but if you force me to search your mind—"

"No," said Knife quickly. "That won't be necessary."

She closed her eyes, still seeing the dazzling imprint of the Queen's magic behind them. "I'll give you what you want."

Cool fingertips brushed her temples, rested there. Knife stiffened, but there was no pain, only a slight probing, until—

Paul climbing the Oak, his child's face alight with wonder . . . His rich voice explaining art to her, and the sure movements of his hands as he sketched her for the first time . . . His muscles taut with fury as he flung the book of photographs to the floor, then slack beneath her hands as she dragged him from the pool . . . His friendship, his generosity, his readiness to help her . . . His excitement at driving her to Waverley, his disappointment when she told him good-bye, and then . . .

Amaryllis snatched her fingers back; the flames around them died. Still dizzy from the onslaught of memories, Knife lifted her head and looked into the Queen's shocked face.

"I know," said Knife. Her lips still tingled with the memory of Paul's kiss; she bit them self-consciously. "But you heard what I told him—it's over. We'll never see each other again."

Amaryllis did not reply. She turned and walked slowly back to her seat, sank down upon it, and folded her hands in her lap. Then at last she said in a voice drained of emotion, "It is too late for that."

"What do you mean?" asked Knife.

"I mean," said the Queen in the same flat tone, "that you have no idea what you have done—to him, to yourself, and to all of us. I had not believed it possible, not with so little magic left to you, but you have bonded to this human boy, heart and soul—and if you remain apart, it can only end in misery and despair for you both."

"But we can't—"

"No," Amaryllis agreed bleakly, "you cannot be together. In your folly you have doomed both him and yourself. You will languish here in the Oak, flightless and powerless; while he suffers the same torment as Alfred Wrenfield and Philip Waverley did before him, a hopeless longing that can be ended only by death."

Tremors of horror ran all over Knife's body, and she leaned back against the wall. "I didn't know," she whispered. "I never meant—"

"Indeed," said the Queen. "Which is why I am prepared to grant you mercy—on one condition. For all your recklessness and disobedience, you are the greatest Hunter the Oak has ever known; and you are still, I fear, the only chance we have of finding other faeries before it is too late. If you do this one thing for me, then I will give back to you the magic you have lost, and your power of flight will be fully restored."

Knife searched the Queen's face, disbelieving, but Amaryllis's gaze remained steady. "And the condition?" she asked.

"It is this," said Amaryllis. "As soon as night falls, you will leave the Oak, armed with the deadliest poison I can give you. You will return to this Paul of yours . . . and you will kill him."

Twenty-one

"No!"

Knife spun away from Amaryllis and dashed for the door. She had to find Paul, warn him— But the archway had vanished, as had all the windows, and she could see no exit.

It's a trick, she thought frantically, *just a glamour, it must be.* But when she pushed at the place where the door had stood, her outstretched hands found only solid oak. She hammered against its unyielding surface, shouting for help. But no one answered her except the Queen herself:

"Even if I were to let you go, you could not save him. There is only one choice . . . but first, there is something I want to show you." Amaryllis waved her hand, and the door sprang open. "Come with me," she said. "And Knife, I would not do that, if I were you."

With a hiss Knife snatched her fingers back from the hilt of her dagger, her hand smarting as though she had clutched a thistle. Robbed of her last defense, she could only follow Amaryllis down the corridor and into the Queen's study, with its desk buried in parchments and dark bookshelves looming on every side.

"I know you mourned the loss of those books about humans," said the Queen. "As did poor Campion. Had I known how much she would suffer, I would have taken her into my confidence. But even if this comes too late to console her, it is not too late for you." She made a sweeping gesture toward the shelves. "Look up, Knife, and tell me what you see."

Grudgingly Knife raised her eyes—and gasped. There stood Laurel's *Human Conventions and Courtesies* with its well-creased spine, the two fat volumes by Juniper entitled *On the Ways of Men*, and all the other books about humans she had thought lost forever. "But how?" she asked. "Campion said they'd been burned—"

"Things are not always as they seem," said Amaryllis. "I ordered the library cupboard emptied, it is true; and at the same time I told Mallow to light the kitchen fire and burn all the fuel I sent her. But the books that Campion saw taken away were mere glamour, more illusion than substance; the originals had already been gathered up by Bluebell at my command and brought safely here." She ran her fingers along the spines in a lingering caress. "Even though I had given up hope that they would ever be needed again, I could not bring myself to destroy them."

"And yet you ask me to murder Paul McCormick." The words were bitter in Knife's mouth. "How can any number of books about humans be worth more than a human life?"

"You forget, Knife, he is dying already. In truth he was doomed even as a child, for by meeting him face-to-face you awakened in him a restless need to create—and then you vanished from his life, your work with him unfinished." She walked slowly around Knife as she spoke. "Still, he might have lived, though never quite happily, had you not sought him out again. You rekindled the spark between you; you fanned it with your friendship and fueled it with a kiss; and now it has become a fire that will surely consume you both . . . unless you do as I bid, and quench it."

Knife turned away, sick at heart. *The Queen is lying,* she tried to tell herself, *she's mistaken, she's wrong. . . .* And yet she could not help but remember Paul's words to her just before they parted: *There's a reason I told you that story about Alfred Wrenfield. What Jane Nesmith gave to him . . . that's what you've given me.*

Wrenfield had drugged himself into an early grave after Jasmine left him; and Philip Waverley also had died young, his potential as a poet unfulfilled. Had she saved Paul from drowning only to condemn him to another, even more hopeless death?

"Your actions forged this bond," the Queen continued, soft but relentless, "so only your hand can break it. And if you refuse to cut the thread that binds your lives together, then you too will wither away and die, as surely as if the Silence had taken you. The crows will return to the Oakenwyld, and we shall all suffer for it; for Thorn has not your strength, your speed, or your courage. There will be no one to seek out other faeries, and in the end we shall all perish—"

"Stop!" Knife clapped her hands over her ears. A teardrop seared her cheek as she whispered, "Enough."

Amaryllis said nothing, only watched her steadily. Knife swallowed back a shard of pain and went on: "You said— you would give me something to—"

"Yes," said the Queen. "I have in my keeping a certain potion, brewed by magic long ago. A single drop in his drink, or in his food, will send him into a sleep from which he cannot wake. He will feel no pain, sense no wrong, never be aware that his heart has stopped. To his parents, it will seem a natural death; and for him, it will be a mercy."

"You swear it?" faltered Knife, and then passionately, "Swear!"

"I do."

"And then . . . when I come back . . ."

"You will be free." Amaryllis laid a hand on her shoulder. "You will mourn him, of course; but like all sorrows, it will pass. I shall restore your wings, and then you shall serve me and your sisters as the Queen's Hunter once more." Her fingers tightened briefly, consoling. "I know your heart cries out against this thing. But I assure you, Knife, it is the only way."

Knife bowed her head. Then she said very quietly, "Yes."

Outside the Oak, twilight had stained the sky indigo, littering it with crumpled rags of cloud and a smudge of vermilion along the horizon where the sun had slipped away. Deep in the forest an owl questioned the night, but received no answer.

Knife slid out the window and walked to the end of the branch, staring blindly out across the Oakenwyld. Then she spread her wings and launched herself into the gathering darkness. In three long glides she crossed the lawn and landed at the back of the House, trembling with the effort of flight. She paused to catch her breath, then thrashed her way up to the kitchen window and crouched there, waiting.

Slowly the minutes passed, until at last the light clicked on and Beatrice McCormick padded into view. Out came the familiar china teacups, clinking onto their saucers; then the milk jug emerged, bowing three times before returning to the depths of the refrigerator. The last item in the ritual was the sugar bowl, and Knife pressed her face to the window, intent as a hunting mink. Two spoonfuls went into the first cup, one in the second, but the third cup remained untouched—Paul's.

Once she had filled the teakettle and plugged it in, Beatrice left the kitchen, but Knife knew it would not be long before the woman returned. Clutching the phial Amaryllis had given her, she ducked through the window and dropped onto the countertop below.

Paul's cup stood innocently before her. Willing herself not to think about what she was doing, Knife pulled out the stopper and tipped the bottle over it. A thread of purple snaked out, traced a dark spiral in the milk, and vanished.

I've done it, she thought in relief. *It's over. I can go.*

And yet her legs refused to move, and the fingers that clutched the phial were slippery with sweat. She felt flushed, dizzy, and her rib cage ached from the hammering of her heart.

I can't do this—

But it's already done—

It's murder—

No, it's mercy—

He'll die if I do this—

We'll both die if I don't—

Knife's fingers uncurled, and the bottle slipped from her hand. Spinning, it tumbled through the air, struck the counter, and smashed to glittering dust.

For a moment Knife stood paralyzed, little explosions of shock firing all over her body. Then with sudden determination she lunged forward, put her shoulder against the poisoned teacup, and pushed. She waited only long enough to watch it teeter over the edge before she whirled and dove back through the window, pressing herself flat against the wall. Panting, she listened to the *thud-thud-thud* of the woman's footsteps, her sharp exclamation at the wreckage littering her kitchen floor.

Do you love him? Wink had asked her only a few hours ago, and Knife had not been sure of the answer. How could she love a human, at her tiny size? It was like falling in love with a mountain, or a tree. Yet for some reason she could not harm Paul McCormick, even in the name of mercy; it would have been easier to carve out her own heart.

Knife clung to the rough brick, calling on all her reserves of strength and courage. It didn't matter what had kept her from killing Paul: Whether it was love or only loyalty, the path before her was the same. She must return to the Oak, and surrender herself to whatever fate the Queen and the Great Gardener might decree. But first, she had to see Paul one last time, and warn him.

She had thought he would be surprised to see her again, especially after the way their last conversation had ended. But as he opened the window he only looked resigned. "You've come back for your book, I suppose," he said as she climbed in.

"Book?" said Knife in confusion. Then blood scorched her cheeks as she remembered Heather's second diary, but Paul had already gone on:

"Look, Knife, I should never have done what I did this morning. I didn't realize—" He stopped, coloring in his turn. "Anyway, it was stupid of me. I know better now."

"Paul? I've brought your tea."

Hastily Knife sprang to her feet and ducked behind the curtain as the door swung wide and Beatrice came in. "It's the oddest thing," she said. "Vermeer's asleep, and we haven't had mice in months. But your cup fell off the counter while I was waiting for the kettle to boil."

"Really," said Paul, and though his voice was relaxed, the line of his shoulders was not.

"Smashed all to bits," his mother mused, "and yet I could have sworn it wasn't anywhere near the edge. It's almost enough to make one believe in poltergeists." When Paul did not reply, she set the saucer down by his elbow and stooped to kiss his cheek. "You've had a busy day, dear. Don't you think you might like to turn in early?"

"I'll go to bed soon. Thank—I mean, I appreciate the tea."

Polite as Paul's voice had been, Mrs. McCormick seemed to understand that she was being dismissed. She heaved a little sigh and plodded out, shutting the door behind her.

Knife stepped out from her hiding place. She opened her mouth, but Paul cut her off:

"The broken cup. Was that you?"

Knife winced. "Yes."

"An accident?"

"No."

"I didn't think so. Why were you in the kitchen?"

"I came to—" she began, and then her eyes welled up. It was a struggle to continue, and when she did, every word felt as though it were clawing its way out of her throat: "The milk, in your cup—it was poisoned. The Queen— my Queen—told me to kill you—but I couldn't—"

"Knife." He reached out and cupped his hand around her, thumb and forefinger warming her shoulders like an embrace. She leaned back against his palm, breathing the scent of his skin, and felt a strange quietness come over her.

"I couldn't do it," she said, when she could speak. "Amaryllis says that without me you'll die of despair, like Alfred Wrenfield and Philip Waverley did. But maybe there's still hope, if—"

"Wait," said Paul. "Why would your Queen order you

to kill me if she thinks I'm going to die anyway?"

Knife could not bear to look at him anymore. She pushed his hand until it dropped away, and walked over to the window. "Because she said that unless you died . . . I'd die, too."

Paul was silent.

"I've ruined everything," Knife burst out, burying her face in the curtain. "I've ruined your life, I've ruined mine— I wish I'd never been born!"

"No!" The word exploded out of him, startling her. "Listen to me, Knife. It wasn't that long ago that I wanted to kill myself. Would have, if not for you. And though I won't pretend I haven't been tempted to try again, especially when I drive past the river and I see them out there, rowing—" He stopped and cleared his throat. "But anyway, I haven't tried, and I don't plan to. I've chosen to live, Knife . . . but I could never have made that choice, if not for you."

"Paul—"

"And now you've saved my life a second time, when you had every reason to take it. I wouldn't blame you if you hated me, after the way I—what I did this morning. I was being stupid, telling myself it wouldn't matter if I kissed you, that you were a faery and couldn't have those kinds of feelings anyway. No wonder you were so upset, especially after what you'd just read about Heather and—"

"Don't," Knife said hastily. "It's all right, you don't have to explain."

"I want to." He shifted his chair closer to the window. "What I mean to say is, I understand why you'd be tempted to kill me, especially if you thought I was already doomed. So I don't blame you for almost going through with it. In fact—Knife, look at me."

Reluctantly she lifted her eyes to his, and he went on: "I want you to understand this as though I were one of your own people. Because that's what it means to me." He drew a deep breath. "*Thank you.* Thank you for your friendship. Thank you for my life."

There could be no doubting the force of those words, or the conviction in his blue eyes as he spoke them. Knife let go of the curtain and sank to the windowsill, over-whelmed.

"Don't go back to the Oak," she heard Paul say, his voice strange and distant in her ears. "Stay here, where your Queen can't touch you."

Miserably she shook her head. "I can't. My people—my friends—they need my help. And you—you have *thanked* me. How could I stay with you, now that—"

"I know," said Paul, sounding resigned. "You think I expect you to feel about me the way that Heather did about Philip Waverley. But I don't, Knife. I know that could never happen, even if—" He broke off, his gaze dropping to his crippled legs. "Well, never mind that. What I mean is, you don't have to worry that I'll make things awkward for you if you stay. I only meant to thank you as—as a friend."

"Oh, Paul," said Knife in a voice that was half wail, "don't you understand? I'm not afraid because I don't love you. I'm afraid because—" She looked up at him, her eyes pleading. "Because I do."

For a moment Paul went absolutely still; then he shook his head. "I told you," he said, "I don't want your pity."

Knife's fist slammed down on the window frame. "And I'm not trying to give it to you! What kind of stubborn—" She broke off in frustration as Paul pivoted the chair and began pushing himself away. How could she make him believe her?

Then her eyes fell upon Heather's second diary, sitting quietly on the bedside table, and she knew.

With one word I have surrendered to Philip the greatest treasure I shall ever own, and yet my heart is content; for I know my secret shall always be safe in his keeping, and that it has comforted him as nothing else could do.

And now, wherever he or I may go, part of me will always be with him.

Knife snapped out her wings and leaped into the air, gliding across to Paul's shoulder. She sat down with one foot braced against his collarbone and slid her arm as far as it would go around his neck; then she whispered into his ear, "Paul McCormick. My name—my true name—is Perianth."

Twenty-two

Paul did not reply, but Knife could feel his pulse quicken, see his throat move as he swallowed. She launched herself off his shoulder and lighted on his knee, looking up into his face.

"Now do you believe me?" she said.

Paul squeezed his eyes shut, his fists clenching on the arms of the chair. "I want to hold you," he said. "But I can't. You're—"

"Too small. I know." She curled her own fingers against her palm, resisting the urge to run to him, to be caught up in his hand and cradled to his heart. "And now that I've used up what little magic I had, I always will be. Which is why I have to leave you now . . . and why I can't come back."

"Then why did you give me your name? I could order you

304

not to go. I could call you from anywhere, and you'd have to come, no matter what your Queen or anyone said—"

"But you won't," said Knife. She reached up and laid her small hand on his. "That's why."

Paul's defiance melted, and he slumped in his chair. "There has to be another way," he said. "It can't just . . . end, not like this."

Knife watched him with aching heart, unable to speak. What could she say to comfort him, when they both knew the situation was impossible?

"You made yourself human before," Paul persisted.

"Yes, but only by accident. And you saw for yourself—it's just a glamour, it doesn't last."

"I know." He leaned forward urgently. "But if you could become really human, and stay that way . . . would you?"

Become human. The thought was both tempting and ter-rifying. To be with Paul always—it was what she longed for. And yet to do so, she would have to leave behind the only home she had ever known, and begin a new life in a world she barely understood; she would be vulnerable, dependent, uncertain—all the things she hated.

And worst of all, she would never fly again.

Knife shifted restlessly. "Yes. No. I don't know. . . . But why are you even asking me? What good is it talking about something that can never happen?"

"Because," said Paul, "I'm thinking that maybe, if we

could strike the right bargain . . . it could."

"You mean—ask the Queen to change me?"

Paul nodded.

I transformed her into a human, said Amaryllis's voice in her memory, *and banished her from the Oak forever.* . . . He was right, Knife realized with a tingling chill. If the Queen had been able to cast such a spell once, she could do it again.

And yet, why should she? The advantage would all be on Knife's side; she had nothing to offer in return. And though she still had the right to ask for one favor, the Queen had specifically said that the request must not put anyone else at risk. It was hard for Knife to see how the loss of their Hunter could do the Oakenfolk anything but harm, and she knew the Queen would see it the same way.

"I'm sorry," she said heavily. "If I thought there was even the slightest chance, I'd ask . . . but it's no use. She'd never agree."

"So that's it?" Paul demanded. "You go back to the Oak, I stay here—and we both die?"

She looked away, unable to bear the anguish in his gaze. "I don't see that we have any other choice." *Unless the Queen is wrong.* But that seemed too much to hope.

"And when you tell your Queen you didn't obey her orders?"

Knife spread her wings and rose into the air. "I'll be all right," she lied, and darted forward to brush her lips against his cheek. "Good-bye, Paul—"

And before he could reach out to her, she was gone.

Never had the journey from the House to the Oak seemed so long. A crow circled overhead, its wings carving black slices from the moon. From the other side of the box hedge came a rustle and a shriek, as a stoat undulated through the grass with a struggling mouse in its jaws. Even the air currents felt treacherous, ready to toss Knife skyward or dash her to the ground the moment her concentration faltered. It took all her strength to make it across the lawn, and by the time she had struggled her way up into the topmost branches of the Oak she felt almost painfully alert, as though her nerves were crawling through her skin.

Even so, she was not prepared for the shadow that dropped down from above, seizing her about the waist and clamping a hand over her mouth. Wings whirred into motion, and before she could even find voice to shout she was yanked backward into the air, plummeting through thirty crow-lengths of leaves and branches to land winded at the foot of the Oak.

"I did it," said a voice in tones of astonished pride, and then as an afterthought, "Ouch."

Knife whirled around to see Thorn standing behind her, massaging her shoulder and wincing. "What do you think you're—" she began hotly, but the other faery cut her off.

"I've already spent half the night out here, waiting for you to stop squawking at that human of yours and get back to the Oak. You're not going back to the Queen without hearing what I have to say first."

"You followed me to the House?" asked Knife, incredulous.

"Well, I had to know if you were going to kill him or not, didn't I?"

Knife put a hand to her forehead. "Wait. How do you know about all this—any of this? I haven't seen you since I left Campion's room."

"You didn't *see* me, no," said Thorn with grim satisfaction. "But I was listening outside the Queen's window the whole time the two of you were talking. I didn't catch all of it, but I heard enough." She eyed Knife's faded wings disapprovingly. "So that's what she was talking about, when she said she'd have to restore your wings. Did you really use up all your magic on that human? Of all the gnat-witted things to do—"

"I love you, too, Thorn," said Knife, and as the other faery spluttered she went on more seriously: "But you have something to tell me, you said. What is it?"

"Campion's getting better," said Thorn, her voice still a little strangled. "Valerian and I weren't sure at first, but when she sat up and asked for something to eat—we knew."

Knife went still, feeling her heartbeat pound through her

whole body. This was it: proof that despite all Jasmine's efforts and the Queen's fears, the Oakenfolk still needed knowledge of the human world to survive. Tragic though it was, Heather's story had spoken to Campion, awakening her mind and reviving her spirits, in a way that all her knowledge of the faery lore had not.

And that meant . . .

"I have something to bargain with," Knife whispered.

"To get your wings back? I hope so," said Thorn. "Believe me, I'm in no hurry to be Queen's Hunter again, but the way you've been floundering about is a disgrace: It's a wonder Old Wormwood hasn't eaten you already."

Knife's mind flashed back to the crow's body, lying stiff and lifeless by the road. She had been so distracted with other things, she had forgotten to share the news. "Old Wormwood is dead. The humans—" Then she stopped short, her breath catching in her throat.

"What?" asked Thorn.

Knife seized her by the shoulders. "Thorn, I need you to do something for me right away, while I go and talk to the Queen. You won't like it, but I swear to you, it's important."

"Enough," said Thorn irritably. "Just tell me what you want."

Knife told her.

Thorn's face went so white that even her lips turned pale.

But then she drew herself up and said stiffly, "All right."

"Thorn, I can't tell you how grateful—"

"Oh, none of that," said Thorn, with a snort that sounded suspiciously like a sniff. "Now stop blathering and get up there. The Queen's waiting."

"I had almost lost hope of your return," said Amaryllis. "What kept you so long?"

Knife folded herself through the window and dropped to the floor, dusting off her hands. "My apologies, Your Majesty," she said. "It took longer than I had expected."

"It is done, then," said the Queen, and then to Knife's surprise she sighed, and put a hand to her eyes. "I could almost wish that you had passed the test," she continued, almost too softly for Knife to hear. "But it is better so."

"Test?" said Knife. "If you mean killing Paul—"

"He will not die," Amaryllis told her. "If he sleeps, it is only to awake refreshed tomorrow. But in your heart you will know that you meant to kill him, and the shame of that betrayal will taint every thought of him hereafter." Knife stared at her aghast as she went on. "Did I not warn you that your friendship with this young human had no future? Now you have proven it for yourself."

"Wait," said Knife. "What if I *didn't* try to kill him?"

"If the bond between you was true," said Amaryllis impatiently, "no threat or persuasion could have made you do him harm. Yet when you took the potion from my hand, I knew that what I had long feared had come to pass, and my people were no longer capable of love."

"Not capable—" Knife's outrage left her speechless. But the Queen had already turned away.

"I do not blame you for the choice you made," she said, her gaze on the window and the rising moon. "You had no power to do otherwise. Ever since the Sundering cut us off from the human world, our people have grown more shallow in their affections, more petty and self-serving. Though I have done what I could to encourage kindness and to reward those few who appeared to possess it, I knew all along that such efforts were in vain. The evil Jasmine did has poisoned the Oak to its very root."

"No," said Knife. "You're wrong. Do you really think that just because we can't go back to the way we used to be, that proves we can never be any better than we are? Besides, you weren't listening when I told you—*I didn't do it.*"

The Queen gave her a sharp look. "Are you telling me that you failed in your mission? That you were unable to carry out my command?"

"I had the opportunity," said Knife, defiant. "I chose not to."

"I warned you that you would die if you did not obey— that only by doing this could you win back your wings and ensure your future as my Hunter. You believed, yet you still held back?" Amaryllis leaned heavily on the table, her face haggard with disbelief. "How can this be?"

All at once Knife understood, and the icy dread inside her dissolved in a hot rush of anger. "You mean that what you said would happen to me, and Paul, was just a test—you *lied*?"

But the Queen did not seem to hear. She went on distractedly: "A true bond. So much better than I dreamed possible . . . and yet so much worse. Has it come to this? And yet what choice do I have left?"

She straightened as she spoke, and Knife stepped back, wary—but too late. Already Amaryllis was reaching out to her, fingers kindling with power even as her red-rimmed eyes silently pleaded forgiveness for it. "You are the only hope I have of saving our people," she said, "yet I cannot trust you so long as your heart is divided. If you cannot forsake this human, Knife . . . then I must make you forget him."

"Wait!" shouted Knife, flinging both arms in front of her face in a futile attempt to shield herself. "You haven't heard—I have to tell you—"

A rushing noise filled her ears, and her thoughts swirled and bled as a ruthless brush swept across the canvas of her mind. Knife staggered backward, cracked her head against the wall and slid to the floor, stunned. The tide of the Queen's magic surged over her, and the image of Paul's face in her memory began to crumble and wash away. . . .

Suddenly her mind snapped like a bowstring, and she felt the spell fly away from her, arrow-clean. The Queen cried out and gripped her head in her hands. "You resisted my spell," she gasped. "How?"

"The same way Heather resisted Jasmine," Knife replied, struggling to her feet. "You can't make me forget Paul, any more than she could forget Philip—because *I gave him my name.*"

"And it is well that she did," came an unexpected voice, "or else Your Majesty would have done a great evil, and all in vain."

They both looked around to see Valerian standing in the doorway, with Wink and a sleepy Linden by her side. Then another shuffled out of the shadows to join them—Campion.

The Queen drew herself up. "What trickery is this?" she said.

"No trickery at all," said Valerian, helping Campion into a chair. "You were told she was dying of the Silence, and rightly so; but thanks to Knife, she is dying no longer." She walked toward the Queen, her stern expression softening. "You are weary," she said, "for you have borne a great burden for many years alone. But to allow despair to lead you into the same path Jasmine took—this is folly, and it does not become you."

"And besides," said Wink, pale and earnest, "if you make

Knife forget, then you'll have to make the rest of us forget, too. I was the one who gave her Heather's diaries in the first place, so it's my fault she read them, and Knife wanting to be with Paul is my fault, too, because I let them meet each other when they were little, and—oh, please don't hurt her anymore. If you have to punish someone, please—" She looked at Knife, and her eyes filled up. "Punish me instead."

Knife moved forward and put her arm around Wink's shoulders. "And you say our people know nothing of love?" she said to Amaryllis. "I don't blame you for thinking me selfish, but Wink deserves more credit than that." She looked down at the Seamstress's bent red head and added softly, "She always has."

The Queen regarded them with amazement. "I underestimated you," she said at last. "All of you, it would seem. Nevertheless—" She broke off as the shutters rattled and Thorn thumped onto the windowsill, her hair windblown and her cheeks red.

"I've done it," she panted at Knife. "He's coming."

Quickly Knife stepped forward, unclasping the ruby pendant from her neck and pressing it into Amaryllis's hand. "I'm asking you this favor," she said. "Come out to the garden with me now, and listen to what Paul and I have to say."

The Queen's fingers closed about the stone. "This is madness," she said. "What use are words now, with

314

the future of the Oak in jeopardy?" But then she caught Valerian's eye, and color tinged her cheeks as she went on, "Yet it is true that I have wronged you, and that you have a right to ask. Very well."

If Paul was glad to see Knife again, he did not show it. "I just want you to know," he said as he wheeled across the lawn to meet her, "that if I lose my mind, it won't be because you left me; it'll be because you kept leaving and then *coming back again*. Although sending that other faery to fetch me was an interesting twist—" His gaze fell to Amaryllis, waiting imperiously at the end of the path. "Is that who I think it is?"

It seemed Thorn hadn't told him what was happening, only that he needed to come out to the garden at once. No wonder he didn't look happy; he had no idea what to expect from this meeting, any more than Amaryllis did.

"Yes," Knife told him, then raised her voice and addressed the Queen: "Your Majesty, we both know the dangers that our people face, and the need for a strong Hunter to protect them. I also understand how important it could be for us to find other faeries if we want our magic back—but I believe that preventing the Silence from killing our people is even more important. Don't you agree?"

"Agreed," said Amaryllis, but she folded her arms as she spoke. "Go on."

"But Paul and I also need each other," Knife continued, "and the Oakenfolk need help that only the humans can give. You saw Campion just now: Valerian said I cured her, but it wasn't really me. It was Heather's story that brought her back, because it told her things she'd never heard before— new ideas, new knowledge. But those diaries won't necessarily help everyone, and even if they did they might not be enough. We have to find more new ideas, of all kinds, to keep the rest of us from sinking into despair as Campion did."

"So what you need," said Paul, his eyes lighting as he began to catch on, "is a go-between—someone with a connection to both worlds, who can take the knowledge my people have and bring it to yours."

"Yes," said Knife, "but even more than that. Someone who can also protect the Oak from harm, and our people from predators, and make the Oakenwyld safe again. As a faery I've done my best, but now I know that I could do it even better . . . as a human."

Amaryllis's lips parted, incredulous. "A *human* Queen's Hunter?"

"Why not?" demanded Paul. "Knife's right—we humans can kill crows, or frighten them away, far more easily than you can. And she wouldn't have to stop hunting food for you, either; she could snare rabbits, gather plants, even bring you things from the House. And I can help your people, too. If there's anything you want or need—metal, cloth, paper—I'll get it for you. I'll even give tours of the House when my parents are out and serve you all tea and biscuits, if that's what you want." His mouth twitched. "But I won't tell anyone else about you, or do anything to threaten your safety. I'll swear that in blood if you like."

The Queen was silent, her head bent. Then she said, "I must speak with Knife about this. Alone."

"What is it?" asked Knife, following Amaryllis to the foot of the Oak. She glanced back over her shoulder to where Paul sat in the middle of the lawn, tense and waiting. "Don't tell me you plan to refuse?"

"I do not," said Amaryllis shortly, turning to face her. "But I cannot accept this offer unless I am satisfied that you, and he, are fully aware of what you are asking. I would not have it said that I made you a false bargain."

"I know what I'm doing," said Knife, impatient. "We both do. We're wasting time—"

"Then do me the courtesy of not interrupting when I speak!" Amaryllis snapped back. Knife reddened, and the Queen went on: "If I make you human, Knife, it will be no easy task. It will require of me all the magic I took from Jasmine, and some of my own as well—power that I can ill afford to spare. If you should regret your decision, I will not be able to help you. You will be trapped as a human forever. Do you understand?"

"Yes," said Knife.

"You will give up your wings, your ageless body, your magical heritage. The Oak will be closed to you, and you will have no one in all the world but Paul, no home that he does not give you. If there is any magical power to the bond between you, it will dissolve, leaving you no guarantee that he will not tire of you and cast you away. Yet as long as the Oakenfolk have need of you, you cannot leave this place, but must live here always." She laid a hand on Knife's arm. "Do not think of this choice as an escape, Knife. If you believe that becoming human will give you more freedom than the Oak can offer, I fear you will be disappointed."

"I used to think I knew what freedom was," said Knife. "To do whatever I pleased, go wherever I chose, and not have to depend on anyone. But now . . ." She lifted her head, resolute. "I know this won't be easy. But I still want to do it."

"I see," said Amaryllis, and took her hand away. "So for yourself, this is what you would choose. But what of Paul? If you become human, your power to inspire him will weaken, if not vanish entirely; he may never achieve his full potential as an artist. And though he cares for you now, there are countless young women in the world; would he still want you if he knew he could claim a far more valuable prize?"

"I don't—" began Knife, but the Queen cut her off.

"Think, Knife. Have you not realized that if I restored your wings, you might still serve both Paul and the Oak as a faery, while the same power that would have made you human could be used for another purpose?"

Knife felt as though a fist had driven into her stomach. "You mean you could—"

"I could, and will if you choose it. He is a worthy human, and such a debt would bind him to the Oak even more surely than his loyalty to you. Why should I not give him what he himself once told you was his dearest wish?"

"Then—" She closed her eyes, and spoke quickly before she could change her mind. "Yes."

"You want me to heal him?"

"Yes."

"Remember, Knife, that the other terms of the bargain still stand. Not only must you continue as my Hunter, but you must also see Paul, and speak with him, on my behalf—even though your feelings for him can never again be expressed, or returned. You will remain a faery, and he a human, forever. Are you willing to endure this, for his sake?"

Knife nodded, too full of grief to speak.

"Very well," said the Queen with satisfaction. "You have chosen wisely, Knife. Now remain here, while I speak to the human."

Knife sat at the foot of the Oak, chin resting on pulled-up knees. Though Paul and Amaryllis were too far away for her to make out their words, she could still hear the Queen's treble rising above Paul's husky baritone; they appeared to be talking on top of each other, and at this rate the sun would come up before either of them finished a sentence. But then Paul broke off and cast a stricken glance at her.

She's told him. The knowledge was as certain as it was bittersweet. *He knows he has the chance to walk again—and that I want him to take it.* She met Paul's gaze, hoping that despite the darkness and the distance between them, he might find reassurance in her face. But his expression remained bleak, and when at last he spoke, his voice was so quiet she could not hear it at all.

Knife felt bruised inside, her heart crushed between hope and misery. She buried her head in her arms, shutting out the world, until she felt the Queen's hand upon her shoulder.

"I could wish the moon were more full," said Amaryllis, sounding weary. "Nevertheless, I will do what I can. Go and stand beside your human."

Mechanically Knife rose and walked across the grass to stand by the wheel of Paul's chair. It would be worth it, she told herself. It would be worth everything to see him rise to his feet and walk again. The Queen had been right: As a human, she had little to offer Paul. But by remaining a faery for his sake, she would give him a gift he would treasure for the rest of his life.

"Perianth," whispered Paul. The sound of her true name nearly broke Knife, and she pressed the back of her hand hard against her lips as he went on: "What did she say to you?"

Knife shook her head, wishing he would not speak. It was too late for words now; already Amaryllis had stepped from the Oak's shadow and opened her arms to the moonlight, the glow of gathering magic swirling about her body.

"What did she say?" Paul demanded. He reached out to her, and in desperation Knife scrambled away, slipped, and fell sprawling on the grass. There was a blinding flash, and a ripple of power passed over her; she heard Paul cry out as though it was hurting him, and she thought dizzily, *It's working.*

Though every muscle groaned and her limbs felt as though they were encased in clay, she managed to push herself back up to her feet. She staggered forward a few steps, swaying like a sapling in the wind. Then her legs buckled, and the darkness swooped down and carried her away.

As she swam back into consciousness, the first thing she heard was Wink's hushed, anxious voice: "Is she dead?"

"No," replied Valerian, "she has only fainted, and already she is recovering. Look."

"I can't see worth a squashed berry," grumbled Thorn. "That flash was so bright, I thought she'd blown herself up and taken the pair of them with her."

Knife stirred, wincing at the pounding in her skull. Despite that and a host of other aches, her back felt warm, and a light blanket had been thrown over her. She supposed Wink had done that: It would be like her. She curled her fingers around the soft fabric and opened her eyes.

As she had expected, Wink, Valerian, and Thorn stood nearby, with Linden still nestled against Wink's shoulder. But they were gathered around Amaryllis's prone body, not hers—and all of them were *tiny*.

Slowly Knife tilted her head back to see Paul gazing down at her in wonder. She could feel the quickness of his breathing against her spine, see his wheelchair lying on its side only a couple of crow-lengths away; he must have heaved himself out of the chair when she fell, and flung his own blanket around her. Then, as her numbed senses began to awaken, she realized why he had done so: She was quite naked.

That meant the change was real, not a glamour. That meant it was permanent. "How?" she demanded. "How could this happen?"

"Well, I don't want to leap to any conclusions," said Paul gravely, leaning on his elbow, "but I think magic may have been involved."

Knife gave a shaky laugh. "You know that's not what I meant."

"Oh, you mean how did they get down here?" He

nodded toward the faeries gathered around the Queen. "I'm not quite sure myself. I'd just got the blanket around you, and when I looked up, there they were. All I know is that the dark-haired one said she'd stab my eye out if I didn't take good care of you, and she looked so fierce that I've been on my best behavior ever since." He gave a rueful grin. "After all, I'm not likely to outrun her."

He spoke lightly, but Knife jolted upright, staring at him. Though his eyes smiled, his face was lined with strain, and he was using both hands for balance—

"Oh," she whispered as her gaze traveled down his body. "Oh, no."

"What's the matter?" said Paul. "I didn't break one, did I?" He pushed himself into a sitting position and reached down to straighten the legs lying slack upon the grass.

"No!" Knife clutched the blanket about her throat, sick with grief and guilt. "You don't understand, Paul. This isn't what I asked for."

"Perhaps not," said Queen Amaryllis feebly as Valerian helped her to her feet. "But as I have been so recently reminded, it is wrong to use magic on others against their will. I had your consent to become human. But he refused to let me make him whole."

"But . . ." Knife turned to Paul in distress. "You could have had your legs back. Why?"

Paul reached out to touch her face. "Listen," he said. "There's a chance that one day the doctors will find a way to help me walk again." He slid his hand behind her neck, drawing her toward him. "But where else will I find a faery who loves me enough to give me her name?"

"Not here, that's for certain," came an irritable voice from below. "And if you two start chewing on each other's faces, *someone's* going to get their eye poked out."

Paul let go of Knife abruptly as Thorn glared up at them. "I suppose you think being a human is all very wonderful," she said to Knife, "but this is a fine mess of hedgehog droppings if ever I saw one. Who's going to drive off the crows now? And I suppose you expect me to do all your hunting, too?"

"Peace, Thorn," said Amaryllis, leaning heavily on Valerian's shoulder. "Those matters have already been addressed—and not even you will have reason to complain of the result." She looked up at Knife. "You have been severely tested this night," she said. "And I would not blame you if you hated me for it. Yet I could not have let you go with this young man were I not certain that you both understood not only love, but self-sacrifice."

"We're not the only ones," said Knife. "You made a sacrifice, too. I can't help you find the other faeries, not any-more—even if I could afford to leave the Oak unguarded that long, they'd never talk to a human. So what will you do?"

"Hope," said Amaryllis. "Now that I have others to help me in my studies, perhaps they will make discoveries and see possibilities that I did not. Campion at least will be glad to assist me, I am sure . . . and perhaps in time, another will arise among us with the will and courage to make the journey." Her eyes flickered to the sleeping Linden as she spoke. "We have that time, now."

Knife nodded. Then, clutching the blanket about her shoulders, she leaned close to the Queen and whispered, "I forgive you."

"My Hunter," said Amaryllis just as softly, and her gaze touched Knife's like a salute before she turned away. Valerian paused to give Knife a respectful nod, then hurried to help the Queen back to the Oak.

"Hmph," Thorn said with a last wary glance at Paul, and moved to follow—but Knife held up her hand. "Wait," she said, and the faery stopped, wings tensed for flight. "Come closer. Please. And Wink—you too."

With obvious reluctance Thorn edged toward her, only to be nearly bowled off her feet by Wink, who rushed forward as though she had been waiting for the summons all along. "Oh, Knife," she said, looking up at her with tear-bright eyes. "I'm going to miss you!"

"You won't have to," said Knife. "I'll be seeing you and Linden—and the others, too—nearly every day. Ask the Queen, when you get back to the Oak; she'll explain."

"Speaking of explanations," began Paul from behind her, but Knife shook her head. "Just a moment," she told him. "I have one last thing to say to my friends." Bending as near to Wink and Thorn as she dared, she said softly, *"Thank you.* I promise you, I will never forget what you have done for me."

Wink hiccupped and flung herself sobbing into Thorn's arms, nearly squashing Linden in the process. Thorn rolled her eyes and thumped the Seamstress on the back, but it was clear that she, too, was touched. "Remember what I told you, human," she said gruffly to Paul. "Take care of her—or you'll answer to me."

"I hear you," said Paul. He laid his hands on Knife's shoulders, and together they watched as the faeries made their way back across the darkened lawn. When they had vanished among the shadows of the Oak, he pulled Knife against him and put his lips to her ear. She closed her eyes, expecting a kiss, but heard instead:

"We have a problem. I haven't the faintest idea what I'm going to tell my parents."

"Oh, Great Gardener," said Knife, twisting around to face him. "I hadn't thought of that."

"Yes, well, I wouldn't have expected you to, with all the other things on your mind. But somehow I think introducing you at the breakfast table tomorrow is going to be awkward." He looked down at her, and even in the fading moonlight she could see his color rise. "Particularly as you'll be wearing my clothes."

Knife brushed back the pale hair from his eyes, then leaned forward and kissed him. "I'm serious!" he objected, when she let him speak. "What am I supposed to say—'I found her lying naked on the lawn at midnight, can I keep her?'" He stopped. "You're shivering. Did I frighten you? Don't worry, I'm sure it'll be all right."

"I'm just a little cold," said Knife, pulling the blanket closer about her shoulders.

Paul wrapped his free arm around her. "It's all right," he said. "I've got you."

"Yes," said Knife, smiling up at him. "You have."

Acknowledgments

This story would never have existed without the help of my many friends on the FidoNet Writing echo, including Dennis Havens, who asked all the right questions about faery biology; the late R. Veraa and Joe Chamberlain, who shared their experiences of living with a spinal cord injury; and my mentors, Patricia C. Wrede and Pamela Dean, who taught me what it means to be a professional author and gave me hope that someday I could be one too.

I am also indebted to Jim, Matt, and Angela, whose demand for new chapters kept me writing steadily until the first draft was finished; to Claire Eddy at Tor for taking an early interest in the manuscript; to Cheryl Klein at Arthur A. Levine for broadening my perspective on readership and teaching me invaluable lessons about revision; to my agents,

Josh and Tracey Adams, for believing in this book and in me as a writer; to my wonderful editor, Catherine Onder at HarperCollins, for showing me how to take Knife's story to the next level—and the next—and the next; to Alec Dossetor for tirelessly reading draft after draft and giving me comments on every one; to Liz Barr, Brittany Harrison, Teri Krenek, and Sylvia Thomas, whose steadfast support helped keep me sane; to Emily Bytheway, Erin Fitzgerald, Claudia Gray, Kerrie Mills, Meg Burden, Seema G., Lisa Inman, Jerie Wills, and Paula Berman, who offered shrewd critiques and encouraging praise; to Emily Friedman and Saundra Mitchell for the delightful fan art; to Laurie R. King for fifteen years of kindness, generosity, and Mary Russell; and to my fellow 2009 Debs on LiveJournal, who are truly a never-ending Feast of Awesome.

Finally, I want to thank my husband for being a wonderful partner; my children and my extended family for putting up with my lunacy; and most of all the One who is both Author and Word, the Beginning and the End, my Lord and my God. As the hymnist Josiah Conder wrote:

Alike pervaded by His eye, all parts of His dominion lie;
This world of ours, and worlds unseen, and thin the boundary between.

—R. J. Anderson 2009